TROUBLE FROM THE START

Books by Rachel Hawthorne

Caribbean Cruising

Island Girls (and Boys)

Love on the Lifts

Thrill Ride

The Boyfriend League

Snowed In

Labor of Love

Suite Dreams

Trouble from the Start

The Boyfriend Project

One Perfect Summer

The Dark Guardian series

Moonlight

Full Moon

Dark of the Moon

Shadow of the Moon

TROUBLE FROM THE START

Rachel Hawthorne

HARPER TEEN
An Imprint of HarperCollinsPublishers

HarperTeen is an imprint of HarperCollins Publishers.

Trouble from the Start

Library of Congress Control Number: 2014950611
ISBN 978-0-06-233071-0 (pbk.)

Typography by Jenna Stempel
15 16 17 18 19   CG/RRDH   10 9 8 7 6 5 4 3 2 1

First Edition

For every girl waiting for her first kiss,
her first boyfriend, her first love . . .

TROUBLE FROM THE START

Chapter 1

AVERY

"You can't just stand here, Avery. You have to get out there and flaunt it."

I wasn't quite sure what Kendall Jones, my best friend since forever, thought I had to flaunt.

"It seems a little late for all that," I told her. "We only have a week left until we graduate."

"Which is exactly why we're here," she said, removing the clip from her red hair, retwisting the curling strands, and securing them back into place. "Jeremy and I had our pick of three parties tonight. I knew this one would have the most people."

Because it was totally without chaperones. Scooter Gibson's parents were out of town and he had the key to his family's lake house so here we were, standing out by a magnificent pool, catching glimpses through towering trees of the moonlight dancing across the calm lake waters. Laughter, screeches, the din of conversation, and raucous cheers as girls stripped before diving into the pool competed with music blasting from speakers on the patio.

"I feel like a party crasher," I told her. "It's not like I was invited."

"You're with us. It's cool."

"I shouldn't have come."

"You're never going to get a boyfriend if you just stay at home."

I had been staying at home more since Kendall and Jeremy Swanson hooked up over spring break. They invited me to go almost everywhere with them, but I often simply felt out of place.

Kendall wrapped her hand around my upper arm. "Look, Avery, I want you to have what I have. But if that doesn't happen, you still need to go on a date. You can't start college never having been alone with a guy. You'll feel awkward."

As though I could feel any more awkward than I did now, standing around, experiencing a rush of hope that I might find a boyfriend of my own every time a cute guy glanced my way, only to be disappointed when he turned back to his friends. I longed for some guy to think I was special enough to kiss.

At seventeen I wasn't kissless but my one kiss had

happened at band camp sophomore year. I still shuddered when I remembered the tuba player pressing his puckered, chapped lips to mine. We'd gotten trapped with a spin the bottle game. I'd thought I would be perceived as cool if I acted like I was up for anything. Instead I discovered that some things just aren't worth it.

"You just need to get out there," Kendall continued. "Let guys know you're interested."

How was I supposed to do that? Wish a flashing neon sign? Not that I thought it would make any difference. I knew these guys, and they knew me. If we hadn't clicked after twelve years of being in school together, what made Kendall think it would happen tonight?

Jeremy was the newest kid in town, and it had taken six months for him and Kendall to start dating, although I noticed the sparks between them way before that.

"Yeah, okay," I said with far more enthusiasm than I felt. "I can put myself out there."

She gave me a quick hug. "You deserve to be as happy as I am."

"Here we go," Jeremy announced, rejoining us and handing us each a plastic cup.

Jeremy's family had moved here in the fall when his dad got a job transfer. He'd been bummed about not graduating with his friends. He'd started hanging around with us, and the three of us grew close. One night when we were all planning to go to a movie together, I'd faked being sick because I suspected he liked Kendall as more than a friend, and I was in the way. That night he'd kissed her, and the rest was history.

"Mmm," Kendall sighed, snuggling against him. "This tastes like an orange dreamsicle."

It did, but it also had a little kick to it. I had a feeling that it wasn't a melted ice cream bar. The two he'd brought each of us earlier had been strawberry something or other.

Jeremy slid his arm around her. He was tall enough that her head fit perfectly into the nook of his shoulder, like fate had made them to go together.

"Let's dance," he said in a low voice near her ear.

She looked at me, one brow arched. "He could be out there."

"Who?" Jeremy asked, clearly baffled.

"The right guy for Avery," Kendall said.

"Oh, yeah, he could totally be out there." Jeremy shifted his gaze to me. "Just avoid the house. It's make-out central in there. Don't want someone to get the wrong idea about what you're looking for."

"I'm not even sure what I'm looking for," I admitted.

"Someone nice like Jeremy," Kendall said. "And you'll have a better chance of meeting him if we're not here. Have fun!"

She handed me her drink and they wandered off.

Self-consciously I glanced around. Everyone else was already separated into groups, based on common interests—which usually involved gossiping about someone *not* in the circle. I didn't really feel like barging in. But I also didn't want to stand here alone like a total loser.

I ambled over to the nearest group of girls. They were giggling hysterically. While I'd missed the joke, I laughed, too, and tried to look like I was part of their gab-fest. Melody Long stopped laughing, which caused the others to stop as well, because she was the alpha in the group. Flicking her long blond hair, she turned ever so slightly and looked at me as though she was considering tossing me in the pool.

"Hi, Melody," I said, plowing ahead, even knowing that I was about to ram into a brick wall. "Isn't this a fun party?"

She narrowed her eyes. "Are you wired?"

"You mean feverishly excited about being here?" I smiled brightly, refusing to let on how much her barb had hurt. It wasn't the first time someone had hinted that I might be a narc. "You bet."

Blinking, she stared at me blankly. It was the same look she wore when we had a pop quiz in history.

"One of the definitions for wired is feverishly excited," I explained, realizing too late that I was making the situation worse, doing my Merriam-Webster's impersonation.

After drinking two fruity somethings-or-other I was finding that my mouth could work without any social filter.

Jade Johnson stepped in front of her. "She means wired like recording stuff for the cops."

"Why would I do that?" I asked, knowing exactly why they thought that and hating that they distrusted the police, that they distrusted me.

As Jade moved in, reminding me a little of a pit bull, she brought with her the fragrance of recently smoked weed, which explained why they were so paranoid. "Because your dad's a cop," Jade said, as though I didn't know what he did for a living. "I think you need to strip down so we know you're cool."

"Yeah," Melody said, brightening as though she'd finally figured out an answer on the pop quiz. "You need to show us you're not wearing a wire."

I thought about pointing out that my clothes—white shorts and a snug red top—weren't designed to hide much of anything. Instead, I just said, "Not going to happen."

Spinning on my heel, I walked away, their laughter following me, and this time I was pretty sure I was the joke.

I passed a group of three couples, but I wanted to avoid twosomes since I would stand out as someone no guy was interested in being with. I spotted two girls and a guy talking. They seemed harmless, but as I neared they began wandering off toward the house. Following after them would have made me appear desperate to be included.

Then I spied Brian Saunders leaning against a wooden beam that supported one corner of a cedar-slatted canopy. He was alone. I created a zigzag path to get to him because I didn't want it to seem obvious I was beelining for him in case he walked away before I got there. When I was three steps away, he was still there, drinking a beer. I noticed a few empty bottles at his feet and it occurred to me that he was still standing there because he was too unsteady to move away. But I was here now.

"Hey," I said brightly, moving in front of him so he blocked the view of the kissing couple stretched out on the lounge chair beneath the canopy.

For a moment he furrowed his brow, blinked, and I was afraid he didn't recognize me.

He blinked again, scowled. "I'll get to the problems tomorrow."

What was he talking about? Then I remembered that I'd given him an extra assignment to work on the last time I tutored him. "Oh, I don't care about that."

He brightened. "So I don't have to do them?"

"They're always optional, but if you work them out then you're more likely to learn the material—God, could I sound any more geekish? I'm sorry. I didn't come over here to talk algebra." Please don't ask me why I came over. *Eager to look like I belonged* wasn't a much better reason.

But he seemed to have forgotten I was even there as he took another sip and shifted his attention away from me. "Do you think Ladasha likes Kirk?" he asked.

I turned in the direction he was looking. I was hardly the one to tutor him in love, although his question seemed to be a no-brainer. Ladasha—who actually spelled her name La-A—always got the leads in the school plays and was moving to New York after graduation to pursue acting. At that particular moment, though, she was in the pool with her legs wrapped around Kirk's waist like he was her life preserver. "Uh, probably," I finally answered.

"She is so amazingly beautiful," he said.

"Yes, she is." She was probably the most beautiful girl in our graduating class.

"I'm going to tell her," he said, and staggered away, leaving me feeling even more self-conscious, as though everyone would figure out that I couldn't hold a guy's attention for two minutes.

Sighing, I returned to the spot where Jeremy and Kendall had left me so that at least they could find me easily. No way I was going looking for them. I wasn't sure all they were doing was dancing. Their relationship had seemed to have gotten intense fast. I was happy for Kendall. She deserved a great guy like Jeremy. He was the one who got invited to the party, and he'd included his girlfriend's best friend. A lot of guys wouldn't be that thoughtful. I'd come because senior year was supposed to be memorable, although at that precise moment I felt stupid and uncomfortable standing all alone while holding two plastic cups filled almost to the top. I chugged down Kendall's. Maybe with a little more alcohol, I wouldn't be bothered by the fact that since I'd spent way too much time studying and not enough partying, I didn't know any of these people well enough that they were going to include me in their little circles.

It had been that way for most of high school. I had so wanted to fall in love, or at least in like, before I graduated. Now I needed to admit that wasn't going to happen, but that was okay. The sea at college would contain a lot more fish, and no one there would know my dad was a cop. He wouldn't be coming to the university to hold assemblies with the theme "Dare to Say No." I loved my dad, loved that he was one of the good guys, but my dating life sucked.

That would all change at college, I was sure. I'd meet someone fantastic and fall in love. That had always been my plan, what I'd dreamed of when no one invited me to dances. I was going to be a late bloomer but I was going to bloom spectacularly.

Glancing around, I spotted a trash can a couple of feet away. I crushed the cup and lobbed it—

Missed. For some reason it irritated me. I should be able to hit a trash can. I wandered over, bent down to pick up the cup. The world spun and I staggered back a couple of steps.

"Whoa, brainiac. Careful." A strong hand gripped my upper arm, steadied me, and managed to send a shiver of awareness through me.

I jerked my head up to find myself staring up at Fletcher Thomas. Staring *up* at him because, at six foot three, he was one of the few guys taller than I was. The lights from the Japanese lanterns circling the pool barely reached him. It was almost as though he hadn't quite escaped the darkness from which he'd emerged. His black-as-midnight hair was shaggy, long. His dark brown eyes were almost invisible in the night. Stubble shadowed his jaw, making him seem unreasonably dangerous, although his reputation managed to do that for him.

I was pretty sure that he would eventually end up in prison. When he bothered to make an appearance at school, he was usually sporting bruises or scrapes, grinning broadly as he said, "You should see the other guy." He seemed to live for getting into trouble.

"Thanks, but I'm fine. I don't need help." Irritated, I worked my arm free of his grasp. How dare he mock my intelligence, which I doubted he had much of? As a member of the honor society, I was obligated to tutor at the school a couple of nights a week. I'd spent many a night waiting for Fletcher Thomas to show up for a math tutorial.

He couldn't be bothered, so if he didn't graduate, he got what he deserved. "And there is nothing wrong with being smart. You should try it sometime."

"Hey now, retract the claws. I was just trying to save you the embarrassment of a face-plant."

"While insulting me at the same time. Or trying to. I'm actually quite proud of my academic record." Could I sound any more like a snob? There went my mouth again, social cues disengaged.

He didn't seem the least bit offended. His eyes were twinkling like he found me humorous, and that irritated me even more. I took a long swallow of my drink, hoping he'd take the hint and go away.

"You know that drink is about three-fourths whipped cream vodka, right?" he asked.

I licked my lips, savoring the taste. "So?"

"So the reason it tastes like candy is to get girls drunk."

"I'm not drunk." I took another long swallow to prove my point, even though I realized I was way more relaxed than I should have been standing in the presence of a guy who had a reputation for showing girls a good time in the backseat of a car. Although I'd never figured out the car part, since he rode a motorcycle. Maybe he took them to the junkyard and found some beat-up vehicle there.

"Isn't this party a little wild for you?" he asked. "Figured read-a-thons were more your style."

"Guess you don't know everything," I said.

"Oh, I know plenty, genius," he said.

"I'm a few IQ points shy of being a genius. Your trying to goad me by referring to my intelligence is a little juvenile."

One side of his mouth curled up into a grin and his gaze swept over me as though he was measuring me up for something that was definitely not childish. My stomach did this little tumble like I was back in gymnastics class—which I'd left behind during seventh grade when I'd shot up to a ridiculous height of five foot ten, well on my way to the six feet I'd finally top out at. Gymnasts are usually small, but then so are most guys in seventh grade. And eighth. And ninth. It wasn't until tenth that some started catching up to me. I hated towering over them.

"You're graduating first in the class, aren't you?" he asked, surprising me with what seemed like genuine admiration in his tone. That and his smile made it hard to hold on to my annoyance with him.

"Third." The announcement had come a few weeks earlier. "Lin Chou and Rajesh Nahar are one and two."

"You got robbed."

Was he sticking up for me? It was kind of sweet, but I also knew that I hadn't gotten "robbed."

"Not really. They're way smarter than I am." Which he would know if he was in any of our advanced classes.

And I didn't mind coming in third. It meant that I didn't have to give a speech during the graduation ceremony, but my grades were still high enough that I could get into any state-funded college I wanted—and the one I wanted was in Austin. I'd been accepted a month ago. I couldn't wait until mid-August when I could head down there and be surrounded by people who cared about academics and grades as much as I did. I took another long swallow of the dreamsicle.

He narrowed his eyes. "You should go easy on that."

"I'm not a novice to alcohol."

"So that's not why you staggered earlier?"

"Just lost my balance."

He brought a brown bottle up to his lips and gulped down beer. I hadn't even noticed he had one until that moment. When I realized I was transfixed by the way his throat worked as he swallowed, I lowered my gaze and noticed how his black T-shirt clung to a sculpted chest, washboard abs, and hard-as-rock biceps. Suddenly I felt warm. Why was I noticing these things? I couldn't deny that he *looked* hot, and while I'd come here hoping to catch a guy's attention, I just didn't want it to be some guy with whom I had absolutely nothing in common. I knew he'd been held back at least one year, so studying wasn't a priority for him like it was for me. Fletcher tossed his empty bottle back into a bush.

"Don't you care about the environment?" I scolded him.

"You're not one of *those*, are you?" he asked.

Ignoring his question, I walked over to the bushes, crouched, and tried to see into the darkness, but I suddenly felt light-headed and dropped to my butt.

Fletcher hunkered beside me, balancing on the balls of his feet, his forearms resting on his jean-clad thighs. How did he manage that? I'd bet money he'd already swigged down way more than I had. "You okay?"

"Yes, just—" I realized that I'd finished off my drink. Everything suddenly looked far away, like I was viewing it through a tunnel. The cup slipped from my fingers and onto the grass.

"You need some fresh air," he said.

"We're outside," I pointed out. "It doesn't get any fresher than that."

His fingers folded around my elbow and I was struck by how large his hand was, how strong, how warm against my skin. With no effort at all, he helped me to my feet. "It's better by the lake."

He curled his arm around my shoulders, pulled me in just a little, and I had this insane thought that we fit together like pieces of a puzzle. I liked his height compared to mine. He made me feel normal, when I often felt like a giant. He guided me over the uneven expanse of land that led down to the lake. When we reached the bank, he didn't release his hold, and while I wouldn't admit it to him, I was grateful because suddenly nothing seemed solid beneath my feet.

I knew I'd had too much alcohol too fast on a too-empty stomach. Snacks weren't nearly as abundant around here as the drinks.

"Take a deep breath," Fletcher ordered.

I did, and I could smell the brine of the lake, the sweetness of the wildflowers, the dankness of the dirt, and Fletcher. His was an earthy fragrance, nothing artificial, all male. With his arm around me, he was overpowering my senses, until he was almost the only thing I was aware of.

"Better?" he asked.

"Yeah." There did seem to be more air here. I could hear the breeze stirring the leaves in the trees around us, feel it wafting over my skin. I turned slightly in his embrace until we were nearly facing each other. His nearness was making me dizzy. His hand came up to cradle the back of my head, and he settled my face into the crook of his shoulder. I had that same crazy faraway thought that we fit. I could hear his heart pounding—felt it thumping through his chest, sending tiny little shivers over my face.

"Don't drink if you can't handle your liquor," he said, his voice low enough that it didn't disturb the chirping crickets. "There is always some guy willing to take advantage."

"Like you?" I asked.

"Exactly like me."

I didn't know why I had this crazy thought that if he leaned down to kiss me, I wouldn't object. He had a reputation for being an amazing kisser. But he wasn't leaning in. Was I really so unappealing that even a guy with no standards wouldn't at least try? Still, I felt obligated to say, "Taking advantage of me would be stupid. My dad's a cop. He carries a gun."

"I'm well aware."

I thought I heard sadness, secrets, in his voice, but that made no sense. Nothing made sense. I was having a difficult time thinking, trying to remember why I was out here at the lake with Fletcher Thomas. The world was spinning, fast, so terribly fast, from his nearness, his scent, his warmth—

No, I realized with horror. Not from anything to do with him. From the vodka and whatever else had been mixed into the drinks. I shoved myself away from him and, to my everlasting mortification, I hurled.

Okay, so I'd lied earlier. I *was* a novice at drinking. I'd had a few sips of beer at other parties, but when your dad keeps a Breathalyzer kit in his car, it's not a good idea to come home in a state that might cause him to use it.

A large, warm hand came to rest lightly on my back. It traveled up my spine and down.

"Breathe deep."

"Deeply," I forced out through my tingling mouth.

"What?"

"Deeply. Adverbs follow verbs."

"Seriously? You're giving me a grammar lesson in the middle of your barfing?"

With as much dignity as I could muster, I straightened. "I'm finished."

And horrified that I'd made such a spectacle of myself in front of him.

"I'll give you a ride home," he said.

Everything in me screamed, "Bad idea!"

Or maybe I was screaming it out loud because he said, "Look, I won't take advantage of you being drunk. Besides, your dad has a gun."

With a wry smile, I peered over my shoulder at him. The world wasn't spinning as fast, but I still felt awful. I wanted to go home. I could probably find Kendall, talk her into leaving the party. Jeremy would take us to her house, and from there, I could walk past the six houses to mine. But why spoil her evening just because drinking too fast had spoiled mine?

"You've been drinking," I pointed out. On second thought, so had Jeremy. I was going to have to call a cab.

"I'm fine to drive."

Bad-boy Fletcher, not drunk? I didn't think so. I backed up a couple of steps. "Close your eyes and walk toward me in a straight line."

"Any line I walk is going to look crooked to you, because you're the one who's drunk."

That was probably true. Maybe. I was finding it hard to think coherently. And I didn't really want to explain arriving home in a cab. "Yeah, okay, I'd appreciate it."

He gave me a long look and that corner of his mouth hitched up again. "So . . . are you a *novice* at riding a motor-cycle?"

I considered lying, but I was past the point of thinking anything I did was going to impress him. Not that I wanted to. "It'll be my first time."

His grin grew wider. "I like taking girls on their first ride."

I flushed. I didn't want to think about how I was one of many he'd given a ride to. Besides he was just being nice because he knew I wasn't feeling well. It wasn't like he was interested in me or anything. I'd just hurled in front of him, after all.

As we walked toward the front of the house, I tried to fire off a text to Kendall to let her know I was leaving. It was easier than trying to find her. Or it should have been. My fingers kept hitting the wrong keys. Normally I could text and walk at the same time. Not tonight. I staggered to a stop and started over.

"What are you doing?" Fletcher asked.

"I need to let Kendall know I'm heading home so she isn't looking for me later. Dang it! Stupid autocorrect."

"Dang it?" He chuckled. "Such harsh language, Grandma. Give it here."

He plucked my phone from me. In spite of the fact that his hands were much larger than mine, his fingers thicker, he didn't seem to have any trouble typing. I heard the *swoosh* of a message being sent. He handed the phone back to me and I glanced at the screen.

Hot guy giving me ride. Catch U l8r.

I released a tiny shriek. "That's not what I wanted to say. And you're so not hot."

"It's eighty degrees out. Course I'm hot."

His hand rested lightly on the nape of my neck, and he led me over to an assortment of coolers near the patio. Some guys standing nearby hooted, whistled, and gave him a thumbs-up.

"What'd you do?" I asked.

"What?" Fletcher asked.

I made a half-wave toward the guys. "They seem excited for you."

"They're drunk idiots. They get excited about every-thing."

Ignoring them, he reached into a cooler and handed me a bottle of water. As we continued on, I swished water around my mouth and spewed it out a couple of times before drinking. It was nice to get rid of any lingering aftertaste from my embarrassing performance by the lake. When we got to where his motorcycle waited, he took the bottle and dropped it into a nearby trash can.

"The environment thanks you," I told him.

"Don't make a big deal out of it. It was right there." Fletcher lifted the helmet off the seat and held it out to me.

"I can't wear that," I said. "It's yours and if we crash—"

"We're not going to crash." His voice held impatience, his hands not so much as he worked the helmet over my head and secured the chin strap. He straddled the bike and patted the area behind him. "Come on, Einstein. You can figure this part out."

Yeah, I could. I settled in behind him. Reaching back, he took my hands and pulled my arms around him. He was so sturdy, all muscle and sinew. Not an ounce of fat. I really wished I wasn't noticing that. It made me sound breathless when I gave him my address.

"Got it," he said. "Hold on tight."

"Tightly," I corrected.

"Whatever, Hemingway." He fired up the bike and the

roar rumbled through me. He revved the engine, and I cringed with the realization so much power was beneath us. "Ready?" he yelled.

I tightened my hold, locked my fingers together so nothing could separate us, nodded, then realized he couldn't see that so I yelled, "Yeah!"

He took off, and I clung to him as though I'd never let him go. I heard his deep laughter echoing around me, felt the wind rushing over my face. The force of it sobered me. I figured this was why he liked giving girls their first ride, because it was at once both terrifying and exhilarating and caused them to hang on tighter. I was acutely aware of the scent of him filling my nostrils, the warmth of his skin seeping through his clothes.

As the world whizzed by, I snuggled more closely against him. It was hard to believe that I was *here*—on his bike. We were on the opposite ends of almost every spectrum known to man. Or at least every "Who's Your Perfect Match?" quiz I took in teen magazines. He would be at the bottom of the list. I wanted someone smart, motivated, nice—

I furrowed my brow. He'd been nice tonight, sticking around when I got sick, giving me a ride home. Straight home. We arrived long before I was ready to give up the experience of riding a bike.

Fletcher pulled into the driveway. I peeled myself away

from him, swung my leg back, and scrambled off the seat.

"Fun?" he asked.

I released a small laugh and smiled. "It was awesome." Much steadier on my feet now, I unbuckled the helmet and held it out to him. He took it and set it down, then gently cradled my cheek with one hand and stroked my lower lip with his thumb.

"You've got a nice smile," he said quietly, as though he was totally surprised by it.

Suddenly I was feeling dizzy again, but it had nothing to do with alcohol, and had everything to do with the way Fletcher was studying me as though he was going to be tested about every facet of my face Monday morning at school and would have to draw it from memory. I knew his reputation, knew girls fell over themselves if he snapped his fingers, and I wondered why he'd approached me tonight. Did he have a secret crush on me? Had he thought tonight might be his last chance to make a move? Was he going to kiss me? Did I want him to? Yes, yes I did.

He sat there so still, the engine rumbling. And the way he was looking at me . . . No guy had ever looked at me so intensely, with such a magnetic pull. Right then, I was pretty sure that he wanted to kiss me. That something special, magical was happening between us.

"I'll wait," he said, and it was like a moment from a movie. *I'll wait until you're ready. I'll wait forever. I'll wait until you're finished with college. I'll be right here.*

"Till you get inside," he finished.

I snapped back to reality.

Obviously I had not sobered at all if I thought Fletcher Thomas was going to wait for me any longer than two minutes. Or that he was even contemplating kissing me. Or that anything special was developing between us. As I backed up, his hand slid away, and I felt this pang of grief, as though I'd lost something. What was wrong with me?

"Uh, thanks for the ride," I said.

"Anytime." He didn't smile, just studied me somberly as though I'd somehow disappointed him.

"Be careful driving," I said, backing up another step.

"Always am."

I took two steps toward the house, stopped, swung back around. "Do you even know my name?"

"Einstein."

I growled. He didn't know my name, didn't know who I was. He'd just seen a girl . . . only he hadn't made any moves. I was pretty sure I was going to be mortified when I was sober.

Then because I really didn't want to leave and I wasn't sure why, I turned on my heel and rushed toward the front door. I took the keys from my pocket, fumbled with them, and had to try three times to get the door unlocked. I stepped inside and closed the door behind me, leaned against it, and waited a minute, two, three—

Finally I heard Fletcher throttle the engine and leave.

And nearly jumped out of my skin when my cell phone barked. Kendall insisted I use that ringtone for her since she loved dogs.

"Yeah?" I whispered, trying to slow down my heartbeat.

"Where are you?" she asked harshly.

"Home."

Mom stepped out of the family room where she'd probably been watching TV while waiting for my return. She always tried to be casual about it, like she couldn't wait another day to watch a particular movie or show, but I knew she was just concerned when I was out late at night.

"Hold up," I said to Kendall. I smiled at Mom and said unnecessarily, "I'm home."

"Did you have fun?"

"Oh, yeah. I'll tell you about it tomorrow. I'm heading to bed."

"Sweet dreams." I couldn't help but smile, because I had a thousand memories of her saying those words to me. She'd probably say them when I was fifty. And they would still fill me with a sense of warmth and security.

Heading up the stairs, I returned my attention to Kendall. "Didn't you get my text?"

"Yes, but it did *not* say the hot guy was Fletcher Thomas."

"How do you know who it was?"

"Someone saw you leave with him. God, Avery, your reputation is toast."

"Nothing happened." I stepped into my bedroom, closed the door behind me, crossed over to my bed, and flopped backward onto it.

"No one is going to believe that. Everyone knows he doesn't give girls free rides."

"Well, he did tonight. I drank too much. Threw up. Trust me. The most desperate-to-get-laid guy at school would not have found me attractive. And Fletcher isn't desperate."

Silence. I could almost hear the wheels turning in her head. Finally, she said, "*Nothing* happened?"

"Nothing."

"Wow, that's not the Fletcher I know."

"Do you really know him?" I asked.

"I know his reputation. Same thing."

Was it? Before tonight I would have agreed with her, but now I wasn't so sure. Because if he expected something in return when he gave a girl a ride—even if it was only a kiss—why hadn't he tried to collect from me? Why was I bothered that he hadn't? "Where are you anyway?" I asked Kendall, trying to get my mind off these disturbing thoughts.

"In the car with Jeremy. I got worried when I heard

about who you'd left with. Why didn't you come find us?"

"I didn't want to ruin your fun. Sounds like I did that anyway."

"No. Jeremy was getting hungry. We're going to hit an all-night breakfast place. Want us to stop by and get you?"

"Thanks, but I'm really tired."

"Okay, I'll see you at school Monday. One more week."

I grinned. "Yeah, one more week."

Setting the phone aside, I stared at the ceiling. I tried not to think about Fletcher, but suddenly he was all I could think about. I'd never really talked with him, but he was kind of funny, and I'd actually enjoyed bantering with him. Although I couldn't figure out why he'd approached me. I was known as being the good girl of school. Had he seen me as a challenge?

Suddenly I was confused. I hadn't wanted him to put any moves on me, but my pride was a little hurt that he hadn't. Even the bad boy of Memorial High didn't want to kiss me.

With a groan I rolled over and covered my head with a pillow. Graduation could not come soon enough.

Chapter 2

FLETCHER

I did know her name.

I'd known it since sophomore year when I'd gotten held back because I'd missed too many classes to meet the state requirement for attendance. Even when the counselor warned me that I couldn't have any more absences, I hadn't cared. I'd been too embarrassed to show up to school with bruises.

When I was a sophomore for the second time, I'd spotted her in the hallway, all bouncy and happy. Pretty in a simple way. She didn't paint her eyes or her lips or her cheeks. She didn't look like a plastic doll. She appeared real and touchable.

She'd said hi to me in the hallway as though I didn't have a reputation for trouble, as though I wasn't a year older than everyone else in the class, as though I mattered.

But then slowly the wariness crept in. I knew she was hearing the rumors, accepting them as truth. The smiles and greetings became fewer. Then they were completely gone.

I didn't know why I'd come to her rescue tonight. The irony was that she'd never realize that I had. Which was probably for the best.

Most girls loved when I gave them attention. But not Avery Watkins. She was smarter than four hundred and forty-eight people in our graduating class. And she threw around fancy words like *novice*. She was probably waiting for Mr. Right—someone equally good, naive, and smart, which I definitely was not.

We hadn't had many chances to talk over the years. Had no classes together, and other girls were usually occupying my time in the hallways. I hadn't expected Avery to stand up to me the way she did. Or maybe it had all been the booze talking, making her daring.

Didn't matter. It wasn't like we'd be crossing paths in the future.

I needed to stop thinking about her, figure out what I wanted to do for the rest of the night. I could always go back to the party, but it had been kind of boring, and none of the girls there had really caught my interest.

Except for Avery. And here I was thinking about her again. Her long, willowy body, the way her head fit in the crook of my shoulder, the way I could slip my arm around her without having to hunch over. I liked that she was tall. I liked the way her blond hair caught the moonlight. There hadn't been enough light for me to see the color of her eyes, and I'd never paid particular attention before. But I'd still seen the irritation in them when I first approached her— and the sparkle when she climbed off my bike.

The sparkle made me want to kiss her. I almost had.

What a mistake that would have been.

Chapter 3

AVERY

The next morning, when I woke up, before I even opened my eyes, I felt like I was being tossed by great rolling waves. I squeezed my eyes shut tighter, but the sensation wouldn't stop. Taking a deep breath, trying to center myself, I realized it was only my bed moving. I groaned. My head was way too fuzzy and my stomach could not handle this movement.

"Hey, squirt, stop it," I ordered, glaring at Tyler. His dark hair did a couple of extra flops into his eyes even after he quit bouncing next to me on the mattress.

"Time for lunch." He gave me a big-toothed grin. "Dad's grilling."

I shifted slowly until I was sitting up and scrubbed my hands over my face. "Shouldn't you be out there helping him?"

He jerked his head up and down, but his big brown eyes were sparkling with mischief. "His summer project is here."

Every summer my dad fostered an at-risk kid, helped them to see that life could be better than what they'd had. It was how I ended up with a brother eleven years younger than me. Tyler's mom had been into drugs. He lived with us a couple of summers ago, stole our hearts, and my parents adopted him. Usually, though, we only served as a halfway house.

"Girl or boy?" I asked, because I could tell Tyler was bursting with the news. Usually Dad waited until school was out. Maybe he wanted this kid to see my graduation as an example of what one could do. Who knew? All I really knew was that I felt too rotten to make nice to some little kid I'd never met before.

"Boy." Tyler beamed. Then he scrunched up his face. "Doesn't say much, though."

"You were quiet when you first came here," I reminded him. "He just needs to get used to being around us."

He shrugged his bony shoulders. "I guess."

Reaching out, I ruffled his dark hair. "It'll be okay. Now I need to get dressed."

"'Kay." He slid off the bed and grumbled, "I don't think he'll play with me."

"He may have never had toys or friends. We'll teach him."

He wandered out of the room and, as usual, failed to close my door. As gingerly as possible, I clambered out of bed, shut the door, and headed into the bathroom that separated my bedroom from Tyler's. Briefly I wondered why anyone thought drinking alcohol was a good idea.

I turned on the shower, stood under a stream of hot water, and let it wash away the cobwebs. As I began to feel like maybe I wasn't going to die, my thoughts drifted to my last moments with Fletcher. Did he ever get within a foot of a girl and not kiss her? So why hadn't he kissed me?

Pressing my forehead to the tile, I wondered if I could be any more superficial—wanting a kiss just so I could say that I had one that wasn't prompted by a dumb game. But it had been more than that. For a few seconds after I got off his bike, it seemed a connection was forming between us. I really thought he was going to kiss me, that he wanted to kiss me. To my utter mortification, I had *wanted* him to kiss me. But why would he when I'd barfed in front of him?

I had to have misread him. He probably had no desire whatsoever to kiss me. I could only hope that I hadn't stood there looking all doe-eyed, like I was waiting for him to make a move. Thank goodness, I would probably never ever cross paths with him again. We had no classes together, and we had only one more week of school. The odds were in my favor that I'd never see him again.

Last night could be forgotten, would never come back to bite me in the butt.

I got out of the shower. After drying off quickly and pulling my blond hair back into a ponytail, I slipped into white shorts, a purple tank top, and sparkly flip-flops. Then I headed downstairs.

I always looked forward to Dad's summer projects. In his line of work, he encountered a lot of kids with less than stellar parents. Even so, being taken away from your family and familiar surroundings—no matter how much they might suck—wasn't an easy thing. The unknown was scary, so we worked to make the kids feel secure. Usually they were preteen. Dad would get them on a baseball team. Mom would take them clothes shopping. Tyler taught them to rock at video games. I took them to museums and parks, read to them, and offered them a sisterly ear whenever they needed it.

I hit the entryway and bounced through the dining room into the bright yellow kitchen. Sunlight streamed in through the windows. I could hear Mom's laughter outside. I opened the door that led onto the back deck and staggered to a stop—

Stared up into familiar brown eyes, although one was decorated with a mosaic of dark bruises that hadn't been there when he'd given me a ride home the night before.

"What are you doing here?" I asked, totally confused.

He'd ridden off—without giving me a kiss. I was never supposed to see him again. Ever.

"Fletcher's staying with us this summer," Dad said.

All the breath left my body. Fletcher Thomas was
Dad's project?

How had that happened? If he were a little kid, I would
smile, hug him, and tell him that I was glad he was here.
But this was Fletcher. A guy who had seen me at my worst.
A guy who attracted trouble.

Keeping his eyes on me but shifting his stance,
Fletcher looked as though he didn't know what to say any
more than I did. My parents were studying us, and Tyler
was looking up at me with expectation. I was supposed to
be setting an example for him, so I smiled brightly and
said, "It's . . . great to have you here."

His eyes never leaving mine, he said, "Thanks."

But what I heard was, "Liar."

Mom touched his shoulder. "Why don't you relax by
the pool while we finish getting lunch ready?"

He shifted his gaze to her. "Thanks."

That seemed to be the extent of his vocabulary this
morning. Not that I blamed him. I felt like I had dropped
into an alternate universe. He probably felt the same. He
gave me one last glance before heading for the pool. Mom
took Tyler into the kitchen, since it was his job to help her
get plates and condiments together. Dad wandered over to

his grill. I followed Dad.

"He's eighteen," I told him as the burgers sizzled while he turned them, the smoke rising to tease my nostrils. "Legally an adult. Not your usual summer project."

"He's not a project," Dad said. "We're just providing him with an opportunity to get his act together. He'll stay in the FROG."

The FROG was our nickname for the apartment over the garage or, as Dad had designated it, Free Room Over Garage. Visiting guests usually stayed there, so they could have a little more privacy.

I glanced over to where Fletcher was sprawled on a lounge chair by the pool. Even though he looked relaxed, I could see his muscles were bunched with tension.

"How well do you know him?" Dad asked.

I jerked my attention back to blue eyes the same shade as mine. I didn't want to reveal how well I'd gotten to know him last night, because I was pretty sure that Dad wouldn't approve of how Fletcher's bringing me home had come about. I shrugged. "We go to the same school, don't have the same classes. I've seen him around. What did you arrest him for?"

"We're not going to discuss how he came to my attention." Dad flipped a burger onto a bun. "Make him feel welcome."

My first instinct was to pull my cell phone from my

shorts pocket and text Kendall. She was not going to believe this.

Instead I wandered over to the pool and sat on the edge of the lounge chair that was next to Fletcher's. He was sporting sunglasses now, but I could still see his bruises fanning out over his cheek. "I should see the other guy, right?"

One corner of his mouth hitched up slightly. "Relax, Big Bang. I won't be staying long."

It took everything within me not to growl. I wasn't ashamed of how smart I was, but it didn't define me. "If that's a reference to *The Big Bang Theory* then I guess you would be Penny."

The curl of his lips hiked up a little higher. "Well played."

I took satisfaction in having bested him. He was the last guy in the world that I cared about impressing, but somehow he totally messed up my thinking.

"Say, listen, you didn't mention to my dad about last night . . . um, you know, the *drinking*?" I had no success not squirming.

"I'm not a snitch."

"Okay." Not that I thought he was, but what did I know about him? "So why did you say you wouldn't be staying long?"

"Got plans."

"What? You mean after graduation? What plans?"

"Heyyyy!" Tyler catapulted himself at me, nearly knocking me off the chair. I was used to his rambunctiousness, though, so I was able to quickly right myself. Scrambling behind me like a little monkey, he peered at Fletcher. "What happened to your eye?"

Fletcher adjusted his glasses on the bridge of his nose. "Got into it with a werewolf."

"Really?" Tyler asked eagerly.

"No," I said. "Werewolves don't exist."

"They might."

"They don't, and you're not supposed to ask questions about someone's ouchie."

"Why?"

"Because it's not polite."

"I got an ouchie, too." He stuck out his leg to reveal a Spider-Man bandage on his knee.

"Looks like it hurt," Fletcher said.

Tyler nodded solemnly. "I cried. Did you?"

"Nah. Didn't hurt that bad."

"You want a Wolverine Band-Aid?" Tyler asked. "It makes ouchies go away."

"Thanks, but my magic sunglasses are taking care of it."

Dad hollered that the burgers were ready. Tyler was rushing to the deck before I even stood up. Fletcher got up, too. One of us misjudged the distance, because we were suddenly standing so close that I could feel the heat radiating off him. I felt a need to say something, anything. "You can use the pool whenever you want."

"Don't have a bathing suit."

"You don't need one."

His eyebrows shot up over the frame of his sunglasses. "You want me to swim nude?"

"What? No! You can wear gym shorts or cutoffs. Or whatever."

My face burning with the misunderstanding, I started walking toward the deck. He fell into step beside me.

"Sooo," he began, "*you* ever go skinny-dipping in it?"

I couldn't look at him. My cheeks were probably apple red by now. "Uh, no. My parents wouldn't approve, and there's a little kid around."

"Late at night, in the dark, who'd see?"

My stomach fluttered as an image flashed through my mind of him and me in the pool late at night sans clothes. But that was never going to happen, especially since he didn't even consider me kiss-worthy. I needed to regain control of this conversation that had somehow jumped the track. "Just because you don't get caught doesn't mean it's not wrong. And before Tyler interrupted us you were on the verge of telling me about your plans after graduation."

"No, I wasn't, but nice try."

"Sit here, Fletcher, sit here!" Tyler cried, patting the seat beside him, which caused relief to swamp me, because that meant Fletcher wouldn't be sitting by me.

Instead, he was across from me. Somehow that was worse. I was all too aware of him watching me. Lunch was burgers, hot dogs, and awkward conversation. Fletcher didn't open up to my parents any more than he opened up to me. But since they were both accustomed to dealing with troubled kids, they gave him space.

Cleanup was my chore. Since we'd used paper plates, it only took me about ten minutes—and it only took me that long because I spent at least a minute watching Fletcher walk in a loose-jointed way to the gate that took him to the side of the house and the studio apartment above the garage that was now designated as his.

Then I texted Kendall and told her I needed a trip to I-Scream—with just her.

"Wait a minute. Fletcher Thomas is your dad's summer project?" Kendall asked as she set her spoon into a malted-milk-balls mixer that included vanilla and chocolate ice cream and stared at me. "Did he know that last night? Is that why he gave you a ride home?"

I considered that, shook my head. "I don't think so. I think he crossed paths with Dad afterward because

Fletcher's face is all bruised like he got into a fight after he dropped me off."

"What a loser." She returned her attention to her ice cream.

I didn't like her harsh assessment. It didn't matter that twenty-four hours earlier I'd probably have thought the same thing. "He's kinda funny."

"What? In a stand-up comic kind of way?"

"No." I took a bite of my sundae. We were sitting in a booth that overlooked the street. I loved this place. Pictures of carousels and carousel horses were everywhere. I wasn't sure how that fit in with the theme of screaming for ice cream, but it was a bright shop that always made me happy. "He just says things that make me smile, even though I know I shouldn't. I never really had a conversation with him before. I mean, I've seen him around, knew who he was, knew his reputation for getting into trouble. But I don't know. He's just different than I expected. And he's really good with Tyler." It had surprised me that he hadn't brushed Tyler off when he was pestering him about his bruises.

"I'm always seeing him with different girls, so he's a commitment-phobe. Unlike Jeremy, who is as loyal as a golden retriever."

I laughed. "Would Jeremy appreciate that comparison?"

"Goldens are great. My favorite dog." She chomped on her crunchy ice cream mixture.

"This week," I teased.

"Yeah, I can be fickle about which dog is my favorite, but not about Jeremy. He is my everything. But we're not here to discuss me. We're here to discuss how you are going to survive a trouble magnet living in your house." Her curly red hair flowed around her shoulders. In spite of her coloring, she didn't have a lot of freckles because she did everything to protect her skin from the sun.

"He's not actually in the house," I explained. "He's in the apartment over the garage."

"Can't blame your parents for taking those precautions. I heard he started shoplifting in middle school."

I remembered hearing that, too. Someone we went to school with had seen Fletcher hauled out of the store by the cops. Now I had to wonder if one of those cops had been my dad when he was still a patrolman.

"I wouldn't want him walking my hallways late at night," Kendall continued.

I shrugged, suddenly uncomfortable with her assessment. "We don't know for sure he shoplifted."

She gave me a pointed stare. "Really?"

"Look, it was a couple of years ago. Whatever. I don't think my parents are worried about him stealing. I think they gave him the FROG so he could have some privacy.

It's difficult living with people you don't know." Every summer I adjusted to a new person within the family. I didn't mind because I knew we were doing some good, but sometimes it was a challenge. This summer especially was going to fit that description. "By the way, I'm not sure Dad wants everyone to know he's living with us, so don't tell anyone. I just told you so that if you come over you won't be freaked out."

"I don't freak out."

"Okay, so maybe I was freaking out and just needed to talk. But still, it's just between us. You know how my parents are about protecting the kids they bring to the house."

"But Fletcher's not really a kid."

"Still, the same rules apply."

"I won't tell a soul, well, except Jeremy, but he won't tell anyone."

I watched my ice cream melting. I wasn't really in the mood for it. "Fletcher says he's not staying long. I probably shouldn't have even told you, but I needed to talk about it because he's not my dad's usual project."

"Just don't make him yours."

I jabbed my spoon into my ice cream and glared at her. "What does that mean?"

"I know you want a boyfriend and I know it's been hard for you since Jeremy and I got together."

I gritted my teeth and took a deep breath. I didn't often

get irritated with Kendall, but her comment had struck a nerve.

"I'm happy for you," I assured her. "And I don't want a boyfriend. I want the right boyfriend. I figure I've waited a long time, so he'll probably be the one and only, someone worth waiting for."

"At college. After this week, we'll start the countdown for that."

I loved Kendall, I really did, but I wanted my life to be more than a series of countdowns.

Chapter 4

FLETCHER

This was such a bad idea.

Last night when Avery's dad had said, "You're coming with me," in that authoritative voice he had, I'd packed my duffel bag without complaint because I understood that the alternative was a lot worse.

Now, sitting on a couch in a room over a garage, I felt like I was losing control over my life. Detective Watkins had laid down rules about curfews and behavior under his roof. I wasn't used to all that. I came and went as I wanted. No one cared. Now suddenly there were expectations. Not that I didn't appreciate what he was doing for me, but he could loosen the chains a bit.

I'd felt really uncomfortable during lunch, with his wife asking me questions about what I was going to do after graduation—like I had plans. My plans usually revolved around just getting through the next day. I hadn't thought much beyond that. I probably needed to. Avery no doubt had.

When she'd stepped onto the deck and seen me, she'd looked horrified. I'd discovered that she had incredible blue eyes. A rich hue that was almost violet, circled in black. I'd never seen eyes like that before.

Although at that particular moment I'd wished I was anywhere other than where I was. I'd wished I wasn't sporting bruises. I'd wished her folks had told her I'd be there before she'd spotted me.

Now I was wishing I hadn't looked out the window when I heard a car drive up twenty minutes after we finished with lunch. I saw Avery take off with Kendall Jones. I could pretty much guess what they'd be talking about. Tomorrow at school, everyone would know I was here.

And that made me want to leave. But I had no choice except to stay.

Chapter 5

AVERY

I tossed the lettuce, tomatoes, cucumbers, and black olives while Mom popped a pan of rolls into the oven. "Should I go ahead and put on the salad dressing?" I asked.

She closed the oven door and set the timer. "No, we'll put out a variety of choices. Don't know what Fletcher likes."

"Do you know anything about Fletcher's dad?" I asked. I knew his mom had died a few years back, but I couldn't recall ever meeting or even seeing his dad.

"That he's pretty much an absent father."

"Is that why Dad brought him here?" I knew Dad would have talked things over with Mom, told her everything, before he offered Fletcher a room over the garage.

"I think your dad just wanted to help him get a good start after high school," she said.

"How did he know about him?"

"Cop stuff."

"Doesn't that make you nervous?" I asked. "Having a criminal so close?" Mom gave me a stare designed to say more about judgment than words ever could. "I know— innocent until proven guilty. But he had to have done something pretty awful to come to Dad's attention."

"People come to your dad's attention for all kinds of reasons. Look at Tyler."

They'd found him in a closet when they raided his crack mom's house. I knew Fletcher hadn't been cowering in a closet. Dad had been open about Tyler's situation. Why was he so closed about Fletcher's? Because of his age? Because I knew him?

"You should go get him," Mom said. "Dinner will be ready in a few."

I stared at her uncomprehendingly for a moment as my mind shifted back to the task at hand.

"Fletcher," she prodded.

"Oh, right."

Less than a minute later, I was standing at the top of the stairs that led to the FROG.

Just because you dread doing something doesn't make you a coward. Just because you do something you dread doesn't make you brave. In my case, I wasn't exactly sure what I was. What I did know was that I really didn't want to knock on Fletcher's door, but since Mom had sent me to get him, I knocked.

The door swung open. With narrowed eyes, Fletcher looked like he was about to commit murder and I would suffice very well as his next victim.

"I'm busy. What do you want?" he asked pointedly.

"Most people greet with a 'Hello. It's good to see you. Come in and visit.'" I had to admit that I wanted to go in and just get a feel for what he might have done with the place. A few years ago when my mom's sister had lost her job, she'd needed somewhere to get back on her feet, so Mom had converted the space over the garage into a little apartment. It had a living area with a bed, a couch in front of the TV, and a desk. There was a bathroom, but no kitchen.

"I doubt you came to visit, so why are you here?" he asked.

"It's time for supper."

"I'm not hungry." He started to close the door in my face. I stuck my foot out, getting a bruised toe in the process, but at least I stopped the door from closing all the way.

"Yeah, that's not happening," I said. "People around here are expected to show up for meals."

"I already ate." He walked into the room, and since the door remained partway open, I took it as an invitation and wandered in.

Fletcher dropped down on the couch, put his booted feet on the short table in front of him, and stared at a baseball game on the TV.

"My mom doesn't like shoes on furniture," I told him.

He just glared harder at the TV, like maybe he thought he could escape into it or something. I was familiar with the tactic. Also knew it never worked. On the table were the empty wrapper from a cream-filled sponge cake, a wadded chip bag, and a package that had once contained salted peanuts. The kind of stuff you picked up from a convenience store.

"This"—I waved my hand over the table—"was your supper?"

"That's some sleuthing there, Veronica Mars."

I came to stand before him, blocking his view of the TV. I knew expressions could be described as storm-clouded. His looked like he was on the verge of erupting into a category-five hurricane. I really didn't care. "My name is Avery. I realize it might be too difficult for you to remember or maybe pronounce, but I'd appreciate it if you'd stop with all the condescending nicknames."

His lips twitched; the storm passed. "Not condescending. I think Veronica Mars is hot."

Was he saying that he thought I was hot? No way, but suddenly I was aware of my face growing warm. I hated that I was probably blushing. Reaching down, I shoved his feet off the table, fought not to cringe at the scratch I'd made. "Look, I didn't want to come get you any more than you wanted to get got, but they expect you at dinner. Let's go."

He studied me like I'd just landed from another planet. His scrutiny made me want to squirm. I didn't know why I was fighting so hard to get him down to supper. If he didn't come with me, Dad would come get him. But for some reason, I didn't want to lose this battle. "Trust me," I said. "It's easier just to do what they expect."

"Easier isn't always the right choice," he said.

I didn't want to discuss philosophy. "In this case it is, but have it your way. I'll leave the door open on my way out since my dad will be here five minutes after I leave."

I headed for the door.

"What did you tell Jones?" he asked.

That stopped me in my tracks. Jones? Slowly I turned. "You mean Kendall?"

"I saw you leave with her. I figured you couldn't wait to start spreading the word that I'm here."

I wanted to tell him that my world didn't revolve around him, but this afternoon it had. "She's my best friend. She spends a lot of time here." Or she did before she started dating Jeremy. "I just didn't want her to be surprised if she ran into you. I'm not telling anyone else."

"Why?"

I blinked. "Why what?"

"Why aren't you Twittering or Facebooking that I'm here?"

I shrugged. "It's nobody's business."

He seemed surprised by my answer, seemed to consider it.

"Look, I'm not judging you," I assured him.

I watched him unfold that long, lean body of his from the couch in one smooth movement that made my heart pound against my ribs.

"You're either a saint or a liar," he said as he sauntered over.

"I'm not a liar."

"Too bad. Liars are way more interesting than saints."

"How would you know?" I asked with what I hoped was a seductive smile. "I doubt you've ever known a saint."

Fletcher dug into Mom's chicken casserole like he thought the apocalypse was about to hit and we'd be without food for eons. Tyler kept peering over at him like he was worried our guest might devour him along with the casserole. Mom asked Fletcher a couple of questions about his classes, which resulted in one-word responses: *Okay. Fine. Fantastic.*

I wondered if he was telling the truth, but if he was, why would he have been assigned to tutoring sessions?

I picked up a bowl. "Green beans?"

He studied me a moment like he was surprised to find me at the table. "No, thanks."

"Do you want some more, Tyler?" I asked.

He shook his head. He loved green beans. Had he said no because of Fletcher? I really hoped he wasn't going to start mimicking our guest. I wondered if Dad had given any thought to the influence Fletcher would have on an impressionable Tyler.

"So I spoke with Pete Smiley," Dad said, his voice suddenly booming out over the table and making us all jump. And I mean all of us, including Fletcher. I didn't figure anything would fracture his calm, uncaring facade. "He's the owner of Smiley's. He's willing to give you a job, Fletcher."

I expected Fletcher to rebel against Dad controlling this particular aspect of his life. Instead he said, "Thanks, 'preciate it."

"Meet me there tomorrow after school. We'll get everything firmed up."

"Yes, sir."

I reminded myself that he wasn't a scared little boy who Dad would handle with kid gloves. He was too old to be influenced by a summer of baseball, hot dogs, and loving arms. Dad was going to be taking a tougher approach. Fletcher no doubt understood the score. If Dad wasn't happy, Fletcher would get booted out, returned to jail, or possibly worse.

"I want a job," Tyler piped up.

Dad grinned. He had a great grin that made his face soften, that made everything about him soften. It was not something he ever took to the office with him. Well, maybe he pulled it out when he was comforting a frightened child. I always knew when he dealt with situations that involved children, because when he came home he hugged me just a little bit harder. "In a few years."

"Yeah, squirt," I said, figuring he was just feeling overlooked by all the attention Fletcher was getting tonight. "Enjoy not working until you have to. Besides, what kind of job could you get? Professional tickler?"

It was funny but when he smiled, I saw Dad's grin. Tyler was adopted but he was taking on Dad's mannerisms. I guess when you love someone sometimes you want to be just like him, and on some things environment can win out over genes.

"I'm a good tickler." Tyler looked up at Fletcher. "What are you good at?"

Fletcher gave Tyler a small smile. "Fixing cars."

I realized Dad had known the answer and that was the reason he'd contacted Mr. Smiley. In spite of the fact that he was sometimes stern, my dad was relatively easy to talk to. It bothered me, though, that he could get information out of Fletcher while I couldn't. "Where'd you learn?" I asked.

As though uncomfortable again, he shifted in his chair. "My dad."

I suddenly wondered how his dad felt about him being here, but I knew he wouldn't answer if I asked with an audience. Probably wouldn't answer anyway. "Yet you drive a motorcycle."

Fletcher went incredibly still and his eyes homed in on me. "It's more fun."

I knew—*knew*—he was thinking about the ride he'd given me and how I'd latched my arms around him as though I'd never let go. My heart did this crazy little thud as I recalled all the sensations I'd experienced last night.

"Can I ride your motorcycle?" Tyler asked.

"Not until you're older," Mom said quickly, as though she thought Fletcher would take Tyler for a ride after dinner. "Much older."

"Why?"

"Because that's the way it is," Dad said, and I fought not to roll my eyes. I hated answers that had no reasoning behind them.

Conversation drifted to Mom's garden, a neighbor who was sick, and the weather. What was noticeably absent was anyone asking anything about Fletcher's dad. Had he gotten caught in layoffs, maybe left town to look for a job elsewhere? Why *was* Dad helping Fletcher out?

When everyone was finished eating, I stood to start clearing off the table. I picked up my plate, Dad's—

"Fletcher, you can help Avery clean up the dishes," Dad announced.

"That's not necessary, Dad," I said. "He's a guest."

"He's not a guest. He's living with us. So he has chores just like everyone else."

I expected Fletcher to toss down his napkin, stand up, and declare that he was out of here. Instead, he stood and followed my lead, grabbing his plate and Tyler's. I was incredibly aware of him walking behind me as I went into the kitchen.

"You can rinse the dishes and put them in the dishwasher," I told him, setting the plates on the counter by the sink. "Everything else requires some knowledge of how Mom likes things done."

Reaching over, I turned on the faucet and grabbed a brush from a mosaic holder I'd made for Mother's Day when I was about six. As I grew older, I realized it was hideously ugly, but Mom still loved it. "Scrape the food into the disposal."

He snagged the brush from my fingers. "Think I can figure it out."

As I watched him scrape food from a plate, I noticed the bunching of his muscles beneath his black T-shirt. I couldn't blame him for being tense again. Dinner had been awkward. I didn't know how to make it easier.

Every now and then, as I put things away, I'd glance over at Fletcher and see him staring through the window that looked out on the backyard and I wondered if he was plotting his escape. His jeans were worn, frayed at the hems. If he had been our usual summer project, Mom would have taken him shopping for clothes. I didn't see that happening. It was weird. I always knew what to expect of my summer. But this summer, I didn't have a clue.

I was wiping down the island, Fletcher the other counters, when Dad walked in. "Avery, why don't you make some popcorn? We're going to have a family movie night."

Fletcher tossed his rag toward the sink and headed for the door.

"That includes you, Fletcher," Dad said.

Fletcher came to an abrupt halt, his sharply defined jaw tightening. "I've got stuff to do."

"It'll wait. We don't get a lot of time to be together during the week, so we make the time Sunday evening," Dad explained. "You're part of the family now." Dad glanced over at me. "Probably ought to make two batches."

Turning on his heel, he strode from the room like everything was settled. He wasn't used to not being obeyed.

Fletcher glared at me like it was my fault that he had

to participate in family night. I shrugged. "It won't be long. Because of Tyler, it'll be a kiddie movie."

"A kiddie movie?" he ground out.

Okay, so maybe that wasn't so reassuring. "Probably something animated."

He shook his head. "I'm not believing this."

"Beats incarceration."

"I'm not so sure."

I headed for the pantry, pointing behind me as I went. "Large bowls are in that cabinet. Why don't you grab a couple?"

I snagged two bags of popcorn, put one in the microwave, and started it up. "So was incarceration an option before my dad brought you here?" I asked casually.

Leaning against the counter, Fletcher crossed his arms over his chest. "What did your dad tell you?"

I rested my hip against the island so we were facing each other. "He won't discuss how he ran into you. Just says you needed a place."

"That pretty much sums it up."

"Your dad's okay with it?"

"Who cares? I'm eighteen."

I couldn't imagine not caring what my dad thought. "You don't get along with him?"

"Look, Twenty Questions, I'm not playing."

The microwave dinged. I pulled out the bag, put the

other one in and began the next process. Shaking the finished bag, listening as the last few kernels popped, I didn't look at him as I said, "Then I'll play. Ask me anything."

I could sense him studying me, and I was already regretting my bold words.

"Are you a *novice* when it comes to guys?" he asked.

I peered over at him and smiled. "Did you learn a new vocabulary word last night?"

He laughed. It was only a short burst of sound, but I liked it. "For the record, I know a lot about guys," I told him.

He looked skeptical. "You ever had a boyfriend?"

"Why the curiosity?" I asked, pouring the popcorn into a bowl.

"Just wondering how much trouble you could have gotten into last night."

I gave him what I hoped was a saucy grin. "Nothing I couldn't have handled."

He seemed to come to attention at that. He gave me an appraising once over. "I heard you'd never spent time alone with a guy."

I wasn't sure how anyone would know that or why it would come up in conversation. The microwave dinged again and I grabbed the second bag. "Not really any of your business."

"So you haven't been alone with a guy."

"I'm alone with a guy right now."

"Not what I meant."

Which I knew, but he was right—playing Twenty Questions was a bad idea. I picked up both bowls. "It's showtime!"

We had a huge flat-screen TV in the family room, and I could tell that Fletcher was impressed. It was hard not to be. Mom and Dad were each in their respective recliners. Tyler was curled on Dad's lap, which left the couch for Fletcher and me to share. If I didn't know better, I'd think my parents were playing matchmaker. But I did know better because my dad was not going to encourage me to get involved with a guy who sported bruises as often as Fletcher did. I knew my parents weren't thinking, were just following habit. Usually I stretched out on the couch.

Fletcher and I sat with a big bowl of popcorn between us. Mom, Dad, and Tyler were close enough to share a bowl. I dragged the afghan my grandmother had made off the back of the couch and draped it over my lap. With a remote, Dad dimmed the lights, then started the movie. *Despicable Me.* Usually I teared up at the end, but this time I was going to have to stay tough. I could just imagine how Fletcher would ride my case.

For the longest time, he sat stiffly at the other end of the couch, his arms crossed over his chest, and glared at the screen, obviously wishing he were somewhere else. Then he started to relax. A scene with the minions made him smile. He dipped his hand into the popcorn bowl where it brushed up against mine.

He went completely still, while my heart thundered inside my chest so hard that I was afraid Dad—or worse, Fletcher—would hear it. The spark that shot up my arm was silly, ridiculous . . . unsettling. The only reason I didn't jerk my hand back was because I figured it would give him some sort of satisfaction. Apparently, completely unaffected, he tiptoed his fingers over mine, before scooping up some popcorn and tossing it into his mouth. His gaze never left the screen, but I had a feeling he wasn't watching the minions as closely, that he was aware of every breath I drew, every tingling nerve ending.

I shifted my body, tucked my legs beneath me, and stared intently at the movie, all the while so incredibly aware of Fletcher. My peripheral vision was suddenly like something a superhero would have. Even in the dimly lit room, I could see how long his eyelashes were. I made out the strong lines of his profile, detected a slight bump in his nose that I'd never noticed before but was more pronounced in silhouette. The remnants of a fight, maybe. I wanted to smack whoever had broken his nose, even knowing that Fletcher had probably started the brawl.

The odd thing was: I thought he was evaluating me just

as closely and it made me want to squirm. At school, he often had his arm slung around some girl's shoulders, and she was usually beautiful. I wasn't slender. I was skinny. Downright skinny, with hollow cheeks and high cheekbones. Freckles dotted a nose that was too big for such a narrow face. I wasn't hideous, but I wasn't drop-dead gorgeous either. Usually it didn't bother me, but then I'd never been scrutinized so thoroughly before.

Why did I care if Fletcher was paying more attention to me than the movie? He wasn't going to make any sort of pass at me. He'd had a chance last night and hadn't taken it. So why was I sitting here wishing we were at a real movie theater, watching a nonanimated flick, sharing popcorn, with his arm around me? This was torture.

As soon as the movie ended, Fletcher shoved himself off the couch like someone had set it on fire. He headed for the door.

"Curfew," Dad barked.

Fletcher turned around, gave a long, slow nod, and said curtly, "Right."

I couldn't imagine that he'd ever had a curfew. On Sunday nights during the school year it was ten o'clock. That was about ninety minutes from now. I figured he could get into a lot of trouble in that time.

He stood there awkwardly, like he thought he should say something more. It made me uncomfortable to see him not exhibiting his usual cockiness. If he had been one of Dad's typical projects, I would have done everything to make him feel at ease in his new surroundings. So why wasn't I doing it?

"Thanks for joining us," I said.

"Sure. Thanks for—" He waved his hand in a semicircle that I figured was meant to encompass the entire day, or at least the movie. "Yeah," he finished, before walking out of the room.

Standing, I folded the afghan and set it over the back of the couch.

"Are you sure this is a good idea, Jack?" Mom asked, once Fletcher was out of hearing range.

"He'll adjust."

Mom looked at me, nodded toward Dad—or more specifically, Tyler, who was still curled on Dad's lap. That was my cue that she wanted to talk without little ears—or my ears—listening.

"Come on, squirt," I said to Tyler as I lifted him in my arms. "Time for bed."

"Read me a story?"

"Absolutely."

A story ended up being three before he finally drifted off, but I didn't mind. Thinking about how much I'd miss him when I went off to college, I wandered into my room. One of my favorite places was the window seat in the corner. One window looked out on the front street, the other overlooked the garage. Sitting on the large purple pillow, I brought my legs up to my chest, wrapped my arms around them, and gazed out at the garage. I didn't think it had been a conscious decision on my part not to turn on the lights, to just let the streetlights and moon illuminate the path I'd taken to the windows, but I did feel a little creepy that Fletcher wouldn't know I was here, wouldn't know I was watching him.

Hunched forward, forearms pressed to his thighs, he was sitting on the top of the steps leading to his apartment. I wondered if he was considering making a break for it. I couldn't blame him. Someone who got into as much trouble as he did probably wasn't used to parental controls. And my dad was all about control.

I watched as he lifted a bottle to his lips, took a long swallow. It looked like a beer bottle. If Dad caught him with that . . .

Wasn't any of my business, but I'd been big sister to about half a dozen kids during my life, and while Fletcher was older than I was, I couldn't quite shrug off my protective nature. With a roll of my eyes and a huff, knowing I was probably going to regret it, I headed outside.

Chapter 6

FLETCHER

I liked listening to the quiet. It wasn't totally without sound, but it was hushed, calm. I could hear the occasional car going down a distant street, a dog barking. I could hear the crickets, the wind rustling leaves in the trees. I could hear the creak of a gate opening, the slap of flip-flops on a cement path.

Avery hesitated at the foot of the stairs. Her reluctance to be here radiated off her in waves. She squared her shoulders and started up. I didn't want to admire her, but I did. She had a strength, a toughness that wasn't immediately visible from the outside. You had to look close. Or closely, I guessed. Verbs, adverbs, adjectives. What did it matter? Words weren't going to change my life.

I'd labeled her a suck-up, a Goody Two-shoes. When the truth was: she was just nice.

I didn't know what to do with nice.

She lowered herself to the step I was sitting on, pressed her shoulder against the railing to put space between us. She was leaning so hard against it that I was surprised the wood didn't splinter and give way. She didn't say anything, just sat there, arms wrapped around her stomach, staring out into the street like it appeared I was doing. Only, I was watching her.

"My dad can be a little overwhelming with his family time," she said softly. "It's his job, I think. There's always a chance when he leaves for work, he won't come back."

"That's morbid."

"But reality. He got shot several years back when he was working undercover, nearly died, so he never takes time with us for granted. I love him, I love that he's attentive, but between you and me, I can't wait to move out, to have some freedom."

I didn't know why my gut clenched at the thought of her leaving. What did I care where she went? Still, I heard myself ask, "When are you going?"

"The fall, when I start college." She seemed to relax, her shoulders rounding slightly. She sighed. "Austin. I'm going to Austin, major in biology, become a doctor. What are you going to do after graduation?"

"Probably get a haircut."

Her head snapped around so fast that I actually heard

her neck pop. Since I was looking at her discreetly, it didn't take much for me to turn my eyes toward her. Her brow was furrowed and her mouth was slightly scrunched up. I didn't think she often looked confused.

"You're kidding, right?" she asked.

I shrugged. "My hair is getting pretty long."

She released a deep sigh and uncurled her body, frustration with me chasing away whatever wariness she'd felt when she first arrived. "Can't you share anything? Why do you have to be so mysterious?"

Because sharing meant opening yourself up to hurt. I wasn't going there, not with her, not with anyone. Instead, I lifted the bottle I held between two fingers and took a deep swig.

"My dad is not going to be happy that you're drinking beer. Where did you get it, anyway?"

"Grocery store." I took another swig.

"How? You're not—" She swiped it out of my hands.

"Hey!" I objected, but I wasn't childish enough to try to get it back.

She examined it more closely. "It's root beer."

"Your powers of deduction are amazing, Sherlock."

She faced me fully. "That's what you were drinking last night. That's why you didn't reek of beer, why you said you were fine to drive."

"You noticed how I smelled?" I asked, although the

truth was that I remembered the strawberry scent of her hair as I held her close.

Ignoring my question, she took a sip, shook her head, released a light laugh that caught on the breeze. "It really is root beer."

"Want me to get you one?" I asked.

"Nah." She offered the bottle back to me.

I finished it off, set it aside. And we both just sat there, looking out. It was a nice neighborhood, nicer than the one I lived in. Mine couldn't even be called a neighborhood really. Just a string of trailers.

"I could cut your hair," she said quietly.

I peered over at her. "Yeah, right, I'm going to let you take scissors to my hair."

She grinned. "Clippers, not scissors. I could use my dad's."

"So I look like a cop? No thanks."

"I wouldn't cut it that short."

"I'll think about it."

"Might help with the job interview tomorrow."

"It's pretty much a done deal, thanks to your dad."

"Yeah, my dad is pretty good at making things happen. Want to know something funny about him?"

I could not imagine there was anything at all funny about her dad, but maybe it would give me some leverage. "Sure."

"He hates donuts."

"He's a cop. They're supposed to live for donuts."

She laughed lightly. "I know, right? But my dad can't stand them, and I love them. When I was little, he'd picked me up from day care and we'd go to the donut shop across the street. We'd sit at the counter. I'd get a donut, he'd get a cup of coffee, and I'd tell him all about my day. The smallest things fascinated him." She linked her fingers together. "I haven't thought about our trips to the donut shop in years."

If I had that kind of memory, I'd think about it every day.

She studied me, and I wondered what she saw. Probably a loser. Most people did.

"I think it's neat that your dad taught you to work on cars," she said. "Is he a mechanic?"

"No, he just liked to tinker. He had a '65 Mustang that he was restoring. I would just sit and watch. One day he let me tighten a nut." I'd been about five. I remembered his hand covering mine on the wrench as he guided my movements. "I was hooked after that."

So maybe I did have some good memories. Like Avery, I'd forgotten to think about them.

"What happened to the Mustang?" she asked.

"He sold it, I guess. I was just a little kid. One day it wasn't there anymore."

"That kinda makes me sad."

Somehow I wasn't surprised. I'd seen her tear up during the movie—over cartoon characters. "My dad isn't sentimental. He probably needed the money. Or maybe it was someone else's car all along. Unlike your dad, he's not a big talker."

"Is that why you don't reveal much? You're like your dad?"

I didn't want to be, but I heard myself say, "Probably."

She sighed. "Yeah, sometimes I think we're more like our parents than we realize or want to be. And on that note, I'll say good night." She stood. "No family movie time tomorrow night."

I wasn't about to admit that I'd enjoyed sitting beside her tonight, watching a sappy movie. I was used to being alone, used to watching out for myself. It was strange to have people around who were trying to take care of me. Meals, chores, movies.

Watching her descend the stairs, I knew I needed to be careful around her. She had a way of making me want to tell her things that I'd never told anyone. That could only lead to trouble.

Chapter 7

AVERY

I didn't know if Fletcher got the notice that we ate breakfast at our house, but he wasn't there when I came downstairs and grabbed a yogurt. As a matter of fact, he wasn't anywhere around and his bike was gone. I couldn't imagine that he'd headed to school early. I told myself it wasn't my business. Maybe he just had stuff to do.

I arrived at school and pulled Trooper—the name I'd given my ancient car because it sounded like it was going to die at any moment but just kept plugging along—into a vacant slot near the back of the parking lot. I grabbed my backpack and walked along the cement path that led to the courtyard where a couple of fountains bubbled.

I didn't spot Kendall on her usual bench, getting in some last-minute kisses with Jeremy—because it was *so* awful not to be with him for three hours before lunch. So I strolled on by. She was probably at her locker. That wasn't too far from mine, and we usually met there to catch up before heading to our first class together. I wanted to tell her that I didn't think Fletcher was as bad as we'd heard. As a matter of fact, I kind of liked him.

Scooter stopped in front of me, blocking my path. "Hey, Avery."

His tone was inviting, friendly. It made me smile. I didn't think he even knew who I was. I'd been at his party but that was because of Jeremy. "Hey, Scooter. Great party Saturday night."

His blue eyes twinkled. "Yeah, I heard you had a good time."

He was talking to someone else about me? He was one of the most popular guys in our class. I had to admit I was flattered. "Loads of fun."

He grinned broadly, his teeth such a bright white that I almost had to put on my sunglasses. "We should hang out sometime."

My jaw almost dropped. He sounded like he really meant it, that he wanted to spend some time with me. "That'd be fun."

He winked. "I'll be in touch." He walked off, those long legs that made him a star on the football field quickly putting distance between us.

I stood there, trying to process what had just happened.

From the moment I'd entered high school, I'd hoped to get some attention from guys. Now, right at the end, a guy was finally showing some interest.

My step was a little lighter as I headed to the building that housed my locker. Wait until I told Kendall about this. She wouldn't believe it.

I was nearly to the door when a guy I didn't know stopped walking and gave me a once-over like he was measuring me for a new outfit. Although he was cute, he made me feel a little uncomfortable. I reached for the door.

"I'll get that," he said. Leaning in, he brushed his shoulder against mine as he pulled open the door. "Avery, right?"

I blinked in surprise. "Right."

"I'm Josh." He grinned. "See you around."

The door closed with us on opposite sides of it before I could ask, "Around what?" That encounter was a little odd. Although I *was* wearing a new blue top that Kendall had assured me was very flattering. . . .

I'd taken four steps inside when Rhys Adams winked at me, like we shared a secret that no one else knew. Our star quarterback doesn't normally wink at me. Maybe he just got something in his eye. Because three guys giving me attention was beyond weird.

Jade—whom he usually winked at—narrowed her eyes at me, or so it seemed. No doubt her contacts were giving her trouble. Or maybe she was still upset from our little encounter at the party. It was hard to tell with her. She seemed perpetually put out with something or someone.

I'd almost reached my locker when Kendall practically barreled into me. "I told you that your reputation would be ruined."

"What are you talking about?"

She grabbed my arm and began propelling me toward the restrooms. "You are not going to believe this."

"What? New toilets in the stalls?"

"Not funny, Avery. So not funny." She shoved open a door, pushed me through. Then seemed surprised that half a dozen girls were standing at the mirrored sinks applying lipstick, eyeliner, or mascara. It was part of the morning ritual for some of them.

"I need to get my books," I told her. "Or I'm going to be late for class."

"What you need to do is listen." She guided me back into the little alcove where the tampon dispenser had been installed, like girls wanted privacy when purchasing feminine hygiene products. "He made a bet with some of the guys at the party. Twenty bucks that he could get into your pants. He collected."

I stared at her. Usually I was good at deciphering what she was saying when she got into one of her speed-talking rolls without her having to repeat herself, but I got stuck on the idea that some guy wanted to get into my pants. "Who?"

"Fletcher," she whispered harshly. "That's why he gave you a ride home."

A cold chill trickled along my spine. My knees went weak. I pressed my back to the tiled wall. I thought about Scooter's smile, Josh's eyes roaming over me, Rhys's wink, Jade's glare. I shook my head. "But like I told you, nothing happened."

"He says it did."

Had I really worried about him last night, gone out to talk with him, comfort him, make him feel welcome? Had I really considered that I could like him?

The girls suddenly rushed out of the bathroom like we were under a zombie attack. But I just stood there like a zombie myself. Even after the first bell rang.

"Come on," Kendall said, shaking me back to life.

"I don't understand why he did that." I staggered for the door, like my brain couldn't connect to my legs. Definitely a zombie.

"Money? Because he's a douche?"

"But we talked. He seemed . . . nice." *He rubbed my back when I threw up.* I grabbed the books I needed for class from my locker, then quickened my pace, grateful that Kendall and I had Advanced Calculus together. And that Scooter, Josh, Rhys, Jade, and especially Fletcher would not be there.

"Well, 'nice is as nice does' is what my mom always says." Her mom often spoke in made-up proverbs. "You need to tell your dad about this. He'll kick him right out of your house. He can't be a project after this. He doesn't deserve your family."

"Don't call him a project here at school. Nobody is supposed to know, remember?"

"Why do you care? He deserves some kind of payback."

"Agreed, but it can't be anything that reflects on my family."

"Fine. My lips are sealed, until I see him. Then I'm going to give him a piece of my mind."

I had a feeling she was going to give him more than a piece.

We stepped into the room just as the tardy bell rang. Why did it sound like it was ringing the death knell on my reputation?

"Almost late, ladies," Mr. Turner said, like it would be news to us.

"Sorry," we both mumbled as we hurried to empty desks at the back of the room.

It was exam week. Because of my grades, I was exempt from every one of the two-hour exams spaced out over four days. I took a novel about a dystopian world out of my backpack and settled in to read as the nonexempts labored over their tests. But after twenty minutes, I hadn't processed a single word. I was thinking about Fletcher, wondering why he'd made that stupid bet. Was everyone imagining me with him? Who all knew? Just the people who were at the party or had word spread through various social networks? Why would people care?

And to think that I'd been flattered that someone like Scooter Gibson had finally noticed me. He'd noticed me for all the wrong reasons. I felt stupid and hurt. And angry.

My reputation was ruined.

I'd always worried about being the good girl, never disappointing my parents, having stellar grades and an untarnished image. Like maybe I thought I would end up in politics or something and didn't want anyone to ever find any dirt hidden in my past. But mostly, I wanted to make my parents proud.

I loved that my parents took in foster kids, that they worked with them, tried to help them acclimate to a life without violence or drugs or abuse. But when they first started doing it, a small part of me had wondered if they were trying to find a replacement for me. If maybe I didn't exactly measure up to their expectations.

Crazy thoughts. I knew that. But it was amazing how I could blow things out of proportion. How something could worry me until it almost became a living, breathing demon that sucked away all rational thought.

"Okay, people, time's up!" Mr. Turner announced. He was a stickler when it came to timing tests or accepting homework. He made no exceptions.

He took up the exams, then settled behind his desk and began calling us up to turn in our books. When he called my name, I walked to the front feeling like I was wearing a big scarlet S for *slut* on my back. I handed him my book.

He marked off my name, then looked at me with huge eyes magnified by his black-rimmed glasses. "Remember, Avery, every problem has a solution. Good luck."

Had he said that to everyone? Did even the teachers know about the bet? "Uh, thanks," I stammered. I'd barely reached my desk when the bell rang.

I snatched up my backpack. Without waiting for Kendall, I hurried out of the room and scoured the hallway for any sign of Fletcher as I strode to my locker, staring down every guy who looked at me like he was imagining me without clothes on, and one girl whose expression said "Slut."

Of course, I had no classes whatsoever with loser Fletcher. And since he never studied or cracked open a book, I seldom saw him in the hallway where the seniors had their lockers. This morning I didn't see him at all. Maybe he hadn't even come to school. Maybe his bike was gone because he'd literally left, moved out. Maybe he was heading out of state. Out of the country would be better.

Kendall caught up with me at my locker. "What was the hurry?" she asked. "We have two hours before the next exam."

"I was trying to find Fletcher."

"I haven't spotted him yet. Lucky for him. I would have punched him."

I grinned. "Thanks."

"Hey, babe," Jeremy said as he joined us. He gave Kendall a quick kiss before looking at me. "Hey, Avery. Why so down? You're exempt from all your exams, right?"

"But not exempt from gossip," I told him. "I just learned about that stupid bet that loser Fletcher made."

"Yeah, that's a crappy way to start the last week of school, but for what it's worth, a lot of people don't believe anything happened."

I knew he was trying to comfort me but all I really heard was that a lot of people knew. Then another thought hit me. Did people think nothing happened because Fletcher wouldn't even bother to make a pass at me? Which he hadn't, but still—I didn't want people knowing that. Or did they think I was strong enough not to be lured in by his curb appeal? I couldn't see any way for me to come out of this on top.

"Have you seen him?" I asked.

"No, I don't have any classes with the guy. Why don't

we get out of here?" he asked. "Go to the Burger Shack for lunch. I'll drive."

"That sounds great," I said. I needed to get off campus.

Of course, a lot of students went to the B.S. Standing in line, I endured their speculative glances. I was so glad when my food was ready and I was able to slip into a back corner booth.

Kendall and Jeremy sat opposite me. After squeezing ketchup over my fries, I shoved one into my mouth. The first good moment of the day: that incredible taste of something designed to clog my arteries.

"At least it's the last week of school," Kendall mused. "And a short one. Exams the rest of the week, we're off Friday, have the ceremony Saturday, and we're done."

"I don't understand why people believe him," I muttered. "That they think I would just jump into the sack with him. I mean, we weren't even on a date. He just offered to give me a ride home."

Kendall lifted a shoulder. "You got on his bike."

"Since when does getting a ride from a guy equal sleeping with him?"

"It doesn't usually," Jeremy told me. "But there was the bet—which I didn't even hear about until this morning or I would have done something about it at the party. Add Fletcher to the mix . . . he has a reputation with the girls."

"But we're standing up for you," Kendall said. "If any-one says anything to us, we're telling them the rumors going around are crap." She looked sadly at her burger as though it had disappointed her. "Although I don't know how much good it does. I mean, I don't know that it's chang-ing any minds."

"That's what makes me so mad," I told her. "Other than making an announcement over the PA system, there's no way I'm not leaving as the slut of Memorial High."

"It's not that bad. Someone with poor judgment maybe, but not a slut. Besides, what does it really matter?" Kendall asked. "You're escaping at the end of summer. It won't fol-low you to college. And you'll probably never see any of these people until a class reunion."

"It's the principle of the thing." Who would have thought an innocent ride home would fill the last week of my senior year with such drama? "What if people haven't forgotten by the time we have a class reunion? What if that's all they remember about me? This stupid rumor that I did something with Fletcher."

"They'll forget. It's only important to them now. More important things are bound to happen to them before a reunion. Or at least I hope they do; otherwise that's sad."

"You're right," I said. "They won't remember." But I would. I'd remember the hurt of being played by a guy who I'd begun to think was nice. How could I have misjudged him so badly? He seemed so nice when really he was scum. Despicable.

"Uh-oh," Kendall whispered, sitting up straighter.

I knew that tone, knew it didn't bode well. Although I didn't see how anything could make this day worse. "What?"

"Fletcher just sat down two tables over, behind you."

I swung my head, peering around the corner of the booth. Oh, yeah, there he was, sharing his table with a blonde and a brunette, shaking salt over his fries, smiling, winking, teasing.

"I'll meet you at the car," I said to Kendall and Jeremy.

"Don't let him chase you out of here," Kendall commanded with conviction in her voice. She was all about standing up for herself. It was a trait we shared.

"Oh, I'm not." I slid out of the booth, grabbed my backpack and my soft drink. I headed for the door, but stopped when I got to Fletcher's table. Without ceremony or comment, I dumped my iced tea over his head.

Sputtering, he stood up so fast that he knocked over his chair. "What the f—"

Then his gaze landed on me, and his eyes widened. A corner of his mouth started to tilt up, but I wasn't in the mood to let him complete that sexy, conniving smile or refer to me as a brainchild or whatever.

"Jerk," I snarled.

He narrowed his eyes and pressed his lips into a hard line.

"Based on your reputation," I continued, "I figured you had experience, but since you apparently weren't aware that we *didn't* have sex Saturday night, let me make it clear for you now: We did not have sex. Look in your biology book, chapter thirteen, if you need a lesson on what sex involves so you'll recognize when it does happen."

Then shifting the weight of my backpack, I stormed out of the almost silent B.S. I was shaking so badly, so much adrenaline rushing through my system, that I didn't know how I managed to keep my legs from buckling as I made my way to Jeremy's car. I felt better, but I was a long way from feeling like this was over.

Chapter 8

FLETCHER

Damn it. Avery knew about the bet.

As I stood there with tea dripping down my face, I couldn't help but admire her spunk, though.

With a steely glare, Kendall Jones walked by me, Jeremy Swanson right behind her. "Not cool, dude," he said as he passed.

Did he think I didn't know that? I'd hoped that she wouldn't hear the rumors going around. I should have known better. There weren't a lot of secrets at our school, which was the reason I was very careful about what I revealed. I thought about going after Avery but now didn't seem like the right time or place. It would just make matters worse. I looked at Ronda and Vicki, the two girls who had asked to join me for lunch.

"I'll be back." I grabbed a stack of napkins because I

knew the B.S. had electric hand dryers, then went into the bathroom and blotted up the sticky tea on my face and in my hair. She would drink sweet tea. Once my black T-shirt dried, no one would know about the incident. Who was I kidding? It would be all over school by the end of the day.

Grabbing hold of the sink, I leaned in toward the mirror. The bruises would be there for a while, but I wasn't sure where I was going to be if Avery told her dad about the bet—which she seemed mad enough to do. If she did, her dad would kick me out, and then where would I go? He might even tell Smiley to fire me before I'd had a chance to start work.

I had to talk to Avery before she spoke to her dad. She wouldn't call him, right? She'd wait until he got home? I'd just have to catch her before then. That wasn't going to be easy since we were on shortened days. After combing my fingers through my damp hair, I headed back out to the dining area. Ronda and Vicki were gone. So was my burger. Someone had cleared our table. The place was nearly empty, and all the students had vanished. I looked at my watch and cursed. I was going to be late to my next exam.

Saturday night, it had all seemed like an easy way to make some cash. Now it could cost me everything.

Chapter 9

AVERY

I was so tempted to skip school that afternoon. I didn't have to take a final but I did have to be there for roll call. I thought about checking in and telling the teacher I was sick, but I'd never skipped in my life. The thought of doing it now, just because of Fletcher, made me angrier.

So I stayed for the afternoon and ignored the whispers I heard around me, trying to convince myself that they didn't have anything to do with me. Why did people even care? Maybe they were just nervous about graduation or finals or not knowing what the future held, and it was easier to focus on gossip than the realities of what happened next.

I was so relieved when the bell rang. Three more days to go. Not that I was counting. Some guy whistled at me as I rushed out the door to the parking lot. I avoided everyone's gazes. All I wanted to do was get home.

When I pulled Trooper into the driveway, I was disappointed to see that Fletcher's bike was already there. How had he gotten home before me? Probably skipped school after he ended up with my sweet tea on his head.

I entered through the front door and was assailed by the aroma of freshly baked chocolate chip cookies. I detoured into the kitchen, coming up short at the sight of Fletcher, wearing a milk mustache, sitting on a stool at the island counter.

"Avery!" Tyler shouted, nearly tumbling off the stool beside Fletcher to come around and give me a hug, leaving cookie crumbs on my jeans. When he'd first come to us, he hadn't known what a hug was, flinched anytime arms went up as though he expected to get hit. Now he gave the best hugs.

"Hey, hon," Mom said. "Come join us for some warm cookies and milk."

I shifted my attention back to Fletcher. He'd apparently taken a napkin to his mouth while I was distracted with Tyler. "No, thanks. I just wanted to let you know I was home."

"As though I wouldn't know that with all the noise that old clunker makes," she said with a smile.

But I wasn't in the mood for jokes. "Trooper gets me where I need to be."

"Trooper?" Fletcher asked.

Ignoring him, I said, "I'm going for a run."

Before Mom could get after me for my rudeness, I turned on my heel and headed through the doorway. I heard Tyler explaining to Fletcher that Trooper was the name I'd given my car. It seemed the bad boy was charming everyone in the family. I refused to admit that he'd looked adorable with the white mustache.

In my bedroom, I slung my backpack onto my bed. I was so tense that I could have screamed. I changed into shorts, a tank, and my running shoes. After pulling my hair back into a ponytail, I slipped on a Texas Astros cap. With my iPhone nestled in an armband, I tucked the earbuds into my ears and headed out through the front door.

Fletcher was standing near the garage and immediately began striding toward me. Guess he'd had his fill of cookies. "We need to talk."

"I don't think so." Normally I stretched out here. Should have done it on the deck or in the backyard. I started out at a jog.

Fletcher, in boots, loped beside me. "Come on."

Reaching out, he grabbed my arm. I wrenched free, jerked the earbuds loose, and jogged in place. "Don't touch me."

"Look, I know you're mad—"

"You don't know anything about me. Let's keep it that way."

I headed off again, my feet pounding the pavement. I could hear the echo of Fletcher's biker boots thumping along beside me. I glanced over. "You are not running with me."

"I want to explain."

"There's nothing to explain. I know about the bet, I know what you told everyone. You think you're important, that you have something to prove. All you did was ruin my reputation. And for what? To be the big man of the hour? You're just small." I lengthened my stride, quickened my pace, and left him in the dust.

I heard his steps slow and fade. I went faster, taking satisfaction in the knowledge that he couldn't keep up with me. I wanted as much distance between us as possible. I thought he'd been nice, looking after me at the party, offering me a ride. He'd just been using me to make money, to prove that no girl was immune to his charms. I felt like such an idiot.

I raced around a curve in the path that led through a stretch of green that intersected the neighborhood. Trees grew tall on either side, the branches forming an arbor that provided shade and warded off the sun. My parents were like the trees, always trying to protect me, but they couldn't protect me from everything. Sure, I could tell Dad about the bet, then Fletcher would be gone, but I was a little old to be tattling, to be expecting my father to take care of matters that I could just as easily take care of.

I was graduating from high school, going to college. I could handle a few weeks of Fletcher underfoot. I didn't have to talk to him. I could be cool during meals, ignore him as we cleaned up after supper. He'd retreat to his apartment over the garage. I'd be in my room. I could make this work.

I circled back around and headed home. I nearly stumbled over my feet when I spotted Fletcher sitting on the steps leading to his apartment. So much for doing my cooldown in the driveway. The backyard would have to do. Habit had me slowing my steps as I went by the stairs. Anger had me ignoring him.

"I didn't tell anyone you slept with me," he said.

Instinct told me to keep going. Instead I stopped dead in my tracks, wished I wasn't breathing so heavily, and glared at him. "That was the bet, and you collected."

He turned his head slightly, and I wondered if my gaze could scorch him. "The bet was that you would leave with me," he said. "You did. I can't help that some people think more happened."

Hands on my hips, I took a step closer. "You didn't hint that something happened?"

"Nope."

"Not even with a sly wink or a nudge? A little knowing smile?"

"No."

He was looking at me through the slats in the railing, his gaze direct, honest.

"Then why are guys putting moves on me?"

"Who?"

"What?"

"Who's putting moves on you?" he asked tersely.

What was he upset about? I was the one whose reputation was in the toilet. "I don't know. Scooter. Rhys. Some guy named Josh who I've never even seen before. Girls are glaring at me. Everyone is whispering."

He cursed. "I guess they just assumed . . . my reputation makes people think they know me, that they have some insight into what I would do."

Was I guilty of that? Thinking I knew him when really all I knew was his reputation? "I know you're a jerk for not telling people the truth."

"What does it matter?"

"It matters." I swung around the railing and went up two steps. "You can emphasize to people that nothing happened."

"They probably won't believe me."

"Why? You also have a rep for being a liar?"

"Why do you care so much?"

"I don't want people believing something about me that's not true."

"Would it be so bad if people thought you liked me?"

"But that's not what they think. They're convinced I hopped on your bike, then hopped into bed with you. That I have no standards."

"Standards? Do you think I'm that far beneath you?"

"No, stop twisting this around. I'm talking about people—guys especially—thinking that I don't have enough respect for myself to believe that I deserve better than some guy who is just passing by. It's about respect. For me. For you, even. For a relationship. I want a guy to ask me out because he wants to get to know me. Because he likes me. Not because he thinks I'm an easy booty call."

Fletcher studied me for a long moment, then nodded. "That's fair, so okay."

Hands on my hips, I glowered. "Okay what?"

"I'll let it be known that nothing happened."

With three days left of school, it might not make a difference. But maybe it would. "Thanks."

The word came out hard and I didn't sound grateful in the least, but I was still upset, and I didn't quite trust that he couldn't have nipped this in the bud earlier.

He shook his head. "I can't believe you spilled your tea over my head."

Crossing my arms over my chest, I leaned my hip

against the railing. "I considered locking you in a choke hold."

He scoffed. "Yeah, like you could do that."

"I know self-defense." My dad had made sure of it.

Silence eased in around us. My anger at Fletcher dissipated. Somewhat. "Why would you make a bet like that?"

"It's what guys do."

"So juvenile."

"Easy money."

The anger sparked again. "I wasn't easy."

I shoved myself away from the railing, started down—

Pain shot through my left calf, my leg folded. I grabbed the railing with one hand, my calf with the other. "Shoot!"

The stairs vibrated as Fletcher flew around me. "What's wrong?"

"Just a cramp." Pressing my toes onto the step, I tried to stretch out the muscle. Not enough room. I shoved on Fletcher. "Move."

"Sit."

"Get outta—"

His hands came around my bare calf, choking back my words. He lifted my leg, giving me no choice except to drop down onto the step. "Fletcher—"

"Do you have to argue with me about everything?" he asked as he nimbly untied my sneaker. "You should have taken the time to cool down."

"Which is what I was going to do when you stopped me."

He tugged off my shoe, dropped it. It bounced before falling between the steps to the ground. He knelt. With just the right amount of pressure, he bent my foot back with one hand while the other gently massaged the knot in my muscle. His hands were large and warm. I almost moaned as the pain began to lessen. He must have felt the knot dissipating because he sat with my leg across his lap and began using both hands to knead the aching muscles. Then I had to bite back a moan of pleasure. It felt so good.

He took half a second to peel off my sock and toss it at me. I snatched it, stuffed it into a pocket, while his fingers returned to working their magic.

"It's okay now," I felt obligated to admit.

"Give it another minute. It could cramp back up."

I was willing to give it ten minutes, thirty, a hundred. I didn't usually notice guys' hands, but something about his was intriguing. Maybe it was the fact that they were caressing my skin with deliberate long strokes interlaced with little squeezes. Every now and then he would return his attention to my foot, bend it, stretch the muscle in my calf.

"You're good," I said.

"Thought *you* thought I was a bad boy."

"I meant that you're good at massaging."

"Lot of practice."

And that pretty much broke the spell he'd been weaving. I didn't want to think about all the girls he'd practiced on. I pulled my leg free. He seemed at once surprised and irritated. I stood. "It's fine now."

He gave me a half-smile. "Just let me know if you need help working out another cramp."

"I think I can manage it."

I started down the stairs. He didn't try to stop me. I slipped under the steps and snagged my shoe. When I straightened, he was standing, watching me, and I was glad that he hadn't had a good view of my butt from where he was. "Thanks for the help with the cramp."

It seemed like I was always thanking him.

"No problem. Like I said, anytime."

"Weren't you supposed to meet Dad at Smiley's?"

"Yeah, I need to head over there, but I wanted to get this straightened out first."

"Why? You'll make a bad impression with Smiley and make my dad mad."

"I called to let them know I'd be a little late."

I considered putting on my shoe so I wasn't lopsided, but let it go. "Why did you want to take care of this first?"

"Because your dad is a cop; he's observant. He would have known something was wrong between us, and there is no way I would have come out of the story looking good and still been welcome here."

"I didn't think you really wanted to be here."

Shrugging, he rubbed his hands on his jeans. "It's not so bad."

"High praise indeed for the Watkins's hospitality."

"I like it when you're not mad. The girls I'm usually with . . . they don't care about their reputations. Or they care but they care about being popular or desired or . . . they don't care about the things you do. You're different."

Before I started to blush, I said, "Everyone's different. And you should go."

"Yep."

With an uneven stride, I walked to the gate. I felt his gaze on me the entire way. Now if I could just forget the way it had felt to have his hands on me.

Chapter 10

FLETCHER

I loved the smell of engine oil and grease. I felt right at home when I stepped into Smiley's garage. Mr. Smiley—or Smiley, as he told me to call him—was an odd-looking guy with big ears and a smile that took up most of his face. He looked really glad to see me and enthusiastically shook my hand when Avery's dad introduced us.

With pride, he took us on a tour of the place. Running my hand over some of the tools reminded me of working on cars with my dad—before my mom died, before he lost his job, before everything went to shit.

"So what do you think?" Smiley asked. "Think you'd like working here?"

I didn't have to look at Avery's dad standing there to know my answer. "Yes, sir. I'd love working here. I could start Friday."

He furrowed a brow that was wrinkled with years. "Graduation is Saturday, isn't it?"

My gut clenched at the reminder. "Yes, sir."

"Let's make it Monday then. Enjoy your last few days of high school."

I could have told him that was impossible. School and I didn't get along, but I didn't see the point. I thanked him. He shook my hand again. Then I walked out with Detective Watkins. He wore a suit. I heard a slight creak of leather and knew he wore a gun holstered beneath his jacket. The first time I'd met him he'd been in uniform and had explained all the various notches, loops, compartments, and other aspects of his duty belt. I'd been twelve at the time. Scared. He'd made me feel safe.

"I was hoping we'd have a few minutes to grab a quick cup of coffee," he said now, "but it's almost time for supper. We should probably head home."

"About that." He stopped walking to face me squarely. I cleared my throat. "I appreciate being included in the family time and everything—"

"It was part of our agreement. You're a member of the family. You eat with us, play with us, and have the same curfew as Avery."

"Yes, sir, but I'm feeling like I can't breathe. I have some school stuff to take care of tonight. You let Avery take care of school stuff, right?"

He studied me a minute, and I wondered if he knew I wasn't being exactly honest about what I wanted to do. "I know it's been an adjustment, but you're right. School comes first. Still, there is a curfew."

"I won't be late." It was so strange to have to check in with someone. I watched him get in his car. I straddled my motorcycle, took my time putting on my helmet, and waited a couple of heartbeats until he'd pulled out and was on the street. Then I took off in the direction of the school. Two lights down, when I knew Detective Watkins could no longer see me, I hooked a right and headed to Joe's Pizzeria. It was a popular hangout and they had the best pizza buffet in town.

The parking lot was already crowded when I arrived. I parked in the area designated for motorcycles and headed in. Travel posters with scenes from Italy dotted the walls. Although I didn't think the owner, Joseph McFarland, had ever been to Italy.

"Hey, Fletcher," Wendy McFarland, his daughter, greeted me. "You here for the buffet?"

We had math together, flirted a little, but had never gotten together. She seemed just a little too nice. She didn't give me a hard time like Avery did. Wasn't sure why it suddenly struck me that I liked the way Avery never cut me any slack.

"Not really." I glanced around, pointed. "I just need to

talk with somebody."

She smiled, winked. "Help yourself to a drink if you want. On the house."

"Thanks, but I won't be here that long."

I sauntered between the tables until I arrived at one that had three couples sitting at it. Grinning at two girls sitting at a nearby table, I asked, "Can I borrow this chair for a minute?"

One smiled brightly. "Sure. You can join us if you want, Fletcher."

"Thanks. I just need the chair." I pulled it out, turned it around, set it beside Scooter Gibson, and straddled it, crossing my arms over the back.

"Hey, Fletch, my man," Scooter said. "I didn't think you were going to make it. Grab a plate, join us."

He'd told me earlier in the day that he'd be here this evening. "Just need to talk to you about that bet."

He gave me a sly smile that made me want to punch him. Had he grinned at Avery like that? "I've got no hard feelings that I lost."

"I didn't think you did, but there seems to be a misunderstanding. The bet was that Avery Watkins would leave with me."

He winked. "Yeah, so how was she in the sack?"

Both my hands fisted into tight balls. "She left with me. That's it. Nothing else happened."

His face dropped like I'd just told him I'd totaled his Corvette. "But when a girl goes with you, something always happens."

Not always, although I was never going to admit that. I had a strict kiss-and-don't-tell policy. Rumors, what the girls told people, I couldn't control. "Nothing happened with Avery. I need you to make sure people know that or I won't be happy." I tapped a finger near my bruises. "You don't want to become the other guy."

He held up both hands. "You don't have to threaten me."

"You'll fix it?" I asked.

"I'll try, sure, but the 'nothing happened' rumors don't travel as fast as the 'something happened' rumors."

I met the gaze of everyone at the table who had stopped eating to watch and listen with interest. Then my gaze landed back on Scooter as I held between my fingers the twenty he and the others had pooled together to cover the bet. I was going to do whatever it took. "Make it right," I ordered.

Nodding, he pushed my hand back. "Keep it. You met the literal terms of the bet. I'll do what I can."

"Thanks." Standing, I returned the chair to its table and sauntered from the restaurant. He was right: it was always harder to undo the damage. I knew that all too well.

* * *

It was strange hearing my footsteps echoing through the hallways. Shadows had begun to fall but it was still light out, would be for another hour or so. I never returned to school after the last bell rang. It was odd being here now. I'd passed two people who were monitoring the hallways and heard a couple of locker doors slam. Then I arrived at Mr. Turner's room.

It was one of the rooms where students could go for math tutoring. There were four tutors, one at each corner. Each one was helping another student. Three of them had their desks arranged so they were facing the person they were explaining things to.

But not Avery. Her desk was right beside Brian Saunders.

Standing just inside the doorway, I watched as Avery explained a problem to him, her finger pointing out one thing and another, her shoulder brushing against his. I didn't want to think about all the nights that I could have been that close to her while she explained things to me.

Because of the way they were facing, I could see the concentration on her face. And more, the passion for what she was teaching. Or was it the act of teaching itself that excited her?

For me, school had always been a chore. Just get the work done, move on. Learn the bare minimum that I needed to get by. I thought about all the times I'd seen

Avery hauling a backpack to and from the parking lot, her shoulders rounded slightly like she was carrying a heavy load. I'd always wondered why she lugged all those books around. It occurred to me that she might not be smart because of her IQ. She might really enjoy learning.

She said something to Brian. He nodded, began making some marks with his pencil. I knew the moment she realized he was going to arrive at the correct answer. Her eyes softened and her lips curled up ever so slightly. I thought about how Brian would feel when he looked up and saw the joy radiating from her face, when he realized he'd gotten it right.

I couldn't stay here. I didn't want to see him grinning at her, see her smile growing even wider, her eyes sparkling even brighter.

I spun on my heel and headed back down the hallway knowing that where Avery was concerned, I seemed capable only of getting it wrong.

Chapter 11

AVERY

"Thanks, Avery," Wanda Ford said, as she shoved her algebra book into her backpack. "If I can just keep all this straight in my head through tomorrow morning, I might make it."

"I would say anytime," I told her, "but we're almost finished with school."

"Thank God. See you around." She hurried out through the door.

She was my last student to tutor, and we'd gone a little long because she was struggling with some of the concepts. As I gathered up my things, I wasn't surprised to see Rajesh Nahar standing near the door. We both tutored in this room, and he always walked me out to the parking lot as though he didn't quite trust the building to be completely empty this time of night. I appreciated the way he watched out for me. We'd been friendly academic rivals through most of our school years.

After turning off the light, he followed me into the hallway and closed the door. I always felt like a lumbering giant next to him because the top of his head didn't quite reach my shoulder. Kendall said I worried about my height too much. Maybe I did. It never seemed to bother Rajesh.

"So do you have your speech written?" I asked.

"Most of it." Although his parents were from India, he'd been born here. "I'm very grateful for the scholarships that I received for graduating second, but I have to admit that I'm really nervous about speaking in front of everyone."

"You'll do great," I assured him. "Although I've heard if you get nervous, you should imagine everyone in their underwear."

He released a small laugh. "I'm afraid they will be imagining me in my underwear."

"They won't. Besides, everyone likes you. They want to hear what you have to say."

He looked askance at me. "Sometimes I wonder if you got an answer or two wrong on an exam just so you wouldn't graduate ahead of me and have to give a speech."

"I'm not brilliant enough to figure out how to scam the system," I told him. Then I smiled. "But you're right. I would have if I could have. No speeches for me!"

He laughed loudly and knocked his shoulder against my arm. He was one of the few people with whom I was comfortable talking about my grades and schoolwork. He studied more than I did. Whenever we could, we'd partnered up for projects because we knew neither of us would slack off.

He shoved open the door and held it while I walked out of the building. Then we were heading for the parking lot.

"I know it makes me a geek," he said, "but I'm going to miss all this."

"Me too," I admitted. "But let's keep it our secret. People already think we're geeks."

The sun was in its final stages of disappearing beyond the horizon; twilight was hovering and would soon give way to darkness. Only a couple of cars remained in the student parking lot. A couple of cars and a motorcycle—parked beside Trooper.

Fletcher was lounging on the hood of my car, his back against the windshield, his ankles crossed.

"Do I need to toss him off your car?" Rajesh asked, and I fought really hard not to laugh. Like little Rajesh could toss buff Fletcher anywhere, although I did appreciate his offer.

"Nah, it's fine," I told him. "But thanks."

"See you tomorrow," he said before heading for his car.

Unable to tear my gaze from Fletcher, I ambled slowly

across the distance separating us, wishing that my heart didn't start pounding like a bass drum. Why did I have to be so aware of him?

"What are you doing here?" I asked when I was near enough that I wouldn't have to shout.

"Wanted to let you know it's fixed." Holding a package of peanuts, he poured some into his palm and popped them into his mouth.

His words made no sense. I studied him, studied my car. Had it broken down somehow without my knowing? "What's fixed? Trooper?"

Fletcher grinned slightly, at my car's name, I guessed. "No, the rumor. I talked to Scooter, a few of the other guys who were in on the bet. Straightened things out. Or at least it's starting to be straightened out." More peanuts, a sip of soda.

I was near enough now to make out the plastic bag flattened by his leg as well as the assortment of nuts, pastries, and candies spread over it. "What is all that?"

He shrugged. "I got hungry waiting for you. Went to the convenience store, grabbed a few things."

"How did you know where I was?"

"There's always tutoring sessions the week of finals. I saw on the list outside the room how late you'd be, so I just decided to wait." He held up a cupcake. "Want to join me?"

I glanced around. Only one other car now. They'd

be locking up the parking lot soon. I should go. Instead I put my foot on the bumper. Fletcher held out his hand. I slipped mine into it and his fingers closed around it. I felt the strain of his muscles as he pulled me onto the hood. I settled beside him, took the cupcake, bit into it, and hit the creamy filling right off the bat. So good. I licked my lips, turned to find Fletcher staring at me like he'd never seen me before. "You okay?"

"Yeah . . . uh, you really like cupcakes."

"Oh my God, did I groan when I took a bite?"

"It was more like a moan."

"Sorry."

"That's okay." Taking another sip of his drink, he turned his attention to the sky. It was almost dark now but the lights in the parking lot had come on so we couldn't really see the stars.

"I'm going to miss school," I said quietly.

"I won't."

Unlike with Rajesh, Fletcher and I had nothing in common. We were silent for a while. "Why did you sign up for tutoring sessions if you weren't going to come?" I finally asked.

"I didn't. Old man Turner signed me up for them. Didn't think it was any of his business."

"He's your math teacher. He was trying to help. He wouldn't have signed you up if he hadn't thought you'd benefit from some extra study."

"You can't make a person learn what they don't want to learn. I mean, really, when am I ever going to plot the roots or, or . . . complete the square or factor an equation?"

He had a point. "A lot of it is brain exercise, figuring things out."

"You like that kind of stuff." He said it like a statement, not a question.

"I enjoy the mental challenge, yes."

He finished off his peanuts, wadded up the empty package. I expected him to toss it onto the ground. Instead he slipped it into the flattened bag. "I saw you tutoring Brian," he said quietly. "You like tutoring."

"I do, yeah. I love that moment when I'm explaining something and the person finally gets it. It's like magic, like seeing a shooting star or a rainbow, this sense of wonder, not really knowing how it happened. Just knowing that it did." I laughed. "God, I sound like a dork."

I glanced over to find him watching me again, so intently that I was having a difficult time drawing in breath. He probably thought I was a total idiot, although he seemed fascinated. Still, I needed to put a little distance between us, so I sat up and wrapped my arms around my drawn-up knees. "You're tall. Why didn't you go out for the basketball team?"

"Being in sports takes too much time. You know, practice and games. Coaches have expectations."

"You might have gotten a scholarship."

"Do I strike you as someone going to college?"

Looking back over my shoulder, I grinned at him. "That's right. I forgot. You're getting a haircut."

He laughed. "That's right." He sobered. "You're tall. Why didn't you play?"

"Would have meant a lot of time away from studying. Grades mattered more to me."

I heard the putter of a golf cart: the custodian trolling the grounds. He came to a stop in front of my car. "You kids need to leave now," he said.

"Yes, sir." I slid off the hood, not surprised that Fletcher was a little slower at it. He really didn't seem to like being ordered around by adults. I wondered how long it would be before he'd had enough of my dad.

The custodian moved on. I unlocked my car. "I'll take the trash."

He held the bag out to me. I took it but he didn't let go. We were both just standing there holding this stupid crumpled plastic filled with garbage, and yet I felt like something else was happening. I just wasn't sure what it was.

He leaned in slightly. "You ever think about doing something you shouldn't?"

"You mean like telling my parents I'm going to one party—that has chaperones—and then going to one that doesn't? Or drinking until I puke?"

"You do that a lot? Tell your parents one thing, then do something else?"

I released a big sigh, not sure why it bothered me that he would be disappointed. I didn't live my life to impress Fletcher Thomas. "No."

"Maybe you should."

"Yeah, because it worked out so well when I did."

"Learning curve. You should know all about those, Einstein."

I didn't know why it didn't sting when he called me that this time. I knew he was mocking my intelligence—or I thought he was. Although the way the word rolled off his tongue didn't really sound like a put-down. It almost sounded like a compliment.

Before I could examine it further, he let go of the bag. "I'll follow you home."

"You don't have to."

He gave me a crooked grin. "I'm going that way."

I smiled. "Yeah, I guess you are."

I got into the car, started it up, and headed out. It was strange, but I'd never thought I could develop a friendship with someone who constantly broke the rules, someone like Fletcher. But whenever we talked, I could almost forget that he lived for trouble, and that I didn't. I could almost believe that we might become friends.

"You just talked?" Kendall asked.

Shortly after I got home, I walked over to her house. Now I was stretched out on her bed, a mound of pillows at my back, while she sat in a chair, tilted back, her feet on the desk. Her room looked a lot like mine. The summer before we started high school, we'd painted our rooms a light purple with one dark purple wall and bought the same white comforters and curtains. We had the same bulletin board, the same lamps. If we could have convinced our parents to buy us new furniture, we would have had that matching as well. I couldn't remember now why we'd decided that we had to have everything exactly the same.

"Just talked," I repeated.

"That is so weird," she said. "I heard Fletcher never *just talks* with girls."

"I can't decide if I should be hurt or feel special because he only talks with me," I admitted.

"Feel special, of course. Because you are."

I smiled. "You are a true best friend to say that."

"I mean it. You don't want a guy to kiss you just to kiss you. You want it to mean something. Kisses don't mean anything to Fletcher. He hands them out like they're candy on Halloween."

Licking my lips, I could still taste the sweetness of the cupcake. I sat up and folded my legs beneath me. "Do we really know that?"

It bothered me to think of Fletcher going after girls' lips simply because he was sexy and could. "What if it's all just a rumor, like the one going around about me sleeping with him? People know the kind of person I am, and yet they believed I'd do something that was totally unlike me."

"But people have seen Fletcher with girls. And we've seen the evidence of the fights he gets into. I'm pretty sure anything we've heard about him is true. But why do you care? You're not starting to like him, are you?"

"He's just a little different than I thought."

"Yeah, because your dad is riding his ass."

Was that it? Was he toning down his bad boy image because of my dad? Why did I want him to be doing it because of me?

"I sure would like to know what Fletcher did," she said, giving me a speculative look. "I bet it was bad."

"He killed someone," I deadpanned.

Kendall jerked upright and dropped her feet to the floor. "Get out!"

I laughed at her reaction, then sobered with the realization that she'd actually thought he was capable of something like that. "Of course he didn't. And whatever he did couldn't have been too bad or Dad wouldn't let him live with us."

She scowled. "Then why did you say that?"

"I don't know. I guess I've become fascinated with how easily people believe things." And bothered by it.

"Well, at least the rumors about you are going to stop," she said.

As soon as I'd walked into her room, I'd told her that Fletcher was taking care of that problem.

"So you can go to the party at the beach with Jeremy and me Saturday night. You won't get hassled."

A lot of kids were heading to the beach after the ceremony to celebrate that we were finally done. I didn't want to go by myself but I didn't want to be a tagalong either. "I don't know."

Kendall gave me a pointed look. "You are not staying home the night we graduate."

"There are other parties."

"Which one do you want to go to? We don't have to go to the beach."

I loved that she included me in things she did with Jeremy, but it was difficult to see her cuddling with him while I was standing there wishing someone would snuggle against me like that. But I didn't want to hurt her feelings or make her feel that since she was with Jeremy I didn't want to be around her. She'd tried so hard not to let him come between us. Friends always came first, she said. Still, there had been a shift in our relationship. I just didn't know how to explain it.

"Let's do the beach," I said. Surely I could find someone there to hang out with.

"Great. It's going to be a blast." She leaned forward slightly. "We're going to find someone for you."

I knew she meant to be encouraging, but I felt like the girl destined to be the bridesmaid and never the bride.

She tapped her chemistry book. "Now I have to study a little more before Jeremy comes over for some smooch time."

"Okay, see you tomorrow." I got off the bed and headed for the door. I'd almost reached it when she called out to me. I stopped and looked back.

"Fletcher's an idiot for not kissing you," she said.

I wanted to believe her, but I had a feeling that I was the idiot for wishing he would.

Chapter 12

FLETCHER

I almost did it again. I almost kissed Avery last night when we were sitting on the hood of her car. And I wasn't sure why. She wasn't beautiful. She wasn't really even pretty. But she did have a fascinating face—the way it lit up when she talked about something she was passionate about. And she was passionate about so many things.

As I strolled down the hallway the next morning, I found it difficult to believe that all we'd done last night was talk. I wasn't used to talking to girls for an extended length of time without working in a kiss or two. Maybe that was the reason I almost kissed her: habit.

I reached my locker and banged my fist on it. That was an insult to her. Habit had nothing to do with it. I knew that. I liked talking with her. I liked the way she smelled. Strawberries. I thought maybe it was her shampoo. What was I doing noticing her shampoo?

Even worse: Sometimes I dreamed about her. I didn't worry about the dreams when I was asleep because I can't control my subconscious. But I dreamed about her when I was awake, especially when I was in class and my mind would start to wander. I seemed to have no control over that and it bothered me big-time. I was wrong for her in every way imaginable. It didn't take a genius to figure that out. And I was no genius.

I spun the combination, freed the lock, and opened my locker. I stared at the algebra book angled there. I had to pass this stupid class. I needed this worthless credit to graduate. I'd never gone to a tutoring session because the idea of needing a tutor made me feel stupid. But the guy Avery had been tutoring hadn't looked as though he'd felt stupid as she leaned in and explained the material. As he'd been working the problem, he'd begun to look triumphant. Leaving the textbook where it was, I slammed the locker closed. Was there any point in even taking the exam?

"Hey, Fletcher."

Recognizing Morgan Anderson's sexy voice, I erased the frustration from my face and turned around. "Hey, Morgan."

She stepped forward, and I leaned back against my locker. Flattening her palms against my chest, she moved in a little closer. I placed my hands on her waist. We'd spent a little bit of time together, usually when she was in between boyfriends. I liked her. She was fun. I never had to wonder what it might be like to kiss her, because she was pretty free with her kisses.

"What are you doing Saturday night to celebrate graduating?" she asked.

I was trying not to think about graduation, what it would mean for everyone else, what it would mean for me. "Haven't decided."

"Scooter is having another party at the lake house— course his parents will be hanging around this time but there are lots of dark places." She bit her lower lip. "If you're there, maybe we can get together, since Biff is being a dumbass."

I took a few strands of her mahogany hair, tucked them behind her ear, and grinned. "So, you're not with him now, then?"

"Nope."

"Then I think you can pretty much count on me being there."

"Great." She slid her hands around my neck, rose up on her toes, and gave me a quick kiss. "I can't wait."

"Me either."

She lowered herself to the ground, her eyes—an unnatural green because of her contacts—sparkling with mischief. "Want to hear something really funny?"

"Sure." I could use something to lighten my mood before my math exam. Although knowing I'd be seeing her Saturday night helped.

"There's a rumor going around that you hooked up with Beanpole at Scooter's party."

Everything within me went still and tense at the same time. "Beanpole?"

"Yeah, you know. Avery Watkins. Tall, skinny chick. Really smart. I've been telling people it's not true."

Which was what I wanted, I wanted people to know the rumors weren't true. Avery wanted people to know, but Morgan was insulting her in the process. I didn't appreciate it. "She's not a beanpole," I said.

"She's almost as tall as you are. And she's skinny."

"She's slender."

Morgan narrowed her eyes. "Did you hook up with her?"

It was strange, but I thought it would actually do Avery's reputation some good if I could answer yes. If I said no, Morgan was going to think I didn't find Avery attractive. My thoughts hit a brick wall. Did I find Avery attractive? If I didn't, I wouldn't keep thinking about kissing her. "I gave her a ride home."

"Oh." Her hands slid away. "She doesn't really strike me as your type."

I almost explained that nothing happened, but I was

afraid Morgan would twist it around and find a way to use it to hurt Avery. I realized Avery would never do something like that, would never deliberately hurt someone. I had a feeling Morgan might, although I didn't know for sure because we never really talked. "I like Avery," I admitted.

"Isn't she a little too smart for you?"

Okay, that hurt, although I had no one to blame except myself for my grades. They weren't stellar and until that moment I hadn't really cared. As long as they were good enough to get me the hell out of high school I was happy. But I was more bothered because Morgan seemed determined to put Avery down. "Yeah, she is, but you know what? Smart is pretty sexy." I dropped my hands from her waist. "I'm probably not going to Scooter's Saturday after all."

"Your loss."

Somehow I doubted that. Morgan turned on her heel and marched down the hallway as I tried to figure out why I'd ever liked her in the first place. The bell rang, signaling that we had ten minutes to get to class. I opened my locker, grabbed my algebra book, and wondered why I thought I'd just made things worse for Avery.

Chapter 13

AVERY

"I hate this hair," Kendall said as she released the clip holding her curly red hair in place. She gathered it all up and reclipped it. "Wish I had yours."

We had a few minutes before our first class. Staring in the bathroom mirror as I brushed my long straight strands, I couldn't help but think how funny it was. No matter what conditioner or shampoo I used, my hair never had any body. I'd give anything to have hers. "Trust me, I can't do anything with it except let it hang or pull it back."

"Maybe we should do something radical," she said. "Get it all cut off."

"Maybe," I responded slowly, my attention caught by Morgan Anderson's reflection in the mirror. She was staring at me like she was auditioning for the role of a ghoul in a horror movie. I turned to face her. "You got a problem?"

"You."

"Yeah, I kinda figured that out, the way you were glaring at me."

Kendall stepped up beside me. For all of her five feet four inches, she could be intimidating when she wanted to be. "You have a problem with her, you have a problem with me," she said. I was a little surprised she didn't then shout, "Bring it on!" Although I truly appreciated her loyalty.

Morgan looked at her. "I don't care about you." Then she shifted her attention back to me. "I know about you and Fletcher. And that really doesn't work for me."

I sighed. She was obviously one of his groupies, although I thought she had a boyfriend. Not really my business. "Look, nothing happened."

"He took you home. And he told me he likes you."

I heard Kendall's jaw pop as it dropped. As for me, I was having a difficult time processing words all of a sudden. The ones she'd just spoken seemed to echo between the tiled walls, between my ears. "What do you mean he likes me?"

"That's what he said." She looked me over like I was a new species. "I don't get it."

"I'm sure you misunderstood."

"I'm sure I didn't." She took a step nearer, seemed surprised that I didn't step back. "I want to go to a party with him Saturday night, so tell him that you don't like him."

She stomped out. Blinking, I stared at the door closing slowly behind her.

"He likes you," Kendall said at the same time that I thought, *He likes me?*

"Is this good or bad?" Kendall asked.

"It's ridiculous." I grabbed my backpack.

"Maybe not. I wish we didn't have to get to class," Kendall said. "We'll discuss it at lunch. See if Jeremy has heard anything."

I walked out into the hallway. "There's nothing to discuss. She's wrong."

"You only think that because he hasn't kissed you. Maybe he doesn't kiss girls he likes."

I glared at her.

"Okay, he probably does kiss girls he likes. We'll talk at lunch."

She hurried down the hallway to her chemistry class. I headed to the front office. During this period I served as an office aide. The tardy bell rang as I walked through the door.

"Morning, Avery," Mrs. Muldrow, the office secretary, said, as she filled out an absentee slip for someone.

"Hi." I went behind the counter where two other student aides were already working and shoved my backpack into a little cubby. I was used to the routine. A few kids were lining up for tardy slips. I filled out the form, including the student's name and excuse, then passed it down to Mrs. Muldrow, for her signature.

The tardies were light this morning. When the waiting area was clear, Mrs. Muldrow released a deep sigh, which was also part of the routine. Then she smiled at us. "Hard to believe another year is over. Cookies are in the copy room."

She was famous for her oatmeal cookies. We all grabbed one and then took seats waiting for our assignments.

"This is our last time to meet like this," Kevin said, as though it was a revelation. He shoved his glasses up the bridge of his nose. Most kids called him Gamer because he hung out in comic book stores and played role-playing games all the time. He'd read every Game of Thrones book.

"I'll miss you guys next year," Sarah-Jane said slowly, like air seeping from a balloon.

She was a junior, and I really liked her, even though she dragged her sentences out into forever. "There's so much to do senior year, you won't even notice we're gone," I assured her.

"I'll notice." She peered over at me, wrinkled her brow. "I heard about you and Fletcher."

I rolled my eyes, shook my head. "He just gave me a ride home."

"I heard . . . he liked you. And he is so hot. You're so lucky."

What did I say to that?

"Sarah-Jane!" Mrs. Muldrow called out.

Sarah-Jane popped up. Mrs. Muldrow assigned her to help one of the counselors.

"You go together," Kevin said quietly.

I looked at him. "What?"

"You and Fletcher go together."

"In what universe?"

He grinned. "In this one."

I blushed, because he often talked to me about his role-playing games. When things were slow in the office he would ask my opinion on various backgrounds he was creating for his characters. "I wasn't making fun of you."

"I know. You're too nice to do that, but you should play the games with me sometime. You'd be good at them."

Mrs. Muldrow called him up and gave him a note to deliver to a teacher. As he was leaving, a woman walked in holding a small paper sack. She spoke with Mrs. Muldrow, who tapped a few keys on her computer before calling me over.

"Need you to deliver this to Andrea Jackson. She's in Mr. Turner's class."

"She's on a special diet," the woman said, and I realized she was probably Andrea's mother. I didn't really need to know the details of what was inside.

"I'll get it to her," I promised.

I left the office and crossed the courtyard, heading to the math and science building. I thought about trying to peer into Mr. Tant's chemistry class to see how Kendall was doing on the exam, but I didn't want to distract her. It was the only exam she had to take and she'd missed getting an A in the class by two points. So I walked on by without stopping.

When I got to Mr. Turner's class, I rapped quietly on the door. Through the window, I saw him get up and approach. I also saw Fletcher, front row, far side of the room. Mr. Turner opened the door. Fletcher glanced up briefly, revealing that storm-cloud expression I'd seen before. That sure wasn't the look you gave someone that you liked. I knew the I-like-her look. I'd seen Jeremy give it to Kendall enough times. It was a slow grin, a crinkling at the corner of his eyes. It was joyous, happy, glad.

"Yes?" Mr. Turner prodded, bringing me back to my reason for being here.

"Andrea's lunch. Her mom just brought it."

Now there were two storm clouds looking at me. "Did she not know she would need lunch before she left home this morning?"

"I'm just the messenger. I think there's a law that prevents you from taking your frustrations out on me."

He sighed. "Just because you aced my class, Miss Watkins, does not mean that you can talk disrespectfully to me."

"I meant no disrespect." I really hadn't, but it wasn't my fault I had a lunch to deliver.

He took the sack, holding it daintily with his thumb and forefinger as though he thought it might contain Ebola or something equally deadly. "Thank you, Miss Watkins. I'll see she gets it when she turns in her exam."

He closed the door. I peered through the window. Fletcher was scribbling again.

I headed back to the office. The time went really slowly. Kevin and I rotated running errands. The entire time, my mind wandered back to Fletcher, then further back to Morgan.

Ten minutes before the bell would ring to dismiss class, I approached the counter. Mrs. Muldrow smiled. "Another cookie?"

"Oh, no thanks. I was wondering if it would be okay if I went ahead and left so I could get an early start on lunch."

"I think you've earned an early dismissal."

After grabbing my backpack, I walked through the door, across the courtyard, and into the math and science building. I knew where Fletcher was. I needed to talk to him.

Chapter 14

FLETCHER

When the bell rang, I was ready. I couldn't escape the four walls of algebra class fast enough. I hated the subject, disliked the teacher. He disliked me.

When I saw Avery, I just kept on walking. She fell into step beside me. There weren't many girls who could keep up with me, but she had legs that went on forever. She had no trouble at all.

"I ran into Morgan Anderson earlier," she said, not even breathing heavily.

"Hope you didn't hurt her too badly."

"What?"

"When you ran into her. I assume you were in your car."

"Can you stop?" she asked.

"Not really. I'm ready for lunch. I'm hungry."

She grabbed my arm. "Morgan said—"

I swung around. She closed her mouth, backed up a step. I could imagine what my face showed. I was pretty sure I hadn't gotten enough problems correct to get the score I needed to pass algebra. Without algebra, I wouldn't graduate. The last thing I wanted to deal with was some stupid reputation crisis.

"She thinks something happened between us," I said. "She doesn't believe that all I did was take you home. What does it matter what she thinks or what she believes or what she's telling people? All of this"—I flung out my arms— "it doesn't mean anything. What all these people think doesn't make any difference. We know the truth of what happened. That's all that matters. Why can't you just care about that?" I wanted someone to punch me in the mouth, to shut me up. People were staring, but I couldn't seem to stop ranting. "In two days you won't ever walk these halls again. After graduation, you won't see most of these people again. Do you really think any of them are going to remember any kind of gossip that was going around about you? Not all of us are smart like you, Einstein. Most of us just want to get through it and get out."

She blinked with those blue eyes of hers, only now they were bigger and rounder than I'd ever seen them. I took a deep breath, let it out through my mouth. Took another. Then glared at the kids standing around. "What are you doing? Get out of here. Go eat lunch."

They scurried. I took another deep breath, plowed my hands through my hair. "Sorry."

She smiled, actually smiled. It wasn't much of one, but it was enough. "We had quite the audience. I'm pretty sure that now no one is going to think anything happened between us."

I scoffed. "Yeah."

She looked down at her feet, her white sandals. Her toenails were painted pink. I didn't know why I noticed. She finally lifted her gaze to mine. "She said you told her that you liked me."

I slammed my eyes closed, opened them. "Don't read anything into that."

"But you did say it."

"She was making some snide comments and I wanted her to know I didn't appreciate it."

"About me?"

I didn't want her to know what Morgan had said, didn't want to have this conversation. "What does it matter?"

"About me." She nodded like she was answering her own question. "She wanted me to make sure you knew I wasn't interested, so she can date you."

"I don't date. I get together with girls, we have a good time. She knows that."

"Do you like her?"

I thought of a hundred things I could have said that would have had her heading down the hallway, but they would have all been lies, and for some reason I couldn't lie to her. "I used to. But again, what does it matter?"

She shrugged. "One more question."

I sighed in resignation. "Sure, why not?"

"Did you blow the algebra test? You looked really unhappy when I was in the room earlier."

Not what I was expecting. Not one I really wanted to answer. "Let's just say it was more complicated than I was prepared for." Like you, I thought.

She nodded. "I'll let you go enjoy lunch now."

"Maybe you should tell me where you're going so I can avoid it. Don't want to end up with tea all over me again."

"You won't. Today I'll be drinking a shake."

She started to walk off. I watched as she pulled her cell phone from her jeans pocket. A couple of seconds later, she was holding it to her ear.

"Hey," I heard her say. "You free for lunch? Okay, see you soon. You know where. Love you."

My gut twinged at the final words. She quickened her pace and I tried not to wonder who she was meeting, who she loved, or why I cared.

AVERY

Jo-Jo's Diner was one of my favorite places, not so much because of the greasy food, but because of the memories I had of the place. When I was much younger, Mom and I would meet Dad here when he took a break from patrolling the streets. Sometimes I still met him here.

He was already sitting in a red vinyl booth when I arrived. He slid out and gave me a hug, before giving me a steely-eyed assessment.

"I'm fine," I assured him before I slipped into the booth and opened the menu.

"You don't have that memorized yet?" he asked as he sat across from me.

"I was thinking of ordering something different." I looked up. "Am I boring because I always order the same thing?"

"You're not boring." Dad was wearing a dark brown suit. He'd been promoted to detective a few years back. Sometimes the patrol officers called Dad in to handle difficult cases. I still wondered how Fletcher had gotten into his orbit, but I didn't think he'd tell me if I asked.

The waitress came over and I asked for the pimento cheese sandwich and potato salad. Strawberry shake. The same thing I always ordered. Dad went with meatloaf and mashed potatoes. Coffee. Sometimes he went with pot roast. After the waitress left, he crossed his arms on the table. "So what's up?"

"Can't I just want to have lunch with you?"

"Avery, you're my daughter. I know you. When you call me for lunch, it's because there's something you want to discuss—usually without your mother around."

We'd met here to plan a surprise party for my mom's fortieth. I'd met Dad here the first—and only—time I got a C on an exam. I'd met him here to discuss guys, grades, and college applications. I'd even met him here shortly after they'd adopted Tyler and I was struggling with no longer being an only child. Eventually I talked everything over with Mom. But Dad was almost always my first stop. Before I could drive, if I called him, he'd pick me up at school. He was always there.

"We won't be able to do this next year, when I'm off at college," I told him.

"Find a diner you like in Austin. You can go there, I'll come here and we can video chat. It'll be almost the same."

Almost. But I wouldn't smell my dad's Obsession aftershave. I wouldn't feel his large, warm hand cover mine with reassurance when the things we discussed were difficult, like when my grandparents died or a guy I was tutoring had overdosed.

The waitress brought us our food. I slurped on my shake, thought of the mess it would make if I poured it over Fletcher's head. He'd gotten off easy with the tea. Although I wasn't sure he'd deserved that either. It wasn't his fault what everyone thought.

Dad was watching me, waiting patiently. He never hurried his investigations. Never rushed me to tell him what was on my mind.

"So how important are reputations?" I asked.

He studied me while he finished chewing his bite of meatloaf, took a sip of coffee. "They're crucial. A good reputation can take you a long way."

"But what if they're wrong?"

"Are you thinking of any in particular?"

There was so much that I didn't want my dad to know about Saturday night—that I'd lied about where I was going, that I'd been drinking, that I'd gotten a ride home with a guy I barely knew. It didn't matter that I knew him better now.

"A rumor was going around school about me. It wasn't true, but people believed it. I couldn't stop it from spreading, and it altered my reputation. It made me wonder if other reputations aren't true."

"There's usually some seed of truth in a reputation," he said.

I could see that. The seed in mine was that I *had* gotten a ride with Fletcher. I wondered what the seed was in Fletcher's, because he just didn't seem as bad as I'd always believed.

"But you shouldn't judge a person solely on their reputation," Dad said. "Take Fletcher, for example."

I sat up straighter. *Yes, let's take Fletcher as an example.*

Dad tapped his fingers on the table, and I knew he was weighing his words. "He has a reputation for getting into trouble, truancy, not always following the speed limit. You have to dig a little deeper. Maybe he just had some tough breaks."

"Like what?" I asked.

Dad gave me his Fort Knox look, which meant I wasn't breaking into his vault of confidentiality.

"I see some ugly stuff, Avery. It's part of the job. A lot of it I can't change. Thought I could change some things with Fletcher. Is it causing problems for you at school because he's living with us?"

"Oh, no," I assured him. "I haven't told anyone." I grimaced. "Well, except for Kendall and Jeremy. They know. But they're not saying anything. I don't think Fletcher has either."

"Yeah, the kid has a lot of pride. Too much maybe. Makes it hard to help sometimes." He grinned slightly. "But we were talking about *your* reputation, I think."

"Kids thought something happened that didn't, and they started looking at me differently, expecting me to behave in ways I never would. I was just wondering if I was worrying about it too much. I won't see these people after graduation. Does it matter what they think?"

"It would help if I knew what they were thinking."

"I'd rather not say."

He mulled it over. "Just do the right thing, stay true to yourself. Your mom and I will always be proud of you."

Which was what I wanted. Or at least what I thought I wanted. A part of me wished I was a little more like Fletcher and didn't care what people thought. It seemed like it would be so liberating.

"So you're almost finished with school," Dad said, taking me away from things I was tired of thinking about. "How does it feel?"

"Great. And speaking of being finished with school, I thought maybe we should renegotiate my curfew once I graduate."

He narrowed his eyes slightly. "In what way?"

"Could do away with it completely," I suggested hopefully.

"I'm not willing to go that far. I don't think your mom will be either."

"But I don't have to get up for class. And in a few months I'll be on my own. Seems like I should be getting ready for that big step. Practicing, setting my own limits for how late I stay out."

He drummed his fingers on the table. "We'll try this. Let your mom know when you think you'll be home. Call if you're running late. But we retain the right to set a curfew anytime we think it's called for."

That was more than I'd hoped for. "Deal."

Then we started talking about sports and reality shows. As ready as I was to graduate, to move on, I also knew I was going to miss this so much.

When I got back to school, I discovered Fletcher leaning against my locker. People were hurrying by, getting to their lockers, heading for their afternoon final.

"Hi," I said as I got closer.

"Hey." He held out a package of cream-filled cupcakes.

I took his offering. "Tell me you didn't have lunch at a convenience store."

"Grabbed a few things. Needed to ride for a bit. I'm sorry about earlier."

"It's okay. I might be a bit obsessive about my reputation, about what people think."

"I probably don't care enough." He shook his head. "Nah, I'm fine not caring what people think."

He glanced around.

"You know people are going to think you like me if you hang around at my locker," I said.

Pushing away from the locker, he swung his gaze back to me. "I do like you."

Then he walked away as though the world still spun on its axis.

"He said he likes you?" Kendall asked.

I'd held it in as long as I could. It was late the next afternoon. She and I had met up after our last class and were presently at a salon sitting beside each other in recliners while we got pedicures. We'd finished the manicures and our fingernails were now sporting purple and white stripes, our school colors, so we were ready for graduation.

"In what way?" she mused.

"I think in the way that I like rain."

"You love rain."

She was right. If it rained every day, all night, I'd be happy. "Okay, that's not a good example. I don't know. The way I like leaves in fall. They're pretty but I wouldn't miss them if they didn't change color."

"How's he been acting since he said that?" she asked.

"That's just it. I haven't seen him. He wasn't at supper last night. And I didn't see him at school today. At all."

She gave me a puppy dog look. "Then, yeah, you're probably an autumn leaf. Did you want to be more?"

I shook my head. "We don't have anything in common. Not like you and Jeremy. You study together, you're going to the same college, you have plans, you talk about things. Fletcher doesn't share things. Sometimes I think he's going to but it's like there's this wall and he just won't go over it."

"He doesn't trust you. You can't have a relationship without trust. That's what my mom says. You need to find someone else."

She made it sound like I'd found Fletcher, like I was breaking up with him or something. One of the nail technicians dimmed the lights. It was time for my favorite part of the pedicure. Sighing, I settled back as she began massaging my feet. My mind started to drift to Fletcher working the cramp out of my calf, kneading my muscles. Why did I keep thinking about him? Especially when I knew Kendall was right. Fletcher wasn't the one. He would never be the one.

Chapter 16

FLETCHER

I'd been avoiding Avery. I had a lot going on in my life and I didn't need complications. Avery would be a complication. Besides, when I'd said I liked her, I'd seen her eyes widen slightly, knew she was giving my words more weight than I meant.

I'd meant that I liked her in the same way that I liked the pot roast Mrs. Watkins had cooked for dinner. Or at least that's what I had intended it to mean.

It was hard to remember that when I was sitting across from her. Her nails were painted with purple and white stripes, the school colors. She really was all about school. She was also comfortable with her parents, talking with them about her teachers, some of the kids at school, movies coming out this summer that she wanted to see. My dad didn't care about any of that stuff. He didn't ask me what I thought about anything. I always felt like a deer caught in the headlights whenever someone here at the table asked me a question.

Avery stood and took her dad's plate. I breathed deeply. I'd escaped tonight without anyone asking me anything. I got to my feet and reached for the little guy's plate.

"You have any plans for tomorrow night, Fletcher?" Detective Watkins asked.

I froze. Okay, maybe not a deer. Maybe someone finally on the other side of the prison fence suddenly having the spotlights hit him.

"We're going out to eat, to celebrate the last day of school," he continued as though he knew I was trying to decide whether to tell the truth or a lie. "We'd like you to join us."

I imagined the kind of place they would go, one that required button-up shirts. All I owned was T-shirts. "Actually I already made some plans."

"Well, if you change your mind, we'll be leaving around six."

I wasn't going to change my mind. I could take only so much family togetherness. "Thanks."

I carried the plates into the kitchen, turned on the water, and started rinsing them.

Avery set the plates she'd brought in down on the counter. "Not a fan of Cheez It Up, huh?"

Furrowing my brow, I looked over at her. It was a place with games, slides, mazes, and a mouse mascot. "That's where you're going? I figured you'd go someplace fancy."

"It's Tyler's last day of school, too. And he squirms a little too much for fancy."

"Yeah, I can see that." It was also fascinating to see how they wanted to do something that included everyone.

"So maybe you'll change your mind," she said.

I shook my head. "No, I really have something to do." Had an appointment with a bag of peanuts at the convenience store.

She left to gather the rest of the dishes and I went back to work. I appreciated the invite, but I was used to being on my own. Things were starting to feel tight. Sometimes when I looked at Avery, it was like there was a huge rubber band around my chest, squeezing. It made no sense.

When she brought in the last of the dishes, she stood with her hip pressed to the counter, watching me.

"Am I doing something wrong?" I asked, not looking at her.

"No, I just . . . I know it's none of my business. I just wondered if you knew how you did on the algebra exam."

I slid my gaze over to her. "Better than I thought."

She smiled brightly. "That's great! It's one of those pesky credits you need to graduate."

"Definitely pesky."

She grabbed a washrag, leaned in, and placed it beneath the running water. Her arms brushed against mine and awareness zinged through me, in spite of the fact that she hadn't done it deliberately. Not like Morgan, not with innuendoes and promises.

She squeezed the rag and started wiping the counter. "So there are a lot of parties going on Saturday night," she said casually. "I'm going to one at the beach. How about you?" Stopping her movements, she met my gaze.

I knew this was my opportunity to let her know that I hadn't meant anything by the like comment. "Probably going to Scooter's."

"Looking to make some more money with another bet?"

"I learned my lesson the last time."

She wiped, turned the cloth over, wiped the same spot again. "Morgan will be there, right?"

"That's what she said."

"You'll have fun."

So why did I feel guilty? "Look, Avery, when I said I like you—"

"I didn't read anything more than friendship into it." She released a light laugh. "And that's probably not even what you meant. You were probably thinking more along the lines of casual acquaintances."

"It's just a little awkward . . . all this." I waved my arm, trying to encompass the kitchen, the house, the neighborhood, the family. "But, yeah, friends . . . that could work."

She flicked the towel, zinged my arm.

"Hey!" I grouched.

She smiled, the smile that wreathed her face, that made what looked plain not so plain anymore. "You should relax some, *friend*," she said. "We don't bite. And if you said no to tomorrow night because of this whole *like* thing between us, you should reconsider. You haven't lived until you've seen my dad dance with a rodent."

I grinned. "He dances with Chelsey, the mascot?"

"He did once. I can't guarantee an encore, but there's always a chance."

"I'll think about it." But mostly I was thinking that she deserved a chance at someone a lot better than me.

Chapter 17

AVERY

Saturday afternoon, I stood before the mirror in my purple gown and cap with the gold tassel. My blond hair, brushed to a sheen, flowed past my shoulders. I couldn't believe the moment had finally arrived.

As I closed my locker for the last time Thursday afternoon I'd felt both excited and sad. Excited to be moving forward, sad to be leaving the familiar behind. Rajesh and I were probably the only two at school who experienced any sadness at all.

Fletcher hadn't joined us at Cheez It Up. He hadn't been at the graduation ceremony rehearsal yesterday afternoon either. I hadn't seen him around today. I had a feeling that while he might have done better on the algebra exam than he'd expected, he hadn't done well enough to pass the class. Maybe he was making himself scarce because he hadn't graduated. And here I was: number three.

I heard a car honk. My keys in one pocket of the capris beneath my robe, phone in the other, I went downstairs and strolled into the kitchen. "Kendall and Jeremy are here, so we're heading over to the school," I told Mom. We had to arrive an hour before the ceremony began so we could be lined up properly for our entrance.

"Gosh, Avery, are you a judge?" Tyler, asked from his place on the stool at the island. He knew all about judges. He'd been in the foster system.

I ruffled his dark hair. "No, squirt. I'm graduating. Remember? This is what you wear when you graduate."

Mom walked over and gave me a big hug. "We'll be in the stands rooting for you."

"All of you?"

She smiled. "Absolutely. Your dad's on his way home now."

Sometimes work kept my dad from attending the school events. We didn't have a lot of crime, but it always seemed to hit when there was something special planned.

I wrapped my arms around Tyler and squeezed him hard. "See you later, squirt. Don't forget to yell when they call my name."

"I won't!"

The horn honked again. I hurried out and slipped into

the backseat. Jeremy took off like we had all night. The guy never went a single mile over the speed limit, which was reassuring to Mom and Dad, but sometimes drove me a little nuts. I thought about the rush of wind going past when I was on the bike with Fletcher. He definitely didn't obey the speed limit.

Kendall twisted around and smiled at me. "Can you believe it? We are about to be officially done with high school."

"After the way my week started out, I am more than glad."

"I think things have died down."

"Pretty much. Fletcher did what he could."

"Speaking of Fletcher, why wasn't he at the rehearsal? Did he not graduate?"

I lifted a shoulder. "I'm not sure. I haven't really had a chance to talk to him. And how would I ask? If he didn't graduate, he's probably embarrassed."

"I can't see him attending the ceremony," Jeremy said. "It's not mandatory. If he let Mrs. Muldrow know he didn't want to do it, she'd take him out of the lineup."

"That's true," Kendall said. "Still, I bet he didn't graduate."

It bothered me that she thought that, even if I was thinking the same thing. If he'd been too proud to let me tutor him, he would be too proud to admit he hadn't graduated. My parents might know, although I couldn't see him sharing that with them either.

"If he's at the party tonight—" Kendall began.

"He won't be. He's going to Scooter's."

"Would you rather go to Scooter's?" Kendall asked.

"No." I looked at Jeremy, trying to decide how much he knew.

"I told him," Kendall said, as though she could read my mind.

I groaned.

"I'm not telling anyone," Jeremy said. "If you want to go to Scooter's, it's fine with me. I don't care which party we go to as long as Kendall's there."

Releasing a small sigh, Kendall reached out and squeezed his shoulder. "I am so lucky."

She was, she really was. "I don't want to go to Scooter's," I told them. "We got the whole like thing straightened out. Basically he was just saying that he didn't dislike me. But there is no interest. Which is good." Because I couldn't see myself with someone who didn't graduate high school, someone who failed classes—either because they weren't smart enough or they weren't trying. And I couldn't see myself with someone who had gotten into some kind of trouble with the police.

No matter how nice he seemed when we talked.

"The beach it is," Jeremy said.

"Great!" Kendall and I said at the same time, then laughed.

Jeremy turned into the school parking lot, pulled into a slot, and turned off the car. Kendall leaned over toward him. "Last kiss as a senior before we graduate."

I doubted that as they locked lips and I got out of the car. I figured they'd sneak in a dozen kisses before we marched onto the field to get our diplomas. The car windows had practically steamed up before they emerged. I could have gone on without them, but Kendall and I had started kindergarten holding hands. It seemed like we should at least walk together to our last big moment of school. Our last names would stop us from sitting together in the chairs that had been set up on the football field, so it just seemed important that we take this final stroll across the parking lot together.

As though she was thinking the same thing, Kendall slipped her hand into mine. "Been a hell of a journey," she said. "Thanks for being there with me through it all."

I squeezed her hand. "Didn't want to be anywhere else."

We walked hand-in-hand into the stadium. Then we separated and I tried to concentrate on the moment so I could hold on to these memories forever. Lining up for the procession in, taking our seats. Listening to the speeches. Rajesh nailed his and got a standing ovation. I was so happy for him.

When the last speech ended, the principal, Mr. Craven, began calling out the names. One by one, students marched across the stage to receive their diplomas. I clapped wildly for Kendall and Jeremy.

For some inexplicable reason, it made me sad when Fletcher's name wasn't called. I'd hoped we were wrong, that I just hadn't seen him in the rush of four hundred and fifty seniors gathering for the ceremony. But he was noticeably absent. I knew he had no one to blame but himself. He hadn't put in the work; he didn't deserve to graduate. That was the way life worked. Effort was rewarded. Laziness wasn't. I tried to imagine him going through another year of high school. He'd be two years older than most of the seniors. I couldn't see him doing it.

I was focusing so much on Fletcher that I nearly missed them calling my name. As I walked up the steps and across the makeshift stage on the fifty-yard line, I could have sworn that I heard Tyler yelling my name. Taking the scroll that wasn't my real diploma—it would come later—I was hit with both a sense of joy and a spark of terror. Years of familiarity would be behind me. Who knew what the future might bring?

Chapter 18

FLETCHER

I stood in the shadows of the stadium bleachers and watched Avery take her diploma. She was wearing that smile, the one that made my gut clench.

I didn't know why I'd come here. Why I was torturing myself like this. Five more points. That's all I'd needed to pass the exam. Five more points and I'd be down there, proving to my old man that I wasn't a loser.

I'd asked hard-assed Turner to give me another problem, to give me a hundred, to give me however many he thought would justify adding five points to my exam. He'd just looked at me with dead eyes and said, "No exceptions, Mr. Thomas. You didn't get enough of the problems that I gave everyone else correct. Why should I be inconvenienced and have to spend my time creating another problem and checking it because you hadn't mastered the material in a timely fashion? I'll see you next year."

Like hell.

I'd listened to the T's being called, inserted my name where it should have been, imagined myself taking that scroll . . .

God, I was pitiful.

The last student name was called. The graduates stood. The alma mater rang out through the stadium as the band played and people sang. When the final words were sung, caps went sailing in the air, applause echoed—

Time to go. I headed for the parking lot. I didn't want to run into anyone, didn't want to be seen. I was stupid to come here. I got on my motorcycle, revved it up, and took off. I wasn't sure where I was going; I just knew that I needed to feel like I was going somewhere.

I rode around until it got dark. I didn't want to go to Scooter's party. Didn't want to go home. Didn't really want to go back to the Watkinses'. But I knew Avery's dad would come looking for me if I didn't eventually show up there, even though it was a curfew-free night because of graduation. I could stay out all night without him getting on my case, but I couldn't think of anything I wanted to do.

Well, I could think of one thing—go to the beach. But that was a bad idea.

I pulled into the driveway, lowered the kickstand, and turned off the bike. I headed for the stairs, heard a door close, and froze. Avery.

I didn't want to talk to her tonight, yet I did. I knew she'd ask me her usual questions—

"Got a minute?" a deep voice asked.

Detective Watkins. Disappointment slammed into me, not so much because he was here but because Avery wasn't. Slowly I turned. "Sure."

He sat down on one of the steps, indicated I should join him. I dropped down, stared at the street, the sky. Too many lights to see the stars. I didn't want to talk to him, had a feeling I knew why he was here.

"Did you think I wouldn't notice that your name wasn't called out tonight?" he asked quietly.

"Thought you were there for Avery."

"We were there for you, too. You're eighteen. I'm not legally your guardian. School isn't going to give me any information. But I expected you to tell me if you had troubles."

"It wasn't trouble. I didn't pass algebra. It's not a big deal."

"I'd argue differently. I think it's important to get your diploma. Do you just lack the one credit?"

I sighed. "Yeah."

"So what are you going to do?"

"Hadn't really thought about it. I want to get my own place. I don't have to have a diploma to fix cars."

"What if you decide at some point you want to go to college?"

I barked out a laugh. "Yeah, right. I'm college material."

"You could be, if that's what you wanted."

"Well, it's not. I hate school."

"So you're going to let high school beat you?"

His words were like a punch. "What do you want me to do?"

"Think about summer school. Get that one credit you need."

"Why do you care? Even in the beginning, way back when I was a stupid kid and you were a patrolman and I got caught shoplifting some sponge cakes and peanuts—why were you nice to me about it?"

Clasping his hands, he dangled them over his knees, studied them. "When I was seventeen I got mixed up in something I shouldn't have. Someone helped me, showed me that I didn't have to keep on the path I was traveling on. It made a difference." He looked at me. "You're not a bad kid, Fletcher. You've had some tough breaks. Right now, life sucks. Probably will suck tomorrow, too. But hopefully one day it won't." He patted my knee. "Think about summer school. You could ask Avery to help you learn all that x variable stuff you'll never use. She took after her mother when it comes to brains."

He unfolded his body and started down the steps.

"Hey, Detective Watkins?"

Turning, he faced me.

"You still see that guy who helped you?" I asked.

He grinned. "Every day. I married her."

Chapter 19

AVERY

I sat on a sand dune, slowly sipping a beer and watching the large pile of driftwood burn. Jeremy and Kendall were nearby but they were paying more attention to each other's lips than to me. Which was fine. That was how it should be.

A couple of guys and a girl were playing guitars and singing. Some people were dancing, some were playing in the surf. When we'd first gotten here, I'd visited with some girls I knew. Everyone was smiling brightly, laughing, looking like a ton had been lifted off their shoulders.

We'd graduated. We were finished with school. The party should have felt different. Instead it kinda felt the same. I felt the same. Uninteresting, a third wheel.

"We're going for a walk," Kendall suddenly said. "Want to go with us?"

I knew her well enough to know she was only inviting

me to be polite. "Thanks, but I'm enjoying the music."

"Will you be okay?"

"I'll be fine." To prove my point, I took another sip of beer. Not sure why I thought that would prove my point, but I did.

They wandered off, and I just absorbed the roar of the surf, the warm breeze, the full moon dancing over the waves. A guy dropped down in the sand beside me, nearly doing a face-plant. Straightening, he looked up at me with a goofy grin, his blond hair flopping into his eyes.

"Hey, I'm Brett."

"I'm Avery."

"I know. I've seen you around school. How did we go through four years and never really meet?" he asked, his words fast then slow, as though he was having trouble keeping up with them. Maybe he was just nervous, although I wasn't sure why he would be.

"Hey, four hundred and fifty kids in our class," I told him, even though he probably knew that. "Can't meet everybody. But we met now."

"Yeah. You're pretty."

"Are you drunk?"

He straightened. "I'm offended." He leaned toward me slightly. "Are you?"

"I don't think so." I held up the bottle. "Well, maybe a little."

For no reason at all my neck began to feel warm, like someone had focused X-rays on it. I glanced around. On the far side of the fire, I saw Fletcher. I wondered when he'd gotten here. More importantly, why was he here? Had things not worked out with Morgan? He was watching me. Or at least it looked like he was. It was hard to be certain. He was standing so still, though, his head aimed in my direction. I turned my attention back to Brett. He was cute in a cuddly puppy kind of way. He seemed like someone who would be fun. Not someone who would be moody. "So where are you going to college?"

That seemed to be the number one question everyone asked these days.

"Community," he said. "You?"

"Austin."

"Cool. That's not too far from here. I could come see you."

I smiled. "You mean like a date?"

"Yeah."

"I'm not going until August."

"That's even better. Wanna walk?" he asked.

"Sure."

He struggled to his feet as the sand shifted beneath him, then held out his hand and helped me up. I did not mean to compare his hand to Fletcher's but I couldn't help it—it wasn't as large, rough, or warm. I had a feeling that he spent a lot of time playing video games. He seemed just a little awkward as we walked toward the surf, his flip-flops slapping the wet sand. I'd taken mine off. I loved the feel of the beach on my bare feet.

"What are you doing over the summer?" I asked.

"Nothing. Just chilling."

"No summer job?"

"Don't need to work."

I probably didn't need to work either, but I didn't want my parents having to pay for everything and I wanted some independence. I was going to work at the Shrimp Hut, a restaurant on the beach not too far from where we were now. I didn't know why I didn't share that with him, why I didn't really want to talk to him. He wasn't creepy or anything. I just didn't feel a connection. I couldn't banter with him, not the way I did with Fletcher.

I squeezed my eyes shut. Why was I suddenly comparing everything to Fletcher?

"Over here," Brett said, taking my hand and leading me away from the fire.

Enough moonlight and stars were out to guide us.

"Probably shouldn't get too far from the party," I said.

"Why?" he asked.

"I came with friends. Don't want them getting worried or looking for me."

He stopped. "I can take you home."

Something about the way he said it made me feel odd. My dad had always instructed me to trust me instincts. "Nah, I'm good going home with my friends."

"I can change your mind."

The next thing I knew his arms were around me, and his mouth was pressing hard against mine, his tongue pushing at the seam between my lips. I shoved him away. He staggered back.

"I heard you were easy," he said.

"You heard wrong."

"I just want a kiss."

"I don't want to kiss you."

He grabbed my arm—

I kicked him hard between his legs, and with a tortured groan, he crumpled into the sand.

Hearing clapping, I spun around. Fletcher was sauntering toward me. "All right, karate kid. I was just on my way to rescue you." He stopped beside me, his grin a flash in the moonlight.

"I told you I knew self-defense," I reminded him. "Just wish I'd had shoes on." I wasn't going to admit it but my big toe was killing me. I might have bruised it.

"I bet he doesn't."

He finally looked up at me. "Bitch."

"Hey, watch your mouth," Fletcher said, "or I'll put my fist into it."

"I just wanted a kiss," Brett whined. "To celebrate graduating, you know?"

"My six-year-old brother doesn't whine as much as you," I told him. "Find a girl who wants to kiss you. Let it mean something."

Shoving himself to his feet, Brett looked over at Fletcher. "I know who you are. You've kissed like a million girls."

"Not that many."

"Give me some tips. What do I do so a girl will let me kiss her?"

My interest was piqued. Maybe I'd even be able to figure out why he hadn't kissed me at Scooter's party.

Fletcher shook his head. "You don't want a girl to *let* you kiss her. You want her to *want* to kiss you."

"How do I make her want to kiss me?"

"Whatever you did tonight? Do the complete opposite."

"Okay, yeah. I think. Thanks."

"And apologize to her."

Brett looked at me. I figured if the sun were out, I would see that he was beet red. "Sorry," he said with contrition, before staggering away.

"What a jerk," Fletcher said.

"I think he had too much to drink."

"If drinking makes him a jerk, he shouldn't drink."

"You say that as though you speak from experience. Is

that why you drink root beer?"

"I like root beer."

"And you like me. Equally?"

"I give root beer the edge."

I laughed. "You could have explained it that way the other night. Makes it really clear. I thought you were going to Scooter's." My abrupt change in topic didn't seem to faze him.

"Decided it wouldn't be all that much fun with the parents around. Didn't figure there would be any here."

"Morgan is going to be disappointed."

"She's pretty resourceful. She'll find someone else."

I almost asked if he'd find someone else. Was he even looking? Did I want to know? We were semi-friends, that was all. I dug my toes into the sand, looked at the way the moonlight washed provocatively over him, wondered why he was really here. Maybe because he needed a semi-friend, not some girl who was just throwing herself at him, wanting to use him.

"You missed the graduation ceremony," I said quietly.

"Wasn't invited."

My heart lurched. He'd tried to keep his voice flat, emotionless, but I heard the fissure of . . . regret, disappointment, sadness. "I'm sorry."

"No big deal."

Turning, he looked out over the surf rolling in. I'd

always assumed he was popular, well-liked. Girls constantly stopped in the hallway, guys greeted him. He was invited to all the parties. So why wasn't he surrounded by friends now? Why was he here alone?

"Was it the algebra?" I asked.

"Yeah." He faced me. "But it's done. Time to move on." His voice was even, detached, as though he couldn't be bothered to care. Yet I suspected he cared a lot. How could he not? Still it would be unkind to linger on the topic.

"You're right. Last party of senior year. We should probably enjoy it."

"Or we could go get a burger."

I smiled brightly. "I like the way you think. I just need to get my shoes."

As we began trudging back toward the party, I knew it wasn't a date, but still I couldn't help but believe that it was *something*. He could be anywhere with anyone. And here he was with me.

We walked along the water's edge. He'd hooked his thumbs in his belt loops. I wanted to think he'd done it to stop himself from taking my hand, then wondered why I wanted him to take my hand. Besides, I was pretty sure that Fletcher was not a hand-taker.

When we reached the area where the bonfire burned, we trudged over the loose sand to the dune where I'd left my sandals. I bent down to pick them up.

"There you are!" Kendall cried as she and Jeremy rushed over. "Where were you?"

Her eyes widening, she came up short at the sight of Fletcher. "Oh, hi."

"Hey."

With a pointed look like she could dig into my brain and retrieve my memories from the last ten minutes, she asked, "Everything okay?"

"Everything's fine," I assured her. "We're hungry, so we're going to grab a burger."

"What a coincidence," she said. "We were just talking about doing the same thing."

"We were?" Jeremy asked.

She elbowed him playfully. "Yes. Remember?"

He still looked a little dazed when he replied, "Oh, yeah, I remember. B.S.'s right?"

"You can ride with us," Kendall told me. "Don't want Fletcher to go without a helmet."

I really wanted to ride with him, but it did make sense for me to go with them. Not that I thought she was at all concerned with Fletcher's skull. She had questions she wanted answered.

"We'll meet you there," I told Fletcher.

"Okay," Fletcher said, and walked away.

"So what were you doing with him?" Kendall asked as he disappeared into the darkness and we headed for the car.

"Just walking around." I wasn't going to tell her the mistake I'd made with Brett. It seemed my ability to judge the good intentions of guys was nonexistent.

By the time we got to the car and were on our way, Fletcher was long gone.

"So how do we play this?" Kendall asked, twisting around in the seat to look at me.

"What do you mean?" I asked.

"Are you interested in him? Is this like a date? Are you getting serious?"

"No, no, and no. We just want a burger, going to the same place."

"It seems like there's more, like maybe he did mean something when he said he liked you."

"It's not more and he didn't mean anything."

"Then what was he doing at the beach?"

"It was a party. He likes parties."

"How do you want to sit?" Kendall asked.

"On my butt. What are you talking about?"

"If we get a booth. Do you want to sit by me or Fletcher?"

"I'll sit by Jeremy."

"What?" she asked.

Jeremy snorted and caught my eye in the rearview mirror. I could tell he thought Kendall's inquisition was as funny as I did.

"You're not taking this seriously," she said. "What message do you want to convey?"

"That I'm hungry."

She gave a little growl. "Do you want him to think you like him?"

"Kendall, I love you, but you're really overthinking this."

"We'll sit at a table," she said with finality. "But we'll sit across from our guys—I know Fletcher isn't your guy, but I'll sit across from Jeremy so you don't have to worry about any awkward touching." Reaching over, she squeezed Jeremy's shoulder. "That's okay, isn't it, babe?"

"Yeah, I'm not a fan of awkward touching," he said.

"You know what I mean. We just need some distance between Avery and Fletcher."

"We don't need the distance," I told her. "He's living with my family, for Pete's sake."

"Which is exactly why you need the distance."

She was my best friend, someone I really enjoyed being with, but she had control issues. "I'll sit by Fletcher," I said.

"At a table. Those booths are small. You can't help but touch in those booths."

The booths were small. I wasn't sure I'd ever really noticed. Fletcher had beaten us to the B.S.—no surprise there—and claimed a booth in a corner. He was sprawled in it, his arm resting along the back. He lifted two fingers in some sort of salute when we walked in.

"We can grab a table," Kendall assured me.

"Booth is fine," I told her, and led our merry little band over. As I approached, Fletcher straightened and moved over slightly. I slid in. My thigh touched his. I was grateful for his jeans and my capris. I worked really hard not to give the impression that I noticed his leg was rock solid.

"So who's going to go place the order?" Kendall asked.

"Fletcher and I will," Jeremy said.

She gave him a smile of gratitude. "Thanks, babe."

I told them what I wanted. Then as I stood to let Fletcher out, I reached into my pocket, pulled out a wad of bills, and began to straighten and count them.

"I've got it," Fletcher said.

"What? No, I pay my own way. This isn't a date."

"I've got it, Katniss."

"This isn't *The Hunger Games*."

"Could be. I'm starving, so let me pay." Without another word, he followed Jeremy to the counter.

I dropped back into the booth and scooted over to the wall.

"Why'd he call you Katniss?" Kendall asked.

"For some reason he's into using nicknames. Although I kinda like that one. She's tough."

"He's a little scary."

I scowled at her. "No, he's not."

"He seems tough, but then I guess that goes with his reputation."

"Ignore his reputation."

"A little hard to do when that's all I really know about him. He's nothing at all like Jeremy."

Looking at the guys standing at the counter, I had to admit they seemed an odd pair. Jeremy's white polo shirt was tucked into his pressed shorts. Fletcher's black T-shirt had apparently shrunk when he'd washed it because it out-lined every muscle. It was untucked and his jeans were snug. His dark hair was long and wild, while every strand of Jeremy's blond hair was in place.

Jeremy said something. Fletcher grinned. He had such a great grin. He was saying something, and Jeremy laughed.

"They seem to get along," I said.

"Jeremy gets along with everyone. My mom says he's going to go far."

I wondered if Fletcher would ever leave the area. What were his plans once he got that haircut?

The guys returned to the table with two trays laden with food. They passed around the burgers and drinks, set two large baskets of fries in the center. Community prop-erty. The booth suddenly shrank when Fletcher dropped down beside me. I refused to hug the wall, which meant that my leg was hugging his. It didn't appear he noticed that he was encroaching on my personal space.

Jeremy lifted his glass. "A toast to our gradua—"

Grimacing, I caught his eye, shook my head before he could continue on with some speech to commemorate our freedom.

He stared at me, shifted his gaze to Fletcher, turned beet red. "Sorry, man."

Fletcher picked up his glass. "To your graduation." He tapped his glass to Jeremy's, to Kendall's—she looked like she wished she were somewhere else—and finally to mine. He winked. "And to less bumpy roads."

My chest knotted painfully with his acknowledgment of our success. I knew how hard it had to be for him. I blinked to hold the tears at bay. "A lot less bumpy."

We all clinked glasses again, drank deeply. I realized there was a lot about Fletcher I'd underestimated.

"So," Jeremy said, "what are you doing over the summer, Fletcher?"

"Working at Smiley's. You?"

"Dad's law office."

"Sweet," Fletcher said.

"Not really. Mostly I'll be filing. Law is not exciting."

"I thought your dad was going to take you to court," Kendall said.

Jeremy grinned. "It's not like on TV. There is never a big aha moment when everyone realizes the wrong person is on trial."

"Jeremy's going to be a lawyer," Kendall said, beaming.

"Maybe," he said. "It's a long way off."

"You'll do it," she said. "I'm hoping to be a vet. I love dogs."

"Don't get her started on dogs," I warned Fletcher. "She does volunteer work for a second-chance shelter. She'll try to talk you into adopting one if you're not careful."

"What's a second-chance shelter?" he asked.

"They rescue dogs from kill facilities," Kendall said. "So they get a second chance."

"I like that," he said.

She blushed slightly, seemed a little confused, and I realized that he was turning out not to be exactly as she'd expected either.

We finished off our burgers while talking about the summer blockbusters that we couldn't wait to hit the theaters. Well, mostly Jeremy, Kendall, and I talked. Fletcher watched as though we were aliens that had just landed, and he couldn't quite determine what to make of us. Although I had to admit that I was observing him as well. He liked lots of salt on his fries but no ketchup. His burger was bun, meat, and cheese. I knew that because nothing else was visible.

When he finished his drink, he got up to get a refill.

"Anyone else?" Jeremy asked, grabbing his glass. Kendall nudged hers over.

Although I was almost out, I just shook my head.

As he walked off, Kendall leaned forward and whispered, "He's a lot different than I thought."

"Jeremy?"

She scowled. "Fletcher. Although it would have been nice if he'd offered to refill your glass."

"Why? I'm perfectly capable of refilling it myself."

"Jeremy always gets my refills."

"He's your boyfriend. Besides, Fletcher isn't Jeremy." She was going into control mode and I wasn't in the mood for it.

"Everything okay?" Fletcher asked when he got back.

"Avery needs some more tea," Kendall said pointedly.

"Okay." Her tone must have gone completely over his head, because he just waited, standing by the table. Waited for me to get out.

"I'm fine," I told him. "This late at night, it'll just keep me up."

He slid in beside me. "You can have some of mine."

"You can't share when it's free refills," Kendall said.

"What difference does it make?" Fletcher asked. "We paid for two drinks. There's no charge for refills."

"But . . ." She seemed stunned by the logic.

Which for some reason I found hilarious. I snatched up Fletcher's cup and took a couple of sips before handing it back.

With a grin, he finished off what was left.

Jeremy returned to the table. A group of boisterous graduates burst through the doors. Some were still wearing their tasseled caps.

"On that note, I think it's time to go," Jeremy said.

We all scrambled out of the booth. Lightly taking my arm, Kendall held me back. "We're not going home yet," she whispered. "Can you get a ride with Fletcher?"

"Thought you were worried about his skull."

"Come on, Avery. Graduation night. I don't have to be home until dawn."

"Sure, let me ask Fletcher."

His reply was simply to hand me his helmet. A guy of few words was Fletcher. I realized as I slid my arms around him that it didn't really bother me. I knew that Kendall and Jeremy spent a lot of time talking. They had so much in common. They enjoyed the same music, video games, television shows, movies. They debated characters, and the best superheroes, and their favorite pizza. I couldn't imagine Fletcher caring about any of those things.

We pulled into the driveway and he cut the engine. Sometimes silence was louder than the roar of an engine. Reluctantly, I swung my leg back and climbed off. I handed Fletcher his helmet and shifted from one foot to the other. "Thanks for the ride home."

"Any time."

"No bets tonight?" I asked.

"No bets."

"See you." Turning, I headed for the front door.

"Hey, college-bound?"

Stopping, I faced him. The outside garage lights washed over him, sitting astride his bike, making him look at once dangerous and welcoming. Why did I always have such conflicting thoughts where he was concerned? "Yeah?"

"Do you always kick guys in the nuts when they try to kiss you?"

Studying him, I angled my head thoughtfully. "Maybe you should try it sometime and find out."

I didn't know what had prompted me to say that. It also seemed that he grew incredibly still straddling that bike. Because I didn't want to offer him the chance to reject me, to laugh, to say *not in a hundred years*, I spun on my heel and strode into the house.

With my back to the door, I took a deep breath and wished I'd had the courage to stay and find out if he wanted to kiss me as much as I wanted to kiss him.

Chapter 20

AVERY

Sunday was a little more relaxed than the one before. Dad was preparing for his usual grilling. I helped Mom bake a carrot cake, my ode to vegetables. The blinds in the kitchen were pulled up, and I had a view of Tyler splashing around in the pool. Although he knew how to swim, he still wore little inflatable floaties around his arms.

Fletcher sat on the edge of the pool. All I could see was his bare back, the ridges of his spine. But I could imagine the individual droplets of water glistening and gliding along his skin. Tyler was taunting him, splashing water at him. Fletcher ignored him.

Then suddenly Fletcher launched himself into the pool. Tyler shrieked as Fletcher grabbed him and held him up. Fletcher's maniacal laugh echoed across the yard.

"You should join them," Mom said.

"What?" And I realized I'd been standing in front of the window like a statue.

"Join them," she repeated as she spread the last of the buttercream icing on the cake, something I was supposed to have helped her finish.

"Are you sure? I was supposed to help you."

"Go have some fun," Mom insisted. "There's not much left to do here."

She didn't have to tell me again. I headed outside. As I neared the pool, I kicked off my sparkly flip-flops, then sat on the edge, letting my feet dangle in the warm water. Tyler circled around Fletcher where he stood.

"Look, Avery!" Tyler called out. "I'm a shark."

"I think you should be a dolphin," I told him. "Wouldn't want you to hurt Fletcher."

Fletcher looked at me, but I couldn't tell what he was thinking because he was wearing his sunglasses. As he glided toward me, Tyler kept pace.

"So what's the movie for tonight?" Fletcher asked.

"I don't know, but I won't be here."

"Big date?"

If I didn't know better, I'd think he sounded jealous. "Work. During the summer, on the weekends, I waitress at the Shrimp Hut."

"I've never eaten there."

"Stop by sometime. Family eats for free."

It was like he had X-ray vision through those sunglasses. I could feel the intensity of his stare. "I'm not family."

So I'd somehow offended him. I shrugged. "You're living here. You're family. Or if you're too proud, you can pay the twenty bucks for a dozen shrimp."

"Seriously? Twenty bucks for shrimp?"

"You should see the price on the steak."

"People pay that?"

"Yep. Jeremy took Kendall there before prom. It was romantic. But put a big dent in his allowance."

"Where did you go before prom?"

"To the bookstore."

Above his glasses, his brow furrowed. He didn't get the joke.

"I spent the night in a dystopian world," I said. "Reading a book," I added, because I wasn't sure if he got it. "Did you go to prom?"

"Can you see me in a tux?"

Actually I could. I thought he would look pretty hot in a tux, but I decided to keep that to myself. "I figured you'd go as a rebel, in a leather jacket and jeans."

"Figured wrong. Couldn't see the point in it. But I can't believe you didn't go."

"When you're a *brainiac*," I said, deliberately using the thoughtless name he'd once applied to me, "sometimes you intimidate guys. Add that your dad is a cop with an arsenal of guns at his disposal, and you're pretty much undatable."

"You've never had a date?"

He sounded endearingly baffled, which made me feel good—that he thought I should be dateable. "No, but that's okay. Gives me something to look forward to when I go to college." I kicked water in his face.

"Hey!"

"You don't strike me as a pool guy."

"The kid kept bugging me."

"I did!" Tyler yelled, splashing water at me. "Come in, Avery."

"Nah. Lunch will be ready soon."

Fletcher leaned down and whispered something to Tyler, who grinned like a fiend and bobbed his head. I could pretty much guess what they were plotting.

"Don't you guys even think it," I warned.

Fletcher propelled Tyler toward me. They both grabbed a leg before I could get away. Tyler hung on like grim death. I tried to kick Fletcher.

He pulled. I toppled over into the water, arms and legs flailing. I came up sputtering, dragging my hair out of my eyes. Tyler was howling with laughter. Fletcher was grinning like a loon, and again something inside me tightened and turned. I thought I might take a hundred dunkings for that smile.

"Jerks!" I yelled.

Lunging to the side, I snatched Tyler up into the air. His shriek nearly burst my eardrum. I looked over my shoulder. Fletcher hauled himself out of the pool in one smooth movement, his muscles rippling while the water sloshed off him. He sat on a lounge chair and pulled a black T-shirt down over his head.

"We won!" Tyler shouted. "We beat you, Avery!"

"Yeah, you won," I admitted, even though I wasn't sure what they'd won. I released Tyler. He plopped back into the water, puttered around. I glided to the edge of the pool and folded my arms over the tile. "You can't get out of the pool after you drag someone else in," I told Fletcher.

"You can if you won and the battle is over."

He looked relaxed. I wished I had been responsible for his ease, but I suspected it was mostly Tyler's doing. The kid had a way of making even the grumpiest people turn into sunny-side-up optimists.

Dad called us to the table. I helped Tyler out of the pool, scrubbed a towel over him, and drew a T-shirt over his head. Holding my hand, he walked with me toward the patio.

"I like him," he said in a whisper loud enough that the entire neighborhood probably heard.

Fletcher was a few steps ahead of us. He slowed his gait.

"He likes you, too," I told Tyler, just before we caught up with Fletcher.

Fletcher swung him up onto his shoulders. Tyler laughed. And all I could think was, *I like him, too.*

The Shrimp Hut was a rustic building that would have been near the boardwalk if the beach had had one. Instead it was just shy of the public area where people sunbathed and rushed into the surf. On the nonbeach side it had a small parking lot, but employees were encouraged to park in the public parking area so the restaurant guests weren't inconvenienced.

I usually arrived at work with shoes filled with sand. I'd learned to wear flip-flops and change into running shoes after I arrived. I hadn't been here since last summer when I worked, but walking into the place was a little like coming home. Fishing nets hung along the walls. Attached to them was an assortment of starfish, crab shells, beach paraphernalia.

"Hey, Avery." Dot greeted me. She was the owner and manager, and not the most creative person in the world considering the moniker she'd given her pride and joy. As far as I knew she'd never married. I didn't think she was much older than my mom but her love of the sun had taken a toll on her. Her skin was darkly tanned and leathery, but she had a smile that lit up the room.

"Hey, Dot. How's business?"

"Getting there. Now that school is out it'll really kick into gear. Speaking of school being out, congratulations on your graduation."

"Thanks," I said, beaming. "Hard to believe."

"It'll get easier. I have a little something for you." She reached beneath the hostess counter and retrieved a small box with a purple bow.

"You didn't have to do that."

"I remember how exciting it was to graduate. Go on. Open it."

Inside was a pewter necklace with a small starfish-shaped medallion at its center. "It's great, thanks!"

"So you don't forget me," she said.

"I could never forget you." Reaching over, I gave her a big hug. "Truly, thank you."

She blushed. "Now go on. I'm not paying you to lolly-gag about. You know the routine."

She didn't pay until I was on the clock so this lollygag-ging was coming out of my pocket, not hers—not that I bothered to point that out. I loved working for her.

"Yes, ma'am," I replied smartly, and went back to the office. I changed my shoes, put my backpack in a locker, and grabbed a white apron. In spite of the prices on the menu, the restaurant was pretty laid-back. Waitstaff wore black shorts and white T-shirts with the restaurant's emblem on them. I pulled my hair back into a ponytail. Then I snatched an order pad from a stack near the door and went to work.

What I loved most about working here were all the different people I met. A lot were from out of town, out of state, out of the country. I also liked the people I worked with. Some were older and they worked here all year long, but many of them were students just catching a job for the summer.

What I hated most about working here were all the different people. The majority were nice but every now and then I waited on someone who was a little difficult: he didn't like the food or the service or the sand. That last type always got to me because they were at the beach. What did they expect?

But I learned to deal with it. If nothing else, it gave me experience at diffusing tense situations. I only had a six-hour shift on Sunday, but my feet were killing me as I trudged to my car after eleven. The sun had gone down two hours earlier. There were no streetlights around here, but I had the flashlight app on my cell phone.

And I wasn't alone. Marc, Jenny, and Katie were also heading to their cars. I'd met them last year when they were seniors in high school. They'd all gone away to college for a year and were now home for the summer.

"The worst part about coming home," Jenny said, "is

that suddenly my dad wants to know where I am every minute of every day. I have to tell him what time I'll be home and he blows up if I'm late. I've spent months with him not knowing where I was or how late I was out." It looked like where she had been was mostly at a tattoo and piercing salon. She had what looked like a constellation inked on her neck. She had nose and lip piercings. The blond hair from last summer was now pitch-black.

"Same here," Katie said, ruffling her fingers through her auburn curls. "My dad practically has me on a leash."

"Must be a girl thing," Marc said. He and I were the same height, but his shoulders rounded like he was always carrying a heavy load. "No one's on my case."

I imagined that it would be difficult to go from almost complete freedom to having to answer to someone again. I wondered if I would experience that when I came home from college. My parents kept such a close watch over me now with curfews, wanting to know where I was going, when I'd be home. All that would change when I went to college. I wondered how I could prevent it from reverting back when I came home for the summer.

"Course it's not as bad as my boyfriend being in Colorado," Katie said with a longing sigh that seemed to drift out over the dunes.

"How did you meet him?" I asked. She'd been boy-friendless last summer. We'd commiserated together.

Obviously we wouldn't be doing that this summer.

"Dorm cafeteria. His uncle's a professor at Tech so that's where he wanted to go. His name's Drew and he's a dream."

"So he doesn't exist?" Marc asked. "Just in your dreams?"

"Funny, Marc," she said. "He exists, and I'm crazy about him."

"He's a long way off," he said. I'd always thought that he kinda liked Katie. "Lot can happen over the summer."

"Nothing's going to happen," she assured him. "Just like nothing happened last summer, if you'll recall."

Ouch! I thought. She'd known he liked her. Maybe she liked him, too, but she had obviously moved on and wanted to shut him down.

"So what about you, Avery?" she asked. "Hooked up with anyone yet?"

"Nope. Saving myself for college." I said it like I'd had a choice.

We reached our cars.

"See you guys tomorrow," I said as I unlocked the door and slid inside. I inserted the key in the ignition, turned it. Trooper puttered and died. "No, no, no."

I tried again. Same thing. I banged my head on the steering wheel. Then nearly leaped out of my skin when there was a knock on the window. I rolled it down.

"You got a problem?" Marc asked.

"Yeah, it won't start."

"I could be all macho and tell you to open the hood, except I wouldn't know what I was looking at, and that could prove kind of embarrassing. But I can give you a ride home."

He lived in a town thirty miles in the opposite direction of where I needed to go.

"I'll be fine. I'm going to call home."

"I'll at least wait until you do that."

"What happened?" Mom asked immediately when she answered. She always expected the worst when I called at night.

"Trooper won't start."

"Okay, I'll be there in a bit."

"Can't Dad come?"

"He got called out."

Which meant she'd have to wake Tyler or find someone to watch him. "Mom, I can get a ride with someone; come back for Trooper tomorrow."

"It'll be fine, honey. Just tell me where to find you."

I told her where I was parked.

"Keep the doors locked, windows up," she reminded me, as though I didn't already know that.

"See you soon," I told her. I looked at Marc. "My mom's coming."

"I'll wait."

"I hate for you to have to do that. It could be a while."

He shrugged. "I'll just go home and binge-watch *Game of Thrones* again."

Smiling, I got out of the car. We sat on the hood. The moon was still a bright orb in the sky. The breeze blowing off the ocean was keeping the bugs away. I could hear the lulling rush of the surf in the distance. I'd love to sleep out here some night. Better yet, in one of the beach houses. Not that I could afford the rent.

"You should have asked Katie out last summer," I said quietly.

Marc groaned. "God, did I look that moony-eyed last year? Did everyone know?"

"My dad taught me to pay attention. When we'd go to the grocery store he'd grill me afterward. What did the lady at the checkout look like? Describe the woman on the ice cream aisle. It was kinda fun." I waited a heartbeat, then asked, "So why didn't you?"

"Was afraid she'd say no."

"Nothing ventured, nothing gained."

"Guys have very fragile egos."

I laughed. "Not the ones I know."

"Maybe you're not as observant as you think."

I lay back and stared at the stars. Because there were so few lights out here, it was like looking at a velvet blanket covered in stardust. "Maybe she's not serious about him."

He hunched forward, elbows on his thighs. "She is." He looked back over his shoulder. "Guess you and I could date."

"Wow, with an offer like that, how could I say no?" I asked.

He groaned. "See, that's why I didn't ask her out. I'm not smooth."

"You don't have to be smooth. You just have to be honest."

"Okay, then. I'd like to go out with you sometime."

"And now I have to be honest. I think we're better as friends."

"Guys hate the f-word. You know that, right?"

"But *friend* is such a good word. It's a good thing."

"Only a girl would say that."

Sitting up, I tucked my legs beneath me. "I think you still like Katie."

"Yeah, I do."

"So we could go out as friends. The whole honesty thing—it won't be a date."

"Fair enough."

The silence eased in around us.

"So that Joffrey's a prick," I finally said.

Marc laughed. "Yeah, he is."

"Have you read the books?"

"Last summer when I should have been asking Katie out."

"You know, you can date and read. One doesn't preclude the other," I chastised. Then we started comparing books made into movies, what worked, what didn't, and what we liked about each format. The time seemed to speed by.

As I became aware of a rumbling, I looked over my shoulder. "Think that's my ride."

"Your mom drives a motorcycle?"

He sounded so impressed that I hated to disappoint him. "No, it's a friend."

"Oh? Must be a good friend to come out this time of night." He nudged my arm playfully. "A really good friend."

I slid off the hood. "He's staying with us."

"I'm intrigued."

"It's no big deal." But I thought if the sun was out that he might see me blushing.

"Don't make my mistake," he said. "Don't be so afraid of rejection that you don't take a chance."

Is that what I was doing? Was I so afraid Fletcher would reject me that I was tamping down any feelings I might have for him?

Fletcher brought his bike to a halt, turned it off, and I could sense him sizing Marc up. Marc doing the same. Honestly, guys could be so juvenile sometimes.

"This is Marc. He works with me," I said. "This is Fletcher."

They each nodded, said nothing.

"So are you going to help me with the car?" I asked Fletcher.

"Yeah, pop the trunk. Your mom said you had some tools."

"Think you'll need a jump?" Marc asked. "I can stay."

"Might. Appreciate it." Fletcher got a flashlight out of the trunk, popped the hood, and shone the light over the engine. "Try to start it."

I did and got the same results as earlier. He fiddled with something, told me to give it another go. Trooper refused to cooperate.

"Okay," he said. "We'll call for a tow truck."

"What about what Marc suggested?" I asked. "A jump."

"It's not your battery and it's too dark for me to get a good look so I can try to fix whatever it is." He turned to Marc. "You don't need to wait."

Marc looked at me. "You sure?"

"I'm sure. Thanks for hanging around."

He took off, while Fletcher called the towing service. After he closed the hood, I popped back onto it to wait. Fletcher stood nearby, sweeping the light from the flashlight over the dunes and weeds, like he was searching for something.

"So who's the guy?" he finally asked.

"I told you. Marc. We work together."

"Do you like him?"

"Sure. He's a nice guy. He realized tonight that he should have asked Katie—a girl we work with—out last summer because now she has a boyfriend, someone she met at college."

He stopped sweeping the flashlight around and sat on the hood. "You know you could have answered that with a yes or a no."

"Unlike you, I'm not a person of few words. And if I answered yes, you might not have understood that we're just friends." For some reason it was important to me that he completely understand that.

"That's good," he said. "You shouldn't date people you work with. Things don't work out, makes it awkward."

"Like you've had experience with that?" I asked.

"I hear things. So how was work?"

"You mean other than the fact that Trooper let me down when I needed her the most? Tiring. My feet hurt. There was one customer—" I growled. "I wanted to charge him a pain-in-the-butt fee. He didn't even leave a tip. Jerk."

Fletcher chuckled. "A pain-in-the-butt fee?"

I looked over at him. I liked the way his smile looked in the moonlight. "Yeah. It should be the law for anyone who has to deal with customers, that based upon their behavior you can charge them additional fees. You just wait until you're dealing with customers at the auto shop."

"I've worked. I know what people are like."

Shifting around, I tucked a foot beneath my leg. Why had I assumed he wouldn't have the gumption to get a job until my dad helped him find one? Why was I never willing to give him credit? "Where did you work?"

He hesitated. Why wouldn't he share anything? "Wait, let me guess. A male strip club."

"That would be interesting," he said.

"To say the least. So really, where did you work?"

"Jake's Tattoos and Piercings."

"The one that went out of business, the one next to the drugstore downtown?" The only one in town, so I wasn't sure why I was asking for clarification. Our town was not known as a hotbed for either tattoos or body piercings.

"Yep, not a lot of people needing tattoos around here. Jake said he was going to Vegas. Don't know if he did."

"Why didn't you go with him?"

"Didn't like doing it, having to get way too close to people."

"I guess you do know about crummy customers."

"Absolutely."

"Think you'll like working at Smiley's?"

"Yeah. Cars are way more interesting than people."

"I don't know that I'd go that far."

"At least cars don't express their disappointment in you."

I banged my fist on the hood. "But they can disappoint you."

"Don't be so hard on the old girl. She must be close to half a century old."

"Not that old," I assured him. "Dad wanted me to have a tank in case I got involved in an accident. Higher chance of survival. I have to admit I was a little insulted that he expected me to have a wreck."

"He probably has complete faith in you. It's the other guy he doesn't trust. Besides, at least he cares."

I wondered if he thought his dad didn't. It was late and I was tired, and here we were with time to kill. "So your dad doesn't mind you living with us?"

"I didn't ask him." He shoved himself off the hood. "Here's the tow truck."

Only then did I hear the rattling and rumbling. I didn't know why those trucks always sounded ominous, as though they needed a tow as badly as the car they were coming to retrieve.

We made arrangements for the tow truck driver to haul it to Smiley's. He'd just leave it there, locked. I rode home with Fletcher. This was getting to be such a common thing that I was contemplating buying my own helmet.

With the wind rushing past us, we couldn't really talk, although I wasn't certain that we ever really did. Each time I thought a bond was developing, he'd step back. Sometimes I thought he liked me, and other times, I felt like he wanted to charge me a pain-in-the-butt fee.

He pulled into the driveway, killed the engine. I got off the bike and handed him the helmet.

"Sorry you had to be bothered to come to my rescue," I said.

"Avery . . ."

His voice held remorse, a fact I almost missed because I was so stunned that he'd actually called me by name. It hit me like a hardball to the solar plexus. I couldn't recall him ever saying my name before. His deep rough timbre had woven around the syllables as effectively as it had around my heart.

"Did you think I wouldn't find you, boy?"

I jerked my head around to see a large guy stumbling out of the shadows at the side of the garage.

"Go into the house, Avery," Fletcher said as he shoved himself off the bike and took a few steps away from it, a few steps toward the rangy, gray-haired man.

"Who is it?" I asked.

"Just go insi—"

Head lowered, the man charged. His shoulder rammed Fletcher in the chest and they both went down.

Fletcher threw him off, scrambled back to his feet, and held his arms out. "Dad, don't."

This was his dad?

With arms and fists flailing, the man came at him again. Fletcher warded off the blows. Then he shoved his father back. The man tottered. He'd barely regained his balance before he charged again and took his son down.

"Mom!" I screamed as I ran to the side of the house. "Call Dad! Call Dad!"

I grabbed the hose, turned on the spigot, and rushed back. Turning the nozzle to full blast, I squeezed the trigger. A powerful stream jetted out, and hit Fletcher's dad in the face. He yelled, scrambled back. I kept the water aimed at his eyes.

Mom tore out of the house, carrying a baseball bat. "Your dad's on his way."

She rushed over to me, dropped the bat, and wrapped her hands around mine. "I've got it."

While she kept the spray going, I knelt beside Fletcher. "Are you okay?"

He held up a hand, looked away. Stupid question. Of course he wasn't. He was bleeding, breathing harshly. Drenched.

I heard tires screeching to a halt. I glanced over my shoulder. Dad leaped out of his car and rushed past Mom.

"You can turn it off now, Mary," he said.

The water fizzled out. Dad turned Mr. Thomas over, handcuffed him.

Hatred burned in the man's eyes as he looked over at Fletcher. "You pressed charges against me!" he growled.

Fletcher shoved himself to his feet. "You didn't give me a choice."

"You're worthless, you know that?" he snarled. "Always have been."

"Shut up," Dad ordered as he heaved the guy to his feet, gave him a hard shake, and started dragging him to the car. "I'm taking him in. Mary, get Fletcher to the hospital. Have him checked over."

"I'm fine," Fletcher said.

After Dad shoved the guy into the back of the car, he walked back over and gave Fletcher a hard stare. "You sure you're okay?"

"Yes, sir."

"I'll add these charges and the violation of his restraining order to the previous ones, but he'll probably still make bail again. Sorry the wheels of justice turn so slowly."

"At least he didn't have a gun this time." Anger simmered in Fletcher's voice.

My stomach dropped to the ground.

"Thanks," Fletcher said, nodding at Mom and me before he turned and headed up the stairs to his apartment.

In shock, I stared after him. "His dad threatened him with a gun?" I whispered.

"Yeah, he's father of the year," Dad said.

No wonder Dad and Fletcher had been tight-lipped about why he was here. I couldn't imagine it, the horror of it.

"Can't you talk to the DA?" Mom asked. "Keep him locked up?"

"I'll do what I can," Dad said. He gave her a small smile. "Good idea to use the hose."

"That was Avery."

Dad hugged me. "I'm torn between being proud of you and telling you if it happens again to run into the house."

"Fletcher told me to, but I just couldn't."

He tucked me beneath the chin. "Yeah, I know. But he won't be bothering you any more tonight."

Dad kissed Mom before heading to the car. As he drove off, Mom put her arm around me and led me into the house. I could barely think; everything I'd seen, heard, and witnessed was spinning around in my head. But I did know one thing: Fletcher wasn't all right.

I went into the bathroom and gathered up a few things before heading back out. I considered just opening the door, but Fletcher had experienced enough intrusions tonight, so I knocked. I was actually surprised when he opened the door.

He sighed. "Look, it's been a long night . . ."

"I know, but you're bleeding." I held up the box. "I brought some stuff."

Sighing again, he opened the door farther. I walked in, set the box on the low table in front of the couch. I grabbed a bowl I'd brought, then went into the bathroom and filled it with warm water. Mom was a nurse. She'd be better at this, but she'd taught me how to take care of minor injuries so Tyler would be left in capable hands when she was at work.

When I walked back into the living area, Fletcher was sitting on the couch, his feet on the table, the TV turned to some movie that had sharks flying through the air. I sat beside him, took a washcloth from the box, dipped it into the water, and gently wiped at the corner of his mouth, where there was a thin trail of blood. His jaw was tight, his eyes focused on the screen.

"When you would come to school, all scratched up and bruised, you would say, 'You should see the other guy,'" I said quietly. I considered my next words. I knew he wouldn't want to hear them, but he couldn't keep holding everything in. "That was him tonight, wasn't it? The other guy? Your father."

Chapter 21

FLETCHER

How do you explain to someone whose dad is one of the good guys that your dad isn't?

I was eight the first time my dad took his fists to me. He was drunk. It only happened when he was drunk. He could go months without drinking and then one night something would set him off and he'd hit the bottle—and after a few he'd decide he needed to hit me as well.

I hated him. And I loved him. It made me feel weak that I loved him. But I didn't want to think about all that so I concentrated instead on Avery: the gentle way she touched the damp washcloth to my busted lip, the way she smelled of fried seafood. The strands of her blond hair that had worked themselves loose from her ponytail and framed her face. The white T-shirt that hugged her like a second skin. Her shorts, her bare legs, so incredibly long, her bare

196

feet, the tiniest toes I'd ever seen.

I noticed all that out of the corner of my eye, because I didn't want her to know I was paying attention to her so I kept my gaze straight ahead, focused on the TV as though the most interesting thing in the world wasn't her but a tornado whipping sharks around.

"When did he first hit you?" she asked.

"I'm not going to talk about it."

"It's not your fault."

"You don't need to tend to me."

"I want to." She took a tube out of her little box, squeezed some clear gel onto the tip of her little finger, and dabbed it at the corner of my mouth, then above my eye, and finally on the bridge of my nose. After wiping her hand on the washcloth, she removed a bandage from the box, tore off the wrapper—

I snatched her wrist. "You are not putting Spider-Man on me."

She smiled and the force of it shot straight to my gut.

"Come on," she said. "It makes ouchies go away."

"You really should leave," I told her, before I did something we were both going to regret.

"I'm not going, not until you talk to me. You can't keep all this in."

"Talking is not what I want to do, and if you don't go—"

"You don't scare me, Fletcher. And you can trust me."

"That's the problem. You can't trust me."

I slid my hand around the back of her head and brought her in for a kiss. I ignored the pain from my busted lip. I wanted to frighten her away. I wanted her to realize I wasn't good for her. I wanted her to know that I was dangerous, that I didn't care about her, that I only cared about me.

Instead, she crawled onto my lap, straddled my legs, took my head in both her hands, and kissed me back.

And I was a goner.

She tasted so good, like key lime pie. She combed her fingers through my hair, stroked her hands over my shoulders. I thought nothing in my life had ever felt so good.

I rolled her over until she was stretched out on the couch and we were pressed together. I loved how tall she was. She fit perfectly against me. I could never get enough of this, never get enough of her. There was comfort in her touch, gentleness, eagerness. She wanted the kiss, wanted it as much as I did.

She scared the hell out of me. The way she cared, the way she smiled, the way she made me laugh. I'd never wanted to kiss a girl as much as I wanted to kiss her. I hadn't liked seeing her sitting on the car with Marc. Jealousy had sliced through me. I'd never experienced jealousy before. I knew I had no right to be jealous now.

She belonged with someone like Marc. Someone who

didn't come with a lot of garbage. She wanted honesty and openness. I'd survived by keeping so much hidden for so long. Embarrassment over the way my old man was. Shame at the thought that maybe I deserved the words and fists he flung at me.

But Avery caring, touching me, wanting me—

It was almost too much, too overwhelming. Yet she was an anchor. So sure of herself.

Breaking the kiss, I lifted my head and gazed into her blue eyes. No pity, no sympathy. I wouldn't have been able to stomach either one. I'd always hated the way people who knew the source of my bruises looked at me as though I couldn't take care of myself.

"You don't have to hide from me," she said.

I pressed my forehead to hers. "He only hits when he gets drunk."

Her arms tightened around me. "Is that why you drink root beer?"

"I'm afraid I'll be like him."

"You're not like him. You're nothing like him."

Her voice held such conviction. I could almost believe her. Swallowing, I rose back up and met her gaze. "You don't know me."

"But I want to."

"I don't fit in your world."

"How do you know? Have you ever tried?"

I shook my head. "I'll just hurt you. I can't be what you want."

"Don't assume you know what I want." She placed her palm against my cheek. "You don't really know me either, Fletcher. Maybe there's a lot we don't know about each other. But what I do know, I like."

I tucked strands of her hair behind her ear. I swallowed hard. "I like you, too."

"We can start with that." She brushed my hair back from my brow. It felt so good to have her fingers going through my hair. "Right now, though, I need to go. Mom knows I came over. She's going to come check up on us at any moment."

"See, I'm the kinda guy a mom checks up on."

She laughed. "All guys are the kind a mom checks up on."

I really liked her laugh. The ease of it.

Reluctantly, I rolled off her. Sitting up, she skimmed her fingers over my face. "I won't tell anyone about the other guy or who he is. Not even Kendall. It's our secret."

She brushed her lips over mine before hopping off the couch and heading for the door.

"Avery."

She stopped, turned. The word lodged in my throat. I'd been on my own for a long time.

"Thanks," I forced out.

"Put on the bandage. I promise it'll make you feel better."

She walked out, closing the door quietly behind her. I looked at Spider-Man, figured what the hell, lifted my T-shirt and placed the adhesive bandage over my heart.

Just so it could remind me that I didn't want to hurt hers.

Chapter 22

AVERY

I'd made it down three steps before I had to sit. My knees were weak, everywhere seemed weak. I pressed my fingertips to my swollen lips. Fletcher's kiss had been nothing at all like the one I'd experienced in band camp. His had started out hungry, rough, and then it had gentled, become slow and thorough as though he was savoring it, savoring me. I'd been so aware of him, but also aware of his pain, his anguish. That his father—

"Avery?"

I looked up to see Mom standing at the foot of the stairs. "You okay, honey?"

"Yeah," I whispered, pushing myself to my feet and descending as quietly as possible the rest of the way.

"How's Fletcher?" Mom asked when I reached her.

I looked back over my shoulder at the door. "I think

he's okay, or as okay as he can be. Busted lip. He's going to have some more bruises tomorrow."

"I should have taken that bat to his father." She slipped her arm around my shoulders, and we began walking to the house. "How are you doing?"

"Still shaken, I think. I don't understand people hurting each other."

She opened the gate. "I know. I don't know if anyone does."

We went through the backyard and climbed the steps to the deck.

"He said his dad had a gun last time. Do you know what happened?"

She sighed. "Yeah. Let's have some tea. It'll help you sleep."

Chamomile tea was my mom's answer to everything. Or maybe she just needed the time to get her thoughts together as she put on a kettle and brewed the tea. She poured the tea into delicate china cups with black roses on them that she had inherited from my grandmother. She arranged a few shortcakes on a plate and set it between us. For comfort.

"Over the years, your dad's been called out to a couple of disturbances at the Thomas place. The first time Fletcher was just twelve. His dad claimed they were just roughhousing. Fletcher wouldn't say.

"Then about a week ago, someone called in that they

heard shots fired. When the officers got there, Mr. Thomas said the gun had gone off accidentally when he was cleaning it. But the officers had heard shouting when they arrived. Fletcher had bruises forming. When the officer took him aside to speak with him, he said he'd only talk to your dad. So they called your dad out."

She took a sip of tea, looked around the immaculate kitchen. "Fletcher was pretty shaken. His father had threatened him with the gun. Your dad talked him into filing charges, and convinced him to come stay with us. Thought he'd be safe here. Then tonight happened."

"What happens now?" I asked, horrified that all this had gone down and I hadn't known. No one at school had known. But then if that were my life, I wouldn't tell people either.

"He'll probably get out on bail, but I'm sure your dad will have a talk with him before that happens."

"Are you scared?"

"No. He's a mean bully. He's not going to hurt us. But you keep the doors locked and you stay alert." She placed her hand over mine. "Police are a phone call away."

I scraped my nail over the countertop. "I believed what people said about Fletcher. I believed it when he said he was bruised because he got into fights. Which I guess he did . . . got into fights. But I just thought he was the one starting them."

"You can't blame yourself. I figured out pretty quickly that he doesn't reveal a whole lot, that he's the master of one-word answers. Your dad was like that when I met him."

My eyes grew large. "Dad?" The same dad I met at the diner when I needed to talk?

Mom smiled. "I know, hard to believe. I think he sees a little of himself in Fletcher."

Dad never knew his father. He'd taken off before Dad was born. He was raised by a single mom. "Like what?" I asked. "His dad didn't beat him. He wasn't around."

"No, but your dad was angry. Didn't trust easily. So he can relate to Fletcher, knows what he needs. We'll help him get over this."

I nodded. "Definitely."

She got up, leaned over, and pressed a kiss to my forehead. "I need to get to sleep. It's going to be a long day tomorrow. Sweet dreams, and don't think about any of this."

She headed to bed, and I sat there for a long time, sipping cooled tea and thinking about all of it. I understood so much more now, but had so many questions. Had Fletcher kissed me because he wanted me or had he just needed the comfort offered by warm lips?

He'd said he liked me. But this time the words seemed to carry more weight, his eyes had held more depth of feeling. Still, I wasn't sure exactly where our relationship stood, but I knew I definitely wanted us to be more than just friends.

"Can we get ice cream?" Tyler asked.

It was a good thing that he was buckled in, because he was a bundle of energy. He loved going on field trips and this one was special. I'd taken Mom to work at the hospital that morning so I could borrow her car.

"If you behave," I said in answer to Tyler's question.

"I always behave."

"How about if you stay calm and don't break anything?"

"I can be calm."

He sat still for a total of three seconds, but that was okay because we'd arrived. Tyler sat up straighter when I stopped the car. Then his brow furrowed.

"This isn't a field trip."

"Sure it is. We're checking on Trooper." And Fletcher. By the time I'd woken up that morning, he'd already left for work. As a matter of fact, his motorcycle revving up was what woke me. After last night, I wanted to make sure he was okay. That we were okay. "I bet Smiley will let you take a tour. You've never been to an auto shop before." Everyone in town knew Smiley. He had huge teeth that made him look as though he might be related to a horse, but he had the biggest, most genuine smile I'd ever seen. His name fit him.

"Are there giraffes here?"

"No."

"Dinosaurs?"

"No."

"I wanted to see dinosaurs."

"The summer is young, my friend."

His brow furrowed even more deeply until his eyebrows touched. "What?"

"Before the summer is over, we'll see giraffes and dinosaurs. Today we're looking at cars."

We got out of the sedan and walked to one of the open bays. There were four, and on the far side was the office. Behind it was a waiting room.

I spotted my car up on a lift. Standing beneath it was Fletcher, wearing a gray jumpsuit with a red rag sticking out of the back pocket. His working uniform. I didn't know why my heart did a little skip. It seemed like he could wear anything and I'd think he looked good.

"Hey, it's Fletcher!" Tyler cried and started to run forward.

I snagged him by the waist and hauled him up into my arms before he'd taken two steps. "No running," I commanded. "And no leaving my side."

"Will a car drop on me?"

A yes would have him hugging my side, but I didn't want to terrorize him or lie to him. "No, but there's a lot of machinery around here so we just have to be careful."

"'Kay."

I put him down just as Fletcher sauntered over, wiping his hands on that red rag. Why did that little action have to look so sexy?

"Hey, munchkin," he said before turning to me. "Checking on your car?"

Checking on you, I thought. His old bruise was yellowing, faded, almost gone, but he had new bruises today and some scrapes. "That and Tyler's never been to an auto shop before."

"I've almost finished fixing the problem from last night but if you could leave it here for a couple more days, I could take care of a few things after hours so you won't be charged for it. I okayed it with Smiley already."

"That seems like a lot of trouble. You don't have to do that."

"Hey, your family is giving me a free room. The least I can do is rotate a few tires."

"Thanks, that would be great. I don't work again until Friday."

"I should be able to have everything finished by then."

"Great then, it's a date." I felt the heat suffuse my face and decided I probably looked as though I was sunburned.

"I didn't mean a *date* date. I just meant a plan, you know, I agree."

The corner of his mouth that I'd tended to last night hitched up slightly. "I know what you meant."

If at all possible, I was probably blushing harder. "Can you give us a little tour?" I leaned in and whispered, "I told Tyler we were going on a field trip."

"Sure."

He took Tyler around, showing him various tools, explaining how the hydraulic lifts worked. My chest tightened with the thought that he'd probably never had anyone to show him around, to take him on little outings.

"Hey, Avery."

Turning, I smiled at Smiley who was as usual grinning broadly. "Hi. I was just checking on my car."

"Fletcher was here before I opened the shop, waiting on me, wanting to make sure he was the one who got to take a gander at it. Don't know where the kid learned his skills, but appears he knows what he's doing. And I like his eagerness and initiative."

"He appreciates having the job."

"Could be a good future for him."

"Hey, Smiley, don't know if we ought to have that kid walking around." A guy with red hair and a short beard interrupted us.

"He's fine. Fletcher's watching him. Avery, this is Don

Johnson. Not the actor." His grin, if at all possible, grew wider. "But my manager. He handles the work area out here, I still handle the office."

"Mr. Johnson," I said, holding out my hand.

He held up oil-smudged hands. "Sorry."

"That's okay."

"It was nice to meet you, though. I'd better get back to work." He walked away.

"Are you planning to retire?" I asked. I couldn't imagine the place without Smiley there.

"No, but I'm starting to take life a little easier, give more attention to the family. Was hoping one of my boys would take over the business, but they have no interest in it."

"I'm sorry to hear that."

He waved a hand like he was swatting at a fly. "Kids are supposed to have their own interests. That's the way we brought them up, to think for themselves."

Fletcher led Tyler back over.

"Can we get ice cream now?" Tyler asked.

"Were you good?" I asked.

"Yes."

I looked at Fletcher. He winked at Tyler, nodded at me. I thought there might be a conspiracy at work, but I said, "Okay, then, we'll go."

"Can Fletcher come with us?" Tyler asked.

"I gotta work, buddy," Fletcher said.

"Take a break," Smiley said. "Life is short. Gotta eat ice cream when you can." He patted my shoulder. "Tell your dad hey."

"I will." As he walked off, I glanced at Fletcher. "Do you want to join us? There's a place just a couple of blocks down."

"Sure. Let me wash up."

He was back in two minutes. When we stepped outside, he slid on his sunglasses and pulled a cap from his back pocket and settled it over his head. I didn't think it was so much to protect himself from the sun as it was to shield his bruises from prying eyes. I thought of all the times he'd swaggered through the hallways at school like those bruises were badges of honor. I'd have given anything for a fireman's hose that I could have directed at his dad last night. The force of it would have knocked him on his ass and brought me some satisfaction.

Tyler was between us, holding our hands. Every now and then he'd lift his feet up and cause us to sway.

"Hey, squirt," I said. "Good behavior all the time on a field trip."

"I want to swing. Can we go to the park?"

"After the ice cream."

Inside the shop, I ordered a strawberry sundae with marshmallow topping, Tyler ordered a brownie sundae, and

Fletcher ordered a banana split with three scoops of vanilla doused in chocolate. At the register, he said, "I got it."

I wanted to argue with him as he pulled out his wallet but I figured after last night, he needed to feel in charge. I found us a booth at the back, near the door that led to a little play area with a slide. I tried not to let it hurt my feelings that Tyler wanted to sit with Fletcher instead of me.

When Fletcher joined us, I said, "Really? They have like fifty flavors of ice cream and two dozen toppings and you go with vanilla and chocolate?"

"It's what I like."

"That's so . . . pedestrian."

"I've got bananas, nuts, whipped cream, and a cherry. You've got ice cream and a topping. Let's not compare boring."

I snagged his cherry.

"Hey!" he groused.

With an innocent smile, I ate it.

"Avery always gets the cherries," Tyler said, setting his on top of my ice cream.

I shrugged. "It's actually my favorite part of coming to the ice cream shop."

"What if it was mine, too?"

"Is it?" I asked.

He shook his head. "Nah. Vanilla and chocolate." He dug in.

I went a little slower. "So how are you liking work?"

"I like Smiley. He seems like a good guy. But the manager, Don Johnson, seems to think I'm a kid playing around or something. He keeps narrowing his eyes at me."

"I think he just has narrow eyes."

Fletcher grinned. "Maybe."

"Smiley's impressed with your work."

He dug his spoon into the ice cream a couple of times without scooping anything out. "Like I told you, I learned a lot about cars from my dad. The way he was last night . . . he's not always like that."

"He should never be like that."

"Like what?" Tyler asked.

How could I forget that little ears were listening? "Like nosey," I said, reaching out and pinching his nose.

"I'm done," he said, shoving his bowl at me.

"How can you be done? You had three bites."

"I want to play on the slide."

"Go on."

Rather than asking Fletcher to move, Tyler slid off the bench and waddled under the table until he came up on the other side and straightened. He shoved open the door and went into the play area. It was enclosed. I could see him and the three other kids in there. He was safe. And feeling independent.

"He's a handful," Fletcher said.

"Yeah, but what else am I going to do with my day?" My cell phone dinged. "Excuse me."

I had a text from Kendall.

Honey getting tickets 4 baseball game Thurs. U in?

I loved baseball, loved Kendall, but I was so tired of being the third wheel. I looked up to find Fletcher studying me as though he was afraid I was getting bad news.

"Hey, would you like to go to a baseball game Thursday night? Kendall has four tickets. She and Jeremy are going. She hates for the others to go to waste."

It was a little lie, but I didn't want him paying for the tickets. I also really wanted him to go with me. I could see the battle playing across his face.

"About last night," he said quietly, "the kiss. It was adrenaline-induced. After everything that happened . . . I just reacted."

"I figured that," I lied as calmly as I could, while disappointment zinged through me. I held up the cell phone. "This isn't a date. Just a ticket that needs to be used."

He studied me for a moment, a long moment that seemed to stretch into eternity. "Okay," he finally said. "I'm in."

Great. I texted back.

Me and Fletcher.

Ding.

Kendall: Seriously?
Me: Yes. NBD
Kendall: We need to talk.
Me: L8r

I shoved my phone into my shorts pocket. "We're on."

"I need to get back to work."

"You should probably go ahead. It'll take me a while to pry the munchkin off the slide."

"Okay, then, I'll see you later."

Watching him walk away, I wished the baseball game was a date. I wished the kiss had meant something. I wished Fletcher wanted to be more than friends.

For someone who was so smart, I was suddenly being incredibly dumb.

"You invited Fletcher," Kendall said as she flopped across the comforter on my bed.

She must have been watching out the window to see me go by because she was ringing the doorbell two minutes after I put Tyler down for his nap.

"He's living with us," I told her. "I couldn't not invite him. It would be rude."

"You didn't invite your parents or Tyler," she said.

"Kendall, don't be difficult." I was sitting in the slider rocker that I'd inherited from my grandmother. Even though it wasn't cold, I'd draped an afghan she'd crocheted over my legs. The chair and afghan always calmed me, and I could tell that Kendall was in a mood to be uncalming. "Oh, and if he should ask, you already had four tickets. I'll pay for his and mine. I just don't want him to know I'm paying for them."

"Oooh." She pursed her lips. "A relationship should not be built on deception."

Her mother's words no doubt. "It's not deception. I wanted him to go and I knew he probably wouldn't if he thought you didn't already have the tickets."

"So do you like him?" she asked.

"Sure. He's nice."

"Nice." She picked up her phone and began tapping keys. "Let me look that word up in my dictionary because I'm not sure it means what you think it does."

"He's a nice guy."

She tossed her phone down. "Well, if you're thinking of liking him, I mean really liking him, you better take him to the public health center and have him tested. Do you know how many girls he's been with?"

"Probably not as many as you think." So much about him wasn't as we'd thought.

"A bunch. Get him tested."

"Are you having Jeremy tested?"

"No, he's not a player. I can't even get him to play with me."

I stopped rocking. "What are you talking about?"

She sat up, then stretched across my bed. *"He's* the definition of nice. He and Fletcher are complete opposites. Jeremy is a virgin. And he wants our first time together to be special, so we haven't"—she flung out her hand—"you know."

"But that's good. That he recognizes that it's an important step."

"I know, I know. I just . . . I don't know."

"You still love him, don't you?"

"Of course I do. More than ever, but sometimes I think a little bad boy might not be so horrible. I mean Fletcher dominated the booth the other night and he didn't even have to do anything. It's just his presence."

"It's him. It's not because he's bad."

"Has he kissed you?"

I felt my face grow warm.

Kendall sat up. "He has. What was it like? Is he a slobberer? No, he wouldn't slobber. But I bet it's intense."

"Focused," I admitted. "Very focused."

"Has he tried more than kissing you?"

"No. He's very much aware of what my dad does for a living."

"But you're of age."

"Yeah," I said sarcastically. "Like that's going to matter to my dad. Besides, Jeremy is right. Something more than kissing should be special. And we're not there yet."

"So where are you?"

"Edging toward friends." Maybe more. I didn't know why I couldn't tell her that. I shared everything with her, but my feelings for Fletcher seemed too new, too raw. Too confusing. Sometimes I liked him, sometimes he irritated me. Sometimes the like went to a whole new scary level—straight into the stratosphere.

"Well, I just don't want you to get hurt."

"I'm not going to get hurt."

I wondered if I sounded as unconvincing to her as I did to myself.

Chapter 23

AVERY

Thursday night, Jeremy drove us to the stadium. Kendall was in the front seat, of course. Fletcher and I in the back.

When we arrived, the place was already teeming with people. Fortunately we found a spot near the back of the lot. We began the long trek to the stadium. Jeremy and Kendall held hands and walked so closely together that their shadow appeared to be some creature with two heads. Not touching, Fletcher and I sauntered along behind. I hadn't seen much of him this week. Apparently we were both honoring the "it was just adrenaline" position regarding the kiss.

Yet I was so aware of him. A worn baseball cap shadowed his face. His sunglasses shielded his eyes from the sun. With both of those, his fading bruises were barely visible. His lip was almost healed. His stride was relaxed, unhurried. I was paying so much attention to him that I lost sight of Kendall. I hadn't noticed that we'd hit the mash of people as they funneled into the entrances.

"I should give you your ticket," I said to Fletcher, "in case we get separated."

"We won't get separated." He placed his arm around my shoulders and snuggled me up against his side as though he were protecting me from an alien invasion from above.

It was a little awkward to move until I slid my arm around his back and hooked a thumb into one of his belt loops. I'd seen other girls do it and always thought it looked cool, like the couple was really together, comfortable with each other.

Because Fletcher was a little taller than I was, I didn't have to shorten my stride, like I usually did when I walked with Kendall. Next to him, I didn't feel like a giant. People jostled us and fought to squeeze around us, as though a limited number of prizes waited on the other side. I didn't even get irritated when people cut in front of us. I liked where I was, nestled against Fletcher's side. I knew as soon as we had room, he'd let me go.

Only he didn't. We got our tickets scanned, walked farther into the area where the crowds quickly dispersed and there was room to breathe again—and he kept his arm around my shoulders. I saw Kendall and Jeremy standing off to the side.

"Over there," I said, pointing.

And still he kept his arm around me as we wandered over, stepping out of the way of people who weren't watching where they were going.

"So," Kendall said when we reached them, "why don't you guys"—she pointed her finger rapidly back and forth between Jeremy and Fletcher—"grab us some dogs and drinks while Avery and I hit the ladies'."

"What ladies and why would you hit them?" Fletcher asked, his face perfectly serious. Although I could see the twinkle in his eye.

Kendall blinked at him. "The restroom."

"Ah." Fletcher winked at me.

"He's teasing you," I told Kendall. "He knew what you meant."

"Huh," she said, giving him a thoughtful look. "You said he was funny. That wasn't very funny."

I thought it was hilarious. "Only because you don't like to be teased."

"True that. We'll see y'all in a bit."

"Sounds good," Jeremy said. "Come on, Fletcher." He took two steps, waited.

I let go of Fletcher's belt loop, and he slowly slid his arm away from me, before heading off with Jeremy.

"That looked cozy," Kendall said as she led the way to the restroom.

"We were just trying not to get separated. I'd forgotten to give him his ticket."

Stopping, she planted her hands on her hips and faced me. "I'm not the dating police."

"Really, that's how it happened." I lifted my shoulders. "But once it happened, it felt . . . nice." Even felt like it was how we belonged.

Kendall let it drop until we were washing our hands at the sink. Then, as she reached for a paper towel, she said, "So are you getting serious about him?"

"I don't know." I leaned toward the mirror, checked my makeup, adjusted my ball cap. "I don't think he's interested in serious."

"But you like him."

I met her gaze in the mirror. "Yeah, I do. But let's not spend the night analyzing every move. Let's just have fun."

The guys were waiting for us, each of them holding a tray with our hot dogs, peanuts, and soft drinks. We made our way to our seats on the third-base line, close to home plate. I sat between Fletcher and Kendall; Jeremy was on the other side of her.

I bit into my hot dog, sighed with happiness. "Ballpark hot dogs taste so good."

"The best," Fletcher said.

Here in the stands, he seemed more relaxed than I'd

ever seen him. His attention was on the game, but every now and then he'd lean over and comment on a play.

It was the bottom of the second. Our team was at bat. The pitch came. The batter didn't swing. The umpire called a strike.

"Ump needs glasses," he said, his voice low near my ear.

I leaned in a little until our shoulders grazed. It was silly to relish the slight contact, but I did. "I know. What's your favorite sport?"

He shifted a little bit, and in spite of his sunglasses, I knew he was looking at me. "Football. Baseball is a close second, though. Never got into basketball."

"Same here," I said, knowing I was reading too much into it, but it was something we had in common. Finally. Something tangible. Kendall and Jeremy had so much in common. I knew it wasn't fair to compare Fletcher and me to them, but I couldn't seem to help myself. And because he'd answered so easily . . . "Favorite superhero?"

"Batman."

I didn't know why but that surprised me. "Why?"

"Because he doesn't have any superpowers. Beneath the mask and cape, he's just a normal guy."

I smiled. "I never thought of him like that. I think he may have just become my favorite, too."

"Nah, I figure you for Superman. He's got it all going:

speed, strength, the ability to fly."

That he'd guessed correctly surprised me, even if he got the reasons wrong. "Actually, it's got more to do with Henry Cavill being such a super sexy Superman."

He chuckled low. "Try saying that three times fast."

I was about to when a loud crack of the bat echoed. With a little screech, Kendall knocked into me. Jeremy jumped to his feet—

And caught the foul ball.

Kendall clapped. Jeremy sat and handed her the ball. I didn't think she could have squealed with more excitement if he'd given her a diamond ring.

She wrapped her arms around him and kissed him. When they broke apart, she showed me the ball like I'd never seen one before. "He's my hero," she said.

She was smiling brightly, so happy. I loved that he could make her so happy.

After that, Fletcher returned his attention to the game. No more questions answered. No more comments. Not even between innings when some silly little skit was going on.

Then right before the top of the fifth inning, kiss-cam flashed on the giant screen. People yelled and clapped. The camera zoomed in on an older couple, who laughed before giving each other a peck on the mouth. It moved on to another couple who kissed, then waved. Couple after couple smiled at the camera and kissed. The audience laughed, encouraged them.

The camera zoomed in on four people.

Kendall screeched, "That's us!"

She kissed Jeremy.

Embarrassed, not sure what to do, I turned to Fletcher. I shrugged, knew the heat of mortification was turning my cheeks a bright red. The camera wouldn't move on. I leaned in to give him a quick buss on the lips—

His hand snaked around the back of my neck and he planted a kiss on me that I thought might melt the camera lens. His other hand came up and cradled my cheek. Somewhere I heard cheering and hooting, but mostly I was just aware of Fletcher, his mouth, his hands, holding me captive. I didn't want to move away, I didn't want to break off from the kiss.

I just sank into it. I let it absorb me. I tuned out everything else until there was only the two of us. I heard the clearing of a throat, but I didn't care about anything except this moment.

Finally he drew back, held my gaze. "My favorite part of baseball," he said.

With a laugh, I realized my hand had knotted in his T-shirt. I didn't remember doing that, but I could have probably run around the bases during that kiss and I wouldn't have remembered it. I unfurled my fingers, tried to flatten the wrinkled material. "I've never been on kiss-cam before."

"Me either."

I liked that, liked knowing it was something unique for both of us. As I settled back into my chair, I noticed Kendall staring at me. "What?" I asked.

"You know the kiss-cam came back to you three times during that."

With a self-conscious laugh, I placed my hand over my mouth. "Really?"

She leaned in and whispered, "That kiss was so intense that I could feel it over here."

Scoffing, I tossed a peanut at her. "You're funny."

"Seriously. I thought they were going to have to call for the fire department."

"Now, you're just being ridiculous."

She was looking at me like she didn't know me anymore. "Just be careful," she warned in a low voice.

Sighing, I turned my attention back to the game, but I couldn't wipe the smile from my face. Sliding my eyes to the side, I saw that a corner of Fletcher's mouth was curled up, as though he'd gotten away with something.

We were supposed to be just friends, but what could you do when the kiss-cam was pointed at you? You made the most of it.

* * *

I told Jeremy to just go to Kendall's house. Fletcher and I would walk home. I wanted a little more time with him and I knew as soon as Mom heard a car pull into our driveway that she would be expecting me to come inside shortly afterward. It wasn't all that late, a little after eleven, so she wouldn't be worried if we weren't home yet.

Fletcher and I ambled slowly along the sidewalk. We didn't hold hands, but every now and then our fingers brushed.

"So how much do I owe you for my ticket?" he asked, his voice a low thrum in the night.

"I told you they had extra that they didn't want to go to waste."

"Yeah, that's not exactly how Jeremy explained it to me."

Okay, so Kendall didn't pass the memo on to her boyfriend. I thought they shared everything. Apparently not.

I sighed. "What can I say? I wanted you to come and I thought you wouldn't if you knew they hadn't bought the tickets yet."

He swung around until he was standing in front of me. "You're always so open, so honest, I didn't think you had a deceptive bone in your body."

"Deception makes it sound so bad. It was just a little white lie."

"And that makes it okay?"

"Didn't you have fun?" I asked, trying to ease my guilt.

"I was miserable."

I felt like he'd slapped me. "I'm so sorry. I thought you'd enjoy it. I thought—"

He touched his fingers to my lips. "I was miserable because all I could think about was kissing you. If it weren't for the kiss-cam, I might have gone crazy."

"I was going crazy, too," I admitted. Was going crazy now. I hoped he was thinking about kissing me again. I really wanted him to. I glanced around. A few of the houses still had lights on. But there was privacy in the shadows. I almost laughed. It seemed a little late to worry about privacy when our last kiss had been in public and televised to an entire stadium.

"The thing is," he said solemnly, "I know kissing you is a bad idea. Us doing anything together is a bad idea."

Not what I'd expected. I'd hoped tonight would prove that we could do things together.

"It was just a baseball game," I said.

"It wasn't and you know it. You wanted it to be a date."

If I was honest with myself, he was right. What an idiot I'd been. I *did* want for us to be more than friends. I wanted what Kendall had with Jeremy.

Fletcher wasn't Jeremy.

"Avery, you're leaving in a few weeks. I'm staying here. You're going to college. I'm not. Hell, I'm still in high school. You're a one-guy kinda girl. I'm not a one-girl kinda guy."

At that particular moment I really didn't like who he was. I thought about trying to convince him differently, but he knew himself a lot better than I did.

"You really read too much into tonight. It was just a night with friends," I said and started walking up the street. Now I was glad the darkness hid my face so he couldn't see my mortification. "I didn't want to be a third wheel, okay? So tonight I decided to use you."

We reached my house. "Don't worry about the cost of the ticket, Fletcher. It was my treat. You know, for the extra work you're doing on my car. When will it be ready?"

"Unfortunately, we had to order a part. It should come in tomorrow but I won't get a chance to install it until tomorrow evening."

"No problem. I'll take Mom's car to work."

"Knock on my door when you get home tomorrow night and I'll take you to get it."

He said it casually, like we were just friends, like I could knock on the door to the room where he slept and nothing was going to happen. "Will do," I said with the same casualness.

"Avery."

I hated when he said my name like that, all soft and low, a rumble that seemed to come up from the depths of his soul. Turning, I faced him.

"I did have fun tonight," he said. "I like you. But I also realize I'm not what you need."

"You don't know what I need, Fletcher. You don't talk to me, so you can't know. You don't share things. You have this wall around you, and all I can do is knock against it."

He gave me a sad-looking smile. "See, you just proved my point. You need someone who will talk to you and share things. That's just not me."

"But it could be if you tried."

"That's the thing, Avery. I don't want to try."

With long strides, he walked over to his motorcycle, put on his helmet, straddled the bike, and started it up. He tore out of the driveway at a speed that probably would have gotten him a ticket if my dad had been around.

I thought about walking back to Kendall's and talking to her about this, but I figured she was still in the car with Jeremy, talking about things that happened tonight, making plans for tomorrow, and sharing doubts, worries, or fears. And kissing him. She would definitely be kissing him. Afterward, he wouldn't make her feel like he wished they hadn't done all that.

I opened the door and went inside. Mom was standing in the entryway. I figured she'd come to look out the window when she heard the motorcycle take off.

"How was it?" Mom asked.

"Great fun."

"Where's Fletcher going?"

"I don't know. He didn't say. It's not really any of my business."

I headed for the stairs.

"Avery, are you sure everything is okay?" she asked.

"Everything's fine," I lied.

In my bedroom, I curled up on the window seat and stared at his door. I couldn't imagine how lonely it would be over there. Even though I was alone in my room, I could sense other people in the house, moving around. Although I wasn't lonely here when no one else was around, but that was because this was my home. I had a place here, my place, with all the things that were personal to me, things that meant something to me. I had memories here.

From what I could tell during the couple of times that I'd been in the FROG with Fletcher, he hadn't brought anything other than clothes. No personal touches, but then his being there was temporary. I guess that was what bothered me the most: there was nothing permanent in his life, except his bike.

I knew Fletcher was right. It was crazy for us to start anything when I'd be leaving for school in August. Long-distance relationships had to suck. And they took a lot of work.

In spite of the way he kissed me, Fletcher and I were

friends. That was all.

I just had to convince myself of that.

A soft rap sounded on my door.

"Yeah?"

It opened, and Mom peered in. "Got a sec?"

"Sure."

She wandered in and sat on the edge of the bed. "Is there something going on between you and Fletcher?"

How did I answer that? I brought my legs up and wrapped my arms around them. "Not really, no."

"Not a lot of conviction in that answer. Maybe you would like for there to be something between you," she suggested.

"No."

She studied me for a moment. She probably could see through the lie. "He has a lot going on in his life, Avery, things he needs to get straightened out. I don't want you to get hurt."

"Fletcher wouldn't hurt me."

"He might not mean to, but he's a lot older than you."

I scowled at her. "He's a year older."

"I'm not talking about a calendar year. I'm talking about experience. He's been independent. He's had to grow up fast. Your dad and I have tried to protect you. For good or bad, we've sheltered you. We'd like to see you with a nice boy, like Jeremy."

A spark of anger shot through me. "Fletcher's nice. What's he done to make you think he's not nice? You taught me not to judge people on rumors. Now you're doing it."

"You're right. He's nice. But his situation, his being part of the family now, you seeing each other so much—mixed in with teen hormones—just don't misjudge your feelings."

I knew she was trying to offer me sage advice. And I knew if Fletcher wasn't living in the FROG that I probably never would have seen him again after I dumped tea on him. I understood that the closeness of his current living arrangement meant we were continually crossing paths. But I also knew that I wanted to know him better, that I wanted to be his friend, maybe more than his friend. It wasn't because I knew about his father. It was because of Fletcher.

"I won't do anything stupid," I said.

Mom laughed lightly. "Famous last words." She got up, crossed over, and hugged me. "Just remember that you have the whole world and a bright future ahead of you."

I couldn't help but think: shouldn't Fletcher have the same?

Chapter 24

FLETCHER

I sat in a back booth at Jo-Jo's and thought about the first time that I'd ever eaten at the diner. I'd been twelve, picked up for shoplifting. I didn't know if all cops would have done it, but Avery's dad had studied the items I'd lifted and decided that I was hungry, so he'd brought me here. He was right. I'd wolfed down the equivalent of two meals before we left.

While I ate, he talked about baseball and cars. He pointed out different breeds of dogs that wandered by. Until then I'd just thought a dog was a dog.

When we were finished, when we were on the sidewalk, I finally got up the nerve to ask him why he hadn't yelled at me.

"Figured you're the kind of kid whose conscience yells louder than I could," he'd said.

He was right. My conscience could nag really loud. Loudly.

"What'll it be, hon?" the waitress asked me now.

"Pimento cheese sandwich, potato salad, strawberry shake."

She walked away and I looked out on the traffic light as it slowly changed colors. Green reminded me of Avery. She was going places. While I didn't even have a high school diploma.

But that wasn't the only reason that I'd put on the brakes tonight, that I'd told her I wasn't a one-girl kinda guy. No girl had ever made me want to be, but she came close. Sometimes I even thought about how nice it would be to have one person who was always there. But I knew how life worked. I knew I had to deserve that. And I didn't.

I might not have realized it if Jeremy hadn't caught that stupid foul ball and without a thought, a moment's hesitation, handed it off to Kendall. I never would have thought to give it to Avery. I would have caught it and thought, "Free ball! Cool!"

Stupid.

Jeremy had barely watched the game. He'd spent most of his time talking with Kendall like they hadn't seen each other since graduation night, although I was willing to bet that wasn't the case.

He was the kind of boyfriend Avery deserved. He knew how to be one.

I didn't have a clue.

That's when my conscience had started yelling: *you could ruin her life.*

The waitress set my order in front of me. I bit into the pimento cheese sandwich. It brought back the memory of sitting here with Avery's dad all those years ago. He was partly responsible for my decision to cool it with her. He'd looked out for me then, was looking out for me now. I owed him. I wasn't going to repay him by bringing his daughter down into the sewer with me.

Chapter 25

AVERY

"So was that your boyfriend the other night?" Marc asked.

I'd already been serving up fried seafood for an hour when his shift started, and those were his first words when our paths crossed. Not even a hello. Just cut right to the chase, even though we hadn't seen each other for several nights.

"No, a friend."

He shook his head. "No way. Not with the vibes that guy was sending. As far as he's concerned, you're his."

I turned in an order for a table of eight and began gathering up their coleslaw. "That is so Neanderthal. Trust me, we're not involved."

Fletcher had made that loud and clear last night.

"Then want to go to a movie next Thursday night?" he asked. "I checked the schedule. We're both off."

I gave him what I hoped was a smile that indicated I appreciated the offer. "Thanks, but I already have plans."

"With him?"

I lifted the tray. "With friends."

I headed through the swinging doors, crossed over to a large table by the window, and handed out the slaw. I didn't have plans, but I didn't want to hurt his feelings. He was a nice guy but I wasn't interested in dating him.

In spite of everything, Fletcher was the one constantly on my mind. Even if he was brushing me off.

"Could hit a matinee," Marc said when I came back through the kitchen to grab a pitcher of tea.

"I have to watch my little brother."

"Convenient."

"Marc—"

"Seriously, that guy sees you as more than a friend, and I think you see him the same way," Marc said. "I'm just trying to get you to admit it."

"By asking me out?"

"If I'm wrong, I've got a date."

"I think you're trying to make Katie jealous. Ask her to the movie as a friend. Who knows? Maybe she'll discover she's with the wrong guy."

I was two hours into my shift when I got to take a break. I walked down to the surf. This was one of my favorite parts of the job: that I could take a break close to the water. I loved the roar of the waves rolling in.

Seeing Jenny standing at the water's edge, I joined her. The sun was low in the sky but sunset wouldn't be for another couple of hours.

"I love working on the beach," Jenny said. "Not at the restaurant but on the beach. I've thought about setting up a shack and renting surfboards because I hate serving food."

"I don't think you'd meet as many people."

"And that's a problem because . . ."

"Have some crummy customers tonight?"

"Yeah. They didn't think I was focused on their need for attention. Honestly, they reminded me of some of the guys I dated at college this year."

"Did you date a lot?" I asked.

"Oh, yeah." She picked up a seashell and tossed it into the water. "A lot of first dates, a few second dates, a couple of third dates. Just no one who really did it for me, you know?"

In a way I was glad to hear that she'd had so many dates in college. I'd been hoping the dating scene would be more active there, although suddenly I wasn't that interested in college guys. On the other hand, her success rate at finding the right guy was disappointing. It sounded a little like playing Whac-A-Mole.

"Did you kiss a lot of them?" I asked.

"Most of them." She looked over at me. "Still no dates?"

I shook my head. Last night obviously didn't count. "No."

She gave me a once-over from my toes to my head. "I don't get it. Guys are idiots. But you will definitely find someone in college."

"It sounded like you dated a lot of them, and none of them were right."

She picked up another shell, studied it. "Right now I'm dating a bunch of frogs, still waiting for my prince. Course even if the prince showed up, I'd probably ditch him, too. Maybe I'm just not ready for a commitment. I like doing what I want to do when I want to do it. Look at Katie. She schedules her breaks for when she knows Colorado is available to chat. I don't want to live my life around a guy's schedule."

"Colorado?" I asked.

"Yeah, that's about all I remember from the oodles she's said about him. That he's from Colorado. I gotta get back."

She might not live her life around a guy's schedule but she did live it around Dot's, and when breaks were over, they were over. I turned and started walking back with her.

"The guys you dated . . . did any of them call things off?" I asked.

"Oh, sure. I really liked a couple of them, but they just wanted to have fun. They practically wore signs that said 'No Serious Relationships Allowed.' Which was fine since I'm not into serious either."

"But what if you had been?"

She stopped walking and studied me. "Is there someone you like?"

I sighed. "There is this guy . . . he keeps putting distance between us."

"Could mean a couple of things. He doesn't like you or he likes you way too much but doesn't want to. In either case, if you keep knocking on that door, you could get hurt."

"So I shouldn't knock."

She started walking again. "I didn't say that. Just understand the consequences. Only you can decide if he's worth the risk. Take Marc. Played it safe last summer. Never told Katie how he feels about her."

"He would die if he knew everyone knows how he feels."

"Even she knows."

"Really?" I asked.

Jenny nodded. "But you know, you can only wait so long for someone, then you gotta move on."

"If Katie knew, maybe she should have encouraged him," I said.

"Love is a complicated business, girlfriend. Sometimes the risk isn't worth the reward."

When I pulled into the driveway, Fletcher was waiting for me—or at least I told myself he'd been waiting for me. He was sitting on the steps outside his apartment, brown bottle in hand. Maybe he was just relaxing. But I was glad to see him. Probably more glad than I should have been.

As I got out of Mom's car, he set the bottle aside, slowly stood up in a sexy kind of way that made my heart start pounding. He sauntered down the steps, reminding me of a panther prowling through the jungle.

"It's kinda late," I said, wondering why I sounded breathless, as though I'd just run from work instead of driving. "I can get the car in the morning."

He rolled his shoulders. "Now's fine. I've got nothing else to do."

We were obviously back at the beginning, where words were considered the enemy and conversation was quick and to the point.

Fletcher straddled his bike and handed me his helmet. I tugged it on, then climbed on behind him and wrapped my arms around him. It was odd, how natural it seemed now, to be this close to him, to inhale his scent, to absorb his warmth. I wished we were doing more than popping into town to pick up my car. I wished we were traveling to

California or Canada. I wished we were going to see the northern lights.

I wished downtown was farther away than it was because we were drawing into Smiley's parking lot before I'd had a chance to finish all my fantasizing. I knew I should be as smart as Katie. I should move on.

But maybe I just wasn't ready yet to give up on what could be amazing rewards.

I spotted Trooper right away. Smiley's had a car wash next door and apparently someone had not only washed my car but waxed it as well.

"Did you make her shine?" I asked, handing Fletcher his helmet.

"It's Smiley's policy to wash every car that's brought in for repairs."

"Right, yeah, I'd forgotten about that." But still it had never shined quite so much.

He dug the keys out of his pocket, dangled them. "Here you go."

I did not want to be Katie. Deciding I needed to take a risk, I swallowed hard. "Fletcher, I'm not really sure what's happening between us."

"Nothing."

"We just kiss for the fun of it?"

A corner of his mouth hitched up. "We probably shouldn't do that anymore."

I didn't want to be back at the beginning. I didn't want the kiss at the ball game to be the last one. I took a step toward him. "And if I want to?"

Without much thought or planning, I leaned forward and pressed my mouth to his. Groaning low, he wrapped his hand around my neck, his thumb caressing the sensitive area just below my chin. I loved the way he took his time, the way he seemed to savor the movements of our mouths.

I propped my hip against the bike, needing some sort of support for my weakening knees. How was it that he could make me feel at once steady and unsteady?

I ran my fingers up into his hair, relishing the fact that right now it was only us, the night, his lips moving over mine.

Drawing back, he stroked my lower lip. "I've got no resistance where you're concerned."

"That's a good thing. I know you like me, Fletcher."

"I'm not good for you, and I'm not going to bring you down to my level."

Is that what last night had been about? Some misguided sense of protecting me? "Shouldn't what's good for me be my decision? And there's nothing wrong with your level. It's not beneath me."

"You're smart, Avery. Scary smart. You're going to college. You're going to meet smart guys—"

"You're smart."

"Not the way you are." He skimmed his fingers along my cheek. "You've got a future. You can do anything—"

"So can you," I interrupted. "You can be anything you want to be. You can have anything you want to have. You just have to be willing to work for it, to do what it takes to make it happen."

"It's not that easy."

"I didn't say it was easy, but someone once told me 'easier isn't always the right choice.' If it was easy, it wouldn't have value." I threaded my fingers through his hair. "I believe in you."

With a low groan, he jerked me forward and buried his face in the curve of my neck. "No one ever has before," he said in a low rasp.

Tears burned my eyes. I couldn't imagine what it would be like to never have anyone in your corner.

"My parents do or they wouldn't have taken you in. Smiley does or he wouldn't have given you a job."

Fletcher leaned back, studied me. "And if you're all wrong?"

"My dad will kick your butt. After I've finished kicking it."

He released a soft chuckle. "You're something else."

"Do you like me?"

"More than I should."

I couldn't stop the joy spiraling through me. "I like you, too."

He jerked his head toward my car. "We need to go. Make sure it works."

Leaning in, I gave him a quick kiss. "We'll talk some more when we get home."

I went to my car, unlocked it, and climbed in. I put the key in the ignition, turned it—

And Trooper purred like it had fallen in love. The car hadn't been this quiet when we bought it. Fletcher had done way more than rotate a few tires. I gave him a thumbs-up before pulling out onto the street. I couldn't believe how smooth it drove. I looked in the rearview mirror. Fletcher was following me.

When I pulled into our driveway, I hopped out of the car. I couldn't wait to thank Fletcher for whatever it was he'd done to Trooper. I wanted to hug him and kiss him.

Instead I just stood there and stared as he whizzed by. No wave, no acknowledgment at all. He just carried on and disappeared into the darkness.

Chapter 26

FLETCHER

I didn't know where I was going. I had no destination in mind. I just knew that I needed to keep riding until Avery was far away and couldn't pull me in. She made me want to believe in dreams and a future and plans worth having. She made me smile. She made me laugh, deep down, where I hadn't even known laughter existed.

Dangerous, so dangerous to forget who I was, to forget where I came from. I wasn't totally stupid. I'd taken biology. I understood genes and how they worked. That our parents contributed to our makeup. I didn't remember much about my mother. I remembered too much about my father.

Sometimes when I looked in the mirror I saw him in my black hair and my dark brown eyes.

I pulled onto a narrow lane and stopped just shy of the

entrance to the trailer park. I turned off the engine and started walking. It was late at night and I knew a lot of the trailers weren't soundproofed very well. I'd wake up half the people here if I drove through. Then they'd look out the window to see who it was and what was going on. I didn't want anyone to know I was here.

So I strolled along. I heard the occasional bark of a dog, a TV turned up too loud, a couple arguing. I hated arguing. I hated loud talking. I hated anger.

Me, who everyone at school was wary of, who everyone thought was so tough—I'd never hit anyone. Shoved on my dad to try to keep him off me, but I'd never hit him. He was my old man, and it just seemed wrong to even think about hitting him.

I stopped and stared at a dilapidated trailer. It was dark, no lights on. I doubted my old man was asleep. He was either out drinking or still in jail. I'd come here to remind myself of what I was. Someone who didn't dream, who didn't believe life got better.

Avery made me want to dream. She made me want to believe everything she said.

When I was with her, I felt different. I felt clean. I felt like she understood me, even though there was no way that she could. How could she understand this when I didn't even understand it?

What if I had inherited whatever it was that made my

dad the kind of man who'd beat on his kid?

    I believe in you, she'd said.

    Four little words.

    They scared the hell out of me.

Chapter 27

AVERY

I took a deep breath, slid beneath the surface of the water, and did several breaststrokes before coming up for air. Beneath the pool, the lights were on, but other than that I was encased in darkness. In the house, everyone was asleep. I told myself that I'd come out here because I wasn't tired, but the truth was that I wanted to be out here when Fletcher returned. He would return. He had to. But even as I thought that, I knew he could keep riding forever.

During my eighth lap, when I came up for air, I heard the roar of a motorcycle, then silence. Relief washed through me because he'd come back. Now I just had to figure out how to act the next time our paths crossed. *How to act.* I hated pretending. I hated having to watch my actions or words. I'd been brought up to believe in honesty, truth, the American way.

I sliced through the water to the edge of the pool. I could see the door to the apartment over the garage. I thought about going to Fletcher, talking to him, but he obviously needed time alone.

I heard his feet echoing on the steps. Then he appeared at the door, stopped, turned. I thought he was looking over the fence into the backyard. He'd see the pool lights on. I didn't know if he'd see me. I thought about waving, I thought about moving to the center of the pool so he'd see my silhouette in the water. But I stayed where I was.

He started back down the steps. Silence. The back gate creaking open.

I watched Fletcher stride across the lawn. He hunkered down at the edge of the pool. The lights cast a blue glow over him.

"You're wearing a bathing suit," he said. "Disappointing."

I welcomed his teasing. Maybe things weren't as bad as I thought. Laughing, I flung water at him. "Of course I am."

He glanced back at the house. "Looks like everyone's asleep. Who would know?"

"I would."

"Which room is yours?"

I realized we'd never given him a tour of the entire house. He was just the guy who lived over the garage. "The one on the second floor with the corner window."

"That looks out on the garage?"

"Yeah."

He turned to me. "So you can see when I come and go."

"If I'm in the window, but it's not my job to keep tabs on you." I felt the need to confess. "But that first night, I saw you sitting on the steps. You looked lonely."

"That's why you came and talked to me."

I pushed myself away from the side, floating back. "Just like you saw me tonight and came to talk. Where'd you go?"

"To my past."

"You didn't stay very long."

"Decided it was best not to."

"I'm glad. The present is better." I glided back and forth. "Why don't you come in the water?"

"No swim trunks, remember?"

"Shorts work, remember?"

"No shorts either." He skimmed his fingers along the surface of the water. Other than that, he was completely still. It was so quiet I could hear the crickets chirping.

I didn't know what to say to get us back to where we had been before last night. Everything suddenly seemed complicated and convoluted. Maybe we could never go back. Maybe we could only go forward.

"Trooper runs really great now," I said. "You did a lot of work on it."

He shrugged. "I like working on cars. I like taking something that's broken and fixing it. Or taking something that's almost broken and making sure it doesn't break. Is that what you're doing with me?"

"What? No." I glided to the edge of the pool and looked up into his face. "I don't think you're broken. I'm not trying to fix you. I like you, Fletcher."

"Enough to tutor me?"

I blinked, stared. Not what I was expecting. I smiled brightly. "Sure."

"Summer school starts Monday."

"What about work?"

"Class starts at eight, so I'll go before work, then stay late to make up for the lost hours. I want this to be the last time I ever see an equation."

"We can make that happen."

He released a strangled laugh. "Where do you get your confidence?"

It was funny. I'd seen him swagger around school and assumed he had way more confidence than me, that he was self-assured and in control. Maybe we all struggled with something. "I don't know all the answers in life, but the beauty in math is that the answer is always there."

He scoffed. "Yet I never seem to be able to find it."

"Maybe you've been looking in the wrong place."

Chapter 28

FLETCHER

Monday night I sat at the table in the dining room, my algebra book opened, and a pad of paper in front of me. Avery sat in a chair beside me, studying the algebra problem I'd solved like it contained the answers to the world. I guess for her it did.

She was so impassioned, so focused. I didn't know if I could ever feel that way about anything.

"Almost," she said. "See here." She used the pencil as a pointer. "You have a negative variable so you want to multiply both sides by negative one. Two negatives make a positive. Most of the teachers I've had don't care about the negative. Turner does."

And he was the one teaching the summer school algebra class. Just my luck. But Avery looked at me with such encouragement. Turner always made me feel stupid, made me not care if I didn't get the variable right. Avery made me see it as a challenge. If I got it right, she'd smile at me. I wanted her to smile.

"I think I've got it," I said. "Let me try the next one."

"Okay, but I want you to write out every step, no matter how small it is. Don't do some of it in your head. No one is impressed with how much 'mental math' you can do, only that the answer is right. My tests are covered with calculations by the time I'm finished. I could do some of it in my head, but what's the point? There's just a better chance I'll mess up."

"But if I can do it in my head, it's a waste of time to write it down."

"This isn't a race. The object is to get the correct answer. I want you to explain your thought process out loud as you work on the problem."

"You've got to be kidding me."

"I know you're not really one for talking, but when you have to vocalize what you're thinking, you'll often catch your mistake. It also helps me identify where you're having issues because I'll know what you're thinking."

"What I'm thinking is that it's stupid."

She gave me an indulgent smile. "Humor me."

I felt like an idiot but I did it, explaining each step as I wrote it down. When I got to the end and announced the answer, I looked at her.

"Very good," she said, and beamed at me. "You got it right."

I scowled at her. "Don't get too excited. That was an easy one. Your brother could have probably solved it."

"I doubt it. He hasn't learned his multiplication tables yet."

She was so comfortable with it. I couldn't imagine looking at all this stuff and having it make sense. "Give me a harder one," I ordered.

She leaned slightly in front of me, and I inhaled the fragrance of strawberries. So distracting. "Okay, let's try a system of equations," she suggested.

I'd asked for harder, and harder was what she gave me. It was two problems with two different variables, and I had to use one to solve the other. I hated these. They seemed to defy logic, and I'd often start one and then keep going in circles until, after about a page of work, I had simply rewritten the problem.

I just stared at it. I couldn't even figure out where to begin.

"It's a car," she said quietly.

"What?" I looked at her. Her eyes contained such earnestness. She really did want to help me.

"Think of the problem as a car," she explained. "It's broken. Knowing the variables will tell you how to fix it. That's all this is. You just want to figure out how to make it work."

"But I know cars."

"You didn't the first time you looked under the hood. You didn't know what all the belts and hoses did, where they went. You learned. An equation is the same thing. You analyze it, you learn what the various parts mean, how they work together. You don't have to look at it and know immediately what the answer is. You solve it. Just like you solved what was wrong with my car. Easy peasy."

"You think fixing a car is easy?"

"Nooo. Not at all. When you pass your algebra class, you can teach me how to repair a car."

I pictured her with grease on the tip of her nose, oil on her cheeks, grime on her hands. I thought about how bright her smile would be when she changed the clunk of a car engine to a purr. "Maybe I will."

She tapped the book. "Math first, though."

"All right." I studied the problem. "So I just want to make this puppy run."

"That's right," she said. "Take your time. I've got all night."

I worked it out, writing down every step, even the obvious ones, and revealing my thought processes, even the profanity. She corrected my steps a couple of times, ignored the profanity. I finally announced the answer.

"You got it!" Her eyes were twinkling, her lips parted in a smile.

My pride had prevented me from having this all year.

"I'm sorry," I said.

Her brow furrowed. "For what?"

"For all the times I didn't show up for tutoring, all the times you were waiting on me."

"Don't worry about it. I didn't have anything else to do."

She should have had plenty to do.

"Ready to try another one?" she asked.

What I was ready for was a kiss, but I couldn't keep running hot and cold with her. I needed a distraction. "Yeah, I'm ready to try another one. The harder the better."

As usual, she gave me exactly what I needed. I wished I could do the same for her.

Chapter 29

AVERY

Tuesday, I was in the kitchen helping Mom prepare dinner. Dad and Tyler were in the den building some kind of Lego city. Fletcher wasn't home yet. I was trying not to worry. We'd exchanged cell phone numbers in case one of us couldn't make a tutoring session. I had this crazy thought that maybe he'd text me some silly nonsense. But of course, he didn't. Unlike Jeremy, he wasn't the type to send little "thinking of you" notes over the phone. He wasn't the type to send notes at all.

The timer started beeping.

"Think that's it," Mom said, wiping her hands on a dishtowel. "Why don't you let your dad and Tyler know it's time to eat?"

"Shouldn't we wait for Fletcher?"

"He called. He's working late tonight."

"At Smiley's?"

"Uh-huh," she said distractedly, pulling a dish from the oven. "Some important job that had to be finished up today."

I had no idea that Smiley had his crew work late to finish up jobs. I wondered if it was a pain-in-the-butt customer or someone important. It just seemed odd.

"Maybe you can put together a plate for him and take it over there after dinner," Mom suggested. "I want to make sure he eats. He's too thin."

Mom thought everyone was too thin. I thought about explaining that he was slender and all muscle, but then she might wonder why I was paying so much attention.

After dinner, I heaped lasagna, two pieces of garlic toast, and Brussels sprouts onto a plate, covered it in foil, and placed it in a quilted casserole carrier. Dusk was settling in as I drove over to Smiley's.

One bay was open. The office windows were all dark. A couple of cars were in the parking lot but they had a numbered card hanging from the rearview mirror, which meant they were in the queue for repair. I pulled in, parked, and grabbed the casserole carrier.

Cautiously I walked to the bay and peered in. Fletcher was working under the hood of a red car. Glancing around, I didn't see anyone else. I just stood there watching his efficiency of movement, the way the muscles played across his shoulders as he tightened, adjusted, repaired whatever needed to be fixed.

Straightening, he turned for the nearby toolbox, stopped, looked at me. "What are you doing here?"

I held up the offering as I wandered farther into the shop. "Brought you some supper. Mom was worried about you eating." And I wondered why I didn't admit that I'd been worried about him, too. "She said there was some job that had to be completed tonight, so why isn't anyone here to help you?"

He dropped a tool into the box. It clanged. He picked up another one. "It's just something I'm doing on my own time. Smiley was okay with it."

"Like when you worked on my car?"

"Yeah, something like that. Let me just finish what I'm doing here."

I leaned against the side of the car, intrigued that he could look into what appeared to be a scramble of parts and know what needed to be fixed. I was also curious, maybe even a little jealous that he was giving time to someone else's car like he had mine. I had hoped I was special. "Whose car is it?"

"Mrs. Ellis," he said through gritted teeth as he struggled with something—tightening, loosening, I didn't know.

"The English teacher?" I asked, surprised. She wasn't that much older than us. Did he have a crush on her?

"That's the one."

"Her husband's serving in Afghanistan."

"That's what I heard. She brought it in for an oil change, but it's just a breakdown waiting to happen. Frayed belts, loose hoses. If her husband was here, he'd probably have replaced them all by now, so I'm just doing it."

"On your own time so she's not charged for labor."

He gave a little awkward shrug.

My chest tightened. I was falling for him. There was a goodness to him that he didn't see. "You're a nice guy."

"Smiley's covering the cost of the parts."

"Okay, so two nice guys."

He grunted as whatever he'd been struggling with gave. With a nod of satisfaction, he looked at me. "So what did you bring me to eat?"

We sat on stools at a workbench where tools hung on pegs. The fragrance of oil and grease wafted around us. I unveiled the plate and handed him a fork. He poked at the Brussels sprouts.

"What's this?" he asked.

"Brussels sprouts. You know . . . vegetables."

With a grimace he shook his head and dove into the lasagna.

"You want to hear something kind of cool?" he asked.

"Of course."

He reached into a pocket, withdrew a key, and grinned.

"Smiley gave me a key to the shop so I could lock up when I'm done." He studied the brass like it was pure gold. "He trusts me with all of this."

"Of course he does," I told him.

Shaking his head, he slipped the key back into his pocket. "I don't know. Makes me feel different."

"It's a good feeling when people trust you, depend on you."

"Yeah." As though suddenly uncomfortable, he turned his attention back to the lasagna. "This is good."

"It's Mom's secret recipe. Noodles from a box, sauce from a jar."

He smiled. "Might be something I could make, then."

"Most definitely. All her recipes are quick and easy. She's not a fan of cooking."

"How about you?"

"I like making desserts. That's about it." Reaching over, I snagged one of the Brussels sprouts from his plate and popped it into my mouth. "I can't believe you don't eat vegetables."

"I can't believe you do. They're gross."

"They're healthy." I glanced around. "You like working here?"

"Yeah. Don't know that I want to do it forever, but it's good for now." He finished off the lasagna and toast.

"How much longer will you be?" I asked as I rewrapped

the plate and slipped it into the cover.

"About an hour."

"That's not too late. We can still get some tutoring in."

Suddenly he looked very uncomfortable. "I know I should have texted you, but I'm . . . uh . . . meeting someone when I'm finished here."

My heart gave a little thud, but I tried to keep my voice level, not to give away how much I was bothered by his announcement. "Oh? Anyone I know?"

"Probably not."

"A girl, I assume."

"Yeah."

"That's good," I said as I hopped off the stool. "Hope you have fun."

I picked up the plate holder. Unfortunately, I hadn't closed it securely. The plate slid out and shattered on the floor. Brussels sprouts rolled all over the place.

"Great," I muttered as I bent down and began picking up the broken pieces.

Fletcher crouched. "I'll take care of it."

"No, I made the mess. I'll take care of it. You need to finish with the car, so you're not late for your date."

"I don't *date*. I get together with girls. Girls who aren't looking for any kind of a commitment. They just want a good time. That's all I'm looking for."

"And I'm not a good time."

He sighed. "I told you, Avery. It would never work with us."

"I get that," I said. "I do. You want easy. And I'm not that."

He sighed. "You are most definitely not easy. Let me clean this up."

I tried really hard not to let his words hurt, but still they stung. "You sweep. I'll hold the dustpan." With my head down, it would give me time to recover before I had to face him.

When the last of the mess was cleaned up, I held the quilted cover to my chest. "Sorry I had to put you to so much trouble," I said to Fletcher.

"Not a problem."

"Liar," I said with a false grin. "See you later."

I knew he was standing in the doorway of the bay watching me as I drove off. I almost waved, but I was too busy kicking myself for coming here with expectations that maybe things *would* work between us. I was also a bit unsettled to discover that I had a spiteful streak. I really, really hoped that he had a lousy time on his date.

Chapter 30

FLETCHER

Her name was Raven. She had short, coal-black hair that spiked in all directions, thick black liner around startling green eyes, a stud in her lip, a ring in her eyebrow, and a 3D tattoo on her hand that made it look like her skin was being peeled back to reveal bone. I knew her from school. She graduated last year and was studying music at a university near Dallas. She was home for the summer.

We'd gone out a couple of times, once last summer, once at Christmas. She'd called my cell phone because she'd stopped by the trailer and a neighbor told her I no longer lived there. It had occurred to me that if I made a point to see other girls, I wouldn't keep thinking about Avery.

So here I was at a club where I shouldn't be since I was

underage. But a fake ID opened a lot of doors.

Raven and I were sitting on a couch. Well, I was on the couch. She was in my lap, swaying to the music that was bound to leave us both deaf.

"I love this band!" she shouted.

She was about six inches shorter than Avery, three inches wider. Why did I even notice that?

"They're good," I yelled back.

"We should dance," she said. Then moved in and kissed me.

This was what I wanted. Easy. A kiss, a dozen of them. The sensations—

But it wasn't Avery's mouth, or Avery's taste, or Avery's sweetness.

Drawing back, Raven slid off my lap and snuggled against me. "Want to go somewhere and make out?" she asked.

"Let's listen to the band for a while." What guy said that? One who felt guilty for being here, one who thought he might have hurt Avery's feelings. But better to hurt her now, to cut things off early rather than later. She was probably glad she didn't have to tutor tonight. She was probably with Kendall and Jeremy, doing something fun.

Why was I thinking about her? The whole reason I was with Raven was so I wouldn't think about Avery.

"Let's dance," Raven insisted. She jumped to her feet, grabbed my hand, and pulled me up.

The dance floor was only about two feet away, so we reached it fairly quickly. Raven started gyrating and was pretty much dancing with everyone in the area. Why were we here?

We'd arrived separately, met up outside. I'd asked her about her courses, her summer job, and the local band she played in. She hadn't asked me about graduation—I would have lied if she had. She hadn't asked me about my job. Hadn't even asked how I was doing. She just wanted someone to have a good time with.

That's what I thought I wanted, too. This was a party place. I should have been having a blast.

Raven was moving away from me. I caught up with her, leaned in, and shouted, "Let's go get something to eat."

"I'm only hungry for the music."

She wound her arms around my neck, and moved against me. She wasn't the girl I'd gone out with before. Or maybe I wasn't the guy she'd gone out with.

I leaned down and shouted, "I gotta go. Have class in the morning."

"Summer school! Getting a jump on those college classes?"

"Something like that."

She put out her thumb and forefinger and mouthed, "Call me."

Then she was gone, lost in the crowd.

I stood there, feeling lost, too.

Chapter 31

AVERY

Wednesday night I worked for Katie because Colorado surprised her by coming to see her. Understandably, she'd wanted the night off to be with him, so she asked me to fill in for her. So it was Thursday before I saw Fletcher again. Right after we cleared the table and cleaned up the kitchen, Fletcher brought out his algebra book.

I sat beside him. I was dying to know how his date went but I refused to give him any satisfaction by asking. "Sorry I had to work last night. They had a situation at the restaurant and I needed to cover for someone."

"Not a problem. You're helping me out here, so we're on your schedule."

"Then you're okay if we only do half an hour tonight?"

"Sure."

"Since we're a little behind why don't you just tell me if

there's anything you're having difficulty with."

"Yeah, this section is confusing me just a little."

"Okay." I spent several minutes explaining it, show-ing different examples, working out some problems. When I looked up, I found him watching me, admiration in his eyes.

"You're really good at explaining things so they're understandable," he said.

I lifted a shoulder. "I love teaching."

His brow furrowed. "But you're not going to school to be a teacher."

"No, I think my parents might be disappointed if I did that."

"Why?"

"Because I'm smart, good at math and science. So it just makes sense that I should go into medicine, be a doc-tor, do research. Make a difference."

"Teaching makes a difference."

"Being in medicine will have more impact."

He studied me. "But it's your life. Shouldn't you do what you enjoy?"

"I want to do what makes them the proudest. Everything I've ever done has been to make them proud."

Turning his chair slightly, he faced me. "I think they'd be proud no matter what you did."

"You don't know them. You may think you do, but you

don't. They have certain expectations—"

"How do you know that they'd be disappointed if you became a teacher?"

It was all right for him to interrogate me, but I couldn't ask questions? I thought about directing us back to the algebra problems, but he'd never expressed such interest in me before, and I didn't want to cut him off the way he always did me. I could teach by example that it was okay to share. "I know what they expect."

"How? Have you ever told them you want to be a teacher?"

"I don't have to. Mom and I have talked about me being a doctor since the first time she let me listen to my heartbeat with her stethoscope."

"How old were you?"

"What has that got to do with anything?"

"How old were you?" he repeated.

"Five."

"You don't think she'd understand if what you wanted to be when you grew up changed in twelve years?"

"What I'm going to study in school really isn't any of your business." Okay, so I pulled out the none-of-your-business card but I knew my parents a lot better than he did. I knew what they wanted, what they expected.

"It's ironic, though, don't you think, that you want me to share more of myself with you—my dreams, my plans—and yet you don't share yours with your parents?"

I gave him a pointed look. "Do you share yours with your dad?"

"No, but then I'm not trying to meet his expectations."

The doorbell rang. I checked the time on my phone. "I've got to go. That's my date." I stood up. "If you want to leave your homework on the table, I'll check it when I get in."

"Your date?"

"Avery!" Tyler yelled as he ran into the dining room. "Marc's here. I like him!"

"Of course you do," I said, ruffling Tyler's hair. "He's nice."

I looked back at Fletcher. "For practice, do page one-fifty, all the even problems."

"The answers to the even problems aren't in the back of the book."

He sounded seriously irritated, and for some reason that made me smile. "Yeah, I know. Just leave them on the table and I'll check them when I get home."

I didn't understand why I was nervous as I walked into the foyer where Mom and Dad were talking with Marc. When I'd shown up for work last night, he'd been there. I'd told him if the invite was still open, I'd love to go to a movie with him. Two could play the dating-others game. And who knew? Maybe away from work, I'd like Marc as more than a friend.

"Hi, Marc," I said.

"Hey." He was standing there, appearing to feel a little awkward. I knew my parents could be overwhelming.

"Marc was just telling us that he's majoring in computer science," Mom said. "That's a good field, lot of potential."

I could see her thinking, *Excellent dating choice.*

"We should go," I said, fully aware that Fletcher was hovering just inside the doorway that led from the dining room. "We don't want to miss the previews."

"We'd like her home by midnight," Dad said. I should have known that tonight he'd exercise his right to set a curfew. I was actually fine with it. Probably a good idea to have a time limit on a first date.

"Oh, absolutely, sir," Marc said. "Not a minute later."

"All right then," Dad began, "you two be careful."

"Have to be," Marc said. "Can't afford to get married. Oh, man." He held up his hands like the SWAT team had just flooded into the room. "That was not cool. I apologize, sir. I have the utmost respect for your daughter, sir."

Laughing lightly, I nudged Marc toward the door, while giving my dad a reassuring look. He didn't have anything to worry about. "It's okay, Marc. He knows you're joking."

When we were outside, I peered back into the foyer and gave my scowling dad a thumbs-up and a smile before closing the door behind us. Marc was breathing deeply. I thought he might hyperventilate. I rubbed his shoulder. "Really, it's okay."

"I've never gone out with a girl whose dad packs heat. Made me a little nervous."

"You did fine."

He took my hand and we walked to the car. When we got there, he opened the passenger door for me.

"Thanks," I said as I climbed in.

"All part of the service." He closed the door, trotted around to the driver's side, and slid behind the wheel. After starting the car, he backed out of the drive. "So I saw Fletcher standing in the doorway. He didn't seem too happy with this outing."

"That's his problem."

"Ah, a woman scorned."

"No, I just . . . okay, yes, I guess. I don't know. Let's talk about something else."

"Okay. What do you want to talk about?"

Well, this was different. I could probably play a thousand questions with Marc and he'd answer every one. "Tell me about your courses."

"Boring to talk about, but if I could show you some of the results of the computer classes, then you might find it a little more interesting. Don't know if your mom would be so impressed if she knew the emphasis of my computer skills is going to be gaming and simulation. You tell someone you want to program games and they think you haven't quite grown up."

Tonight was going to be more fun than I expected. Marc talked using multiple sentences. "Are you grown up?" I asked.

"Absolutely not. Look at the movie I chose for our date: *The Avengers*. How grown up is that?"

"I like superheroes," I told him, and tried not to think about Fletcher and our discussion of superheroes. That all seemed so long ago.

The lines weren't too bad, but Marc had purchased our tickets ahead of time. We got a big tub of buttered popcorn to share and two small drinks.

"My favorite part of going to the movies is the previews," Marc said once we were settled in our seats.

"Mine, too."

It was such a relief not to have to prod him for information. He shared so openly. And he didn't talk during movies. Not a word. Which worked for me because I always immersed myself in the story.

Although tonight I was thinking about the conversation I'd had with Fletcher earlier. Had I misread my parents' expectations regarding my career choice? I'd never thought about being anything other than a doctor, but was that what I wanted? Fletcher had given me something to think about.

When the movie was over, Marc and I went to an all-night pancake house.

"So," he began, as I poured warm syrup over my buttered pancakes, "should I assume that our going out tonight was a one-time event?"

I looked up. "I had a good time. I'm having a good time. The date's not over yet."

"But you're not sitting over there hoping I'll kiss you."

I looked up at the ceiling. I wasn't.

"It's okay," he said. "Don't be insulted, but I'm not thinking about kissing you either."

I laughed. "You are so open. I wish I were thinking about kissing you. You're nice, Marc. I really like you. And I really have had a fun time."

"How many times did you think about him during the movie?"

He didn't have to clarify who the *he* was. "A dozen, maybe more. I wasn't really counting."

"However many minutes long the movie was, that's how many times I thought of Katie."

Reaching across, I placed my hand over his. "I'm so sorry. I know you like her so much."

"I do, but the odd thing is, I just want her to be happy. I hope Colorado makes her happy, that he's good to her."

"You're really a good guy, Marc."

"What else can I do, you know?" He held up a finger. "But I'll tell you . . . the first video game I create and program . . . you can bet it's going to have a character named Colorado who is a lousy mercenary and gets his butt kicked all the time."

I laughed. "You can have some fun programming characters."

"You bet."

It was a couple of minutes before midnight when Marc pulled into the driveway. "Is that Fletcher?" he asked.

He was sitting on the top steps just outside his apartment. "Yes."

"He's not going to attack me, is he?"

"No. He doesn't care that I had a date."

"Like I said, his expression earlier said different."

"Trust me. You misread it."

Marc got out, came around, and opened the door for me. Taking my hand, he began walking toward the door. Just before we reached the shadows, before we were out of Fletcher's line of sight, I stopped. Marc faced me.

I nibbled on my lower lip, knew I had no right to ask, but heard myself say, "Will you do me a favor? Will you kiss me?"

He was perfectly still, only his eyes shifting to the stairs. "You mean where he'll see?"

"Yes."

"You're sure he won't come down and rip me apart?"

I smiled. "I'm sure."

As Marc cupped my face in his hands and leaned in, I realized for the first time that he was my height. His lips touched mine. I moved in and wrapped my arms around his shoulders. The kiss was nice, pleasant. No fire, passion, or hunger. It was better than the one I'd experienced at band camp. Not as good as the ones Fletcher gave me.

I thought it probably had nothing to do with technique. It had everything to do with chemistry—that unidentifiable element that wasn't on any periodic table but made two people sitting in a movie theater together think about someone else.

Marc drew back, smiled. "Thanks for tonight, Avery. I needed it. I had fun."

"Me too." He walked me to the door. I slipped inside, peered into the dining room. No homework papers on the table for me to check.

Mom popped out of the den. "How was it?"

"Fun."

"He seemed really nice."

"He is. Listen, Fletcher is still up. I'm going to pop over and make sure he doesn't have questions about his homework."

"Okay, I'm going to bed now that you're home." She gave me a hug. "See you tomorrow."

I went outside, crossed the driveway, and started up the stairs. Something about Fletcher seemed different, but I couldn't quite figure out what it was.

I'd almost reached him when he said, "Forty-five seconds, not bad."

"What?"

"The kiss. Forty-five seconds."

"You were timing it?"

"Yep."

Leaning forward a little bit, I could smell yeast, hops, barley. "Are you drunk?"

"Yep."

Near the door, I could see two six-packs with empty bottles in every slot except one.

"I cared about the environment," he said. "For you."

I looked over just as he lifted a brown bottle to his mouth. I snatched it from his grasp, looked at the label, sniffed the contents. "How did you get this?"

"Fake ID. Had it since I was sixteen, for clubs and stuff."

I noticed now that his words were slightly slurred. He was sprawled on the steps more than sitting on them. "My dad will explode if he finds out about this."

"He's not the boss of me."

"He is if you're living under his roof."

He pointed to the house. "That's his roof." He pointed

to his apartment. "That's . . . mine."

"Not really, no. Come on, you need to get inside." Dropping the bottle into its designated slot, I picked up the six-packs, opened the door, and walked in. I set them on the small table and turned around. Fletcher hadn't followed me in.

I marched back out onto the landing. "Fletcher."

He swiveled his head around. "I should have known. You were dressed so nice. I should have figured you had a date."

"Fletcher, you need to get up and come inside."

"Don't think I can walk. Need my bike."

"Yeah, I'm going to haul your bike up here so you can ride it into your apartment." I crouched in front of him.

"I like you in red," he said, and touched the shoulder of my red lacy top. "And blue and puple . . . pup . . ."

"Purple?"

He gave me a goofy grin and nodded. "Yep. Every color."

"You are so drunk."

His head wobbled, which I took to be a yes. "Every . . . thing moves funny."

"It's spinning?"

"Yeah."

"I'm going to help you up and get you inside. Come on now."

I locked my arms around his chest. I pulled, he pushed. He grabbed the railing and pulled, too. Eventually he was standing, a lot of his weight on me. God, he was heavy.

"I like that you're tall," he said.

"I'm a giant."

"You're willowy." He grinned. "I bet you didn't think I knew that word. I am not a novice at vocabulary."

I almost laughed. I wasn't sure what he was trying to say exactly.

We shuffled inside. I thought about depositing him on the couch, but we'd worked up enough momentum that I was able to get him to the bed. He flopped down on it.

I tugged off his boots and his socks. He had such large feet. I didn't know why I was surprised or why it seemed like such a personal thing to know. Something hit me in the face. His T-shirt. Somehow he'd managed to get it off, which left me staring at a very fine chest. I'd seen it before when he was playing in the pool with Tyler. But like his feet, it just seemed more intimate to see it now, when he was sprawled across the bed.

He was struggling with his belt.

"I'll get the belt," I told him. "The jeans stay on."

"'Kay."

I worked the belt through the loops and tossed it aside. I put a pillow beneath his head before flicking a sheet over him. I grabbed a glass, then went to the bathroom and filled it. When I came back out, I set it on the bedside table.

"Come on, you need to sit up. You need to drink some water before I go."

I got him sitting up with a pillow behind his back. I handed him the water. "Drink it. All of it."

He drank half of it. I decided to give him a couple of minutes before I made him finish it. "Have you ever been drunk before?" I asked.

Slowly he shook his head. "Never had beer before tonight." He leaned toward me. "It's not that good."

"Yet you kept drinking it."

He smiled, nodded. "Do you like him?"

My stomach tightened. "You mean Marc? I do like him."

He nodded, shook his head, finished off the water. I got him some more. "He's just a friend," I felt compelled to say. Besides, he probably wasn't going to remember any of this in the morning.

"You kissed him," he said.

"You and I are friends. We kiss . . . kissed."

"Yeah. I like kissing you."

"I like kissing you, too."

He grinned again.

"I think you're going to feel terrible in the morning," I told him.

"Yeah."

I helped him lie back down, tucked him in.

"Thanks," he said.

"So what did you hit tonight?" I asked.

He looked at me blankly. "Huh?"

"You're drunk, like your father. So what did you hit?"

He shook his head, furrowed his brow. "Didn't hit anything."

"So you're not like him." Leaning down, I pressed a kiss to his cheek and whispered near his ear, "Think about that."

Chapter 32

FLETCHER

I woke up. Wished I hadn't.

My head was so heavy that I didn't know if I'd be able to lift it off the pillow and it hurt. I was queasy. It would probably be a month before I could eat anything. And there was this persistent beeping in my ears, a tremor near my hip—

My alarm.

I dug my phone out of my jeans pocket and shut it off. I squinted at the time. Who was the idiot who thought it was a good idea to register for a class that started before most people had their coffee? Oh, yeah, me.

I hadn't wanted to be a loser. I sure felt like one now. Why had I started drinking last night? I squeezed my eyes shut. Because of Avery's date. I couldn't be mad about it. I'd had a date earlier in the week. But I had been . . .

I'd been mad. I'd thought about following them. Instead

I'd ridden to the next town over, where no one knew me, stopped at a convenience store, flashed my fake ID, and walked out with the beer. Having dark stubble helped make me look older. Then I'd returned here and started the guzzle-fest.

Marc looked exactly like the kind of guy Avery should date. So clean-cut, he probably squeaked when he walked. Her parents had been impressed with him, despite his stupid idiotic joke. After Avery left, they'd carried on about what a nice guy he was. I'd almost barfed.

With a groan, I dropped my legs off the bed and rolled to a sitting position. Class was definitely out today. Burying my face in my hands, I pressed my fingers to my temples. How did I even get to the bed?

Avery. She'd helped me. She'd also kissed computer whiz. I couldn't get upset about that either, but I was. Why did it matter so much? Because I liked her. I liked her a lot.

I had a vague memory of her helping me undress. I smiled. Had to keep the jeans on, though. I remembered the light brush of her lips on my cheek, the words she'd whispered.

I lifted my head, stared around the room. I'd gotten drunk but I hadn't broken anything, torn anything up, hurt anyone. I wasn't my dad.

My dad wouldn't have finished his algebra assignment before getting drunk. I shoved myself to my feet. I needed to get that turned in. Hard-assed Turner did not accept late homework. Turn it in on time or get a zero.

I needed a hot shower first. I'd be late to class, but it was better than not showing up at all.

I wasn't my dad, I thought again. I didn't have to be a loser.

Chapter 33

AVERY

I'd been not only surprised but impressed Friday morning when I spotted Fletcher leaving for school at an ungodly hour. The last thing I'd expected was for him to make the effort when he had to be feeling rotten.

I didn't get a chance to see him before I left for work either Friday or Saturday. I was hoping I might see him Sunday, although maybe he'd be hooking up with someone else. At least I'd see him when I tutored him Monday.

At the Shrimp Hut, summer was in full swing and Saturday night work was crazy busy. It was always the night when we had the most customers. People came to the beach, stayed late, didn't have to get up and go to work the next morning. Or at least most of them didn't. Plus a lot of people rented houses or condos or stayed in the nearby hotels, so the population on Saturday exploded.

"You have a hot guy at table sixteen," Jenny told me when she came into the kitchen to get her order.

Along my arm I was balancing plates for a family of four. "Thanks."

"If you don't have time, I'll be happy to take care of him, although I hear he asked specifically to be seated in your section."

Picking up the plate, I smiled at her. "First crush of summer, you think?" It wasn't unusual for guys to come in and flirt with us, and then request our section the next time they dropped by. Or girls for that matter. Marc had quite a following.

"First crush for me this summer," she said. "Seriously, if you don't have time, I've got your back and will break the news to him gently. I'll even offer comfort after we close tonight."

"Down, girl, down!" I teased. "I've got it."

Intrigued, I pushed my way through the swinging doors and my gaze skipped over to table sixteen. It was the last table in the corner by the window. Sitting there was Fletcher. My heart gave a little thud, but I didn't have time to examine it. I focused my attention on my other customers first. I delivered the order of broiled flounder to the mom, fried shrimp to each of the kids, shrimp étouffée to the dad. Grabbed ketchup, extra tartar sauce, refilled glasses.

"Can I get you anything else?" I asked, bouncing slightly on the balls of my feet, ready to turn to table sixteen.

"Looks good," the dad said, and I left them to enjoy their meal.

I wended my way between the tables, checking quickly on my customers as I went, making sure no one needed anything, making mental notes of glasses that would soon need to be refilled. I stopped beside Fletcher's table. "What are you doing here?"

He lifted a shoulder casually like it was no big deal. "You came to see me at work. Thought I should return the favor."

"You working is way more interesting than me working."

"I don't know. You have to juggle a lot of balls."

"More like plates and glasses. It's Saturday night. Shouldn't you be out partying somewhere?" I thought I succeeded at not saying it cattily.

"Need to eat." He obviously hadn't taken offense. He tapped the menu. "I'll take the large fried shrimp platter."

I pulled out my order pad. "That's two dozen shrimp. It's a lot."

"I can handle it."

"Fries or baked potato?"

"Fries."

"Salad or coleslaw?"

He shook his head. "You know I don't eat things that are green."

I did know. It made me feel all warm and soft inside to realize that I did know things about him. Intimate things that others probably didn't know. Then I shoved those cozy feelings down because we were back to being friends. "How about some extra fries then?"

"That'll work. I'll have sweet tea."

"Okay, I'll get some cheese biscuits out to you."

"Don't suppose you get a break."

"Not right now, not while we're this busy."

He peered out at the surf in the waning light. "I'll be here for a while."

It seemed an odd statement for a guy who earlier in the week had told me that he was seeing girls. Seemed like there would be plenty available on a Saturday night, but it was a riddle I'd have to consider later. I couldn't afford a distraction right then. I had customers who needed my attention and hot food waiting to be served. I returned to the kitchen.

Jenny wiggled her brows at me. "Told you."

"Told her what?" Katie asked.

"Hot dude at table sixteen."

"Oh, yeah, I noticed him," Katie said, reaching for her latest order. "I'd give up my boyfriend in Colorado for him."

"Thought he was your true love." I hooked Fletcher's order on the pin and grabbed a basket of biscuits.

"A girl can change her mind."

"Not when it comes to true love," I said.

"So did you catch his name?" Jenny asked.

I winked at her. "Fletcher." Then I headed out to deliver his biscuits.

I felt badly that he was eating alone, wished that I could have joined him. I always wondered about the stories that revolved around the diners who came alone: were they widows, still hurting from a recent breakup; loners, seeking solitude? Were they bothered to be sitting at a table with no one to talk with? Some brought books. Some punched away at their tablets. Some gazed out on the surf.

Fletcher just watched me. Every now and then I'd look over at him, and he'd meet my gaze, maybe give me a nod. I wasn't self-conscious about him observing me. I figured he'd get bored after a while and leave.

The crowd began to thin out around ten. We were open until midnight, but we would begin closing sections off so we could start all the prep needed to close up for the night. I grabbed a slice of key lime pie from the fridge, walked out into the dining area, and set it in front of Fletcher. "On the house."

He arched a brow. "Really?"

I rolled my eyes. "Okay, on me. It's one of the perks.

Unlimited pie so I can give you one, no problem. Want some coffee or something else?"

"This is great."

"And your tab is on me, too. Well, not really on me. I'm not going to actually pay for it, but I get some free meals so I'm crediting one to you. Whenever you're ready to leave, you can just go."

"I'll stay until you close."

I shifted my stance. "It'll take us about an hour to clean up after we lock up."

"I'll sit out on the deck and wait. Since I'm here, I might as well follow you home."

"Did something happen?" I asked. "You know with your dad or work or—"

"Nope."

Okay, so he was going to be his usual communicative self. With a smile, I told him I'd see him later. Then I went back to serving my few remaining tables and doing what I could to finish up early.

I was wiping down a table when Marc came over to help me. "Looks like the kiss got his attention," he said with satisfaction in his voice.

I slammed my eyes closed. "I'm so sorry for using you like that."

"As far as ways to get used, that ranks near the top of my favorites list."

I laughed. I wished I could be crazy about him. He was a nice guy.

"I don't know about it getting his attention, though. I'm pretty sure he's here as a friend," I said.

"On a Saturday night?" he asked. "That's more than being a friend."

"He didn't have anything else to do."

He gave me a pointed look. "That guy? He could have not only found something to do, but found some chick to do it with."

I knew that well enough. "Really, Marc, it's not a big deal." Maybe Fletcher just wanted to unload about being drunk the other night. I hadn't seen him since I'd put him to bed.

"Maybe not to you, but it is to him."

When the last of the customers had left and the doors were locked, Jenny and Katie came up to me and spun me around. I felt the ties on my apron loosened, a tug on my hair as my hairclip was removed. One of them whipped away my apron.

"What are y'all doing?" I asked as they spun me back around. They were grinning like mad.

"Hot guy is waiting for you," Jenny said.

"Get out of here," Katie said. "We'll finish cleaning up."

"But it's my job, too."

"Not tonight it's not," they both said as they shoved me toward the office where my things were stored in a locker.

"Go," Jenny said. "We'll want deets tomorrow."

I didn't want to disappoint them, but I didn't know if the details would be that salacious. I had no idea why he was here. And that made me a little nervous because I didn't know quite how to act. To anticipate being with him or to prepare for another brush-off. "Thanks, guys."

I clocked out and grabbed my bag from the locker. I quickly ran a brush through my hair, reapplied mascara and lipstick—which I realized was a little silly since it was dark out—but still, it made me feel more put-together.

Dot was waiting for me at the door. "Have fun," she said as she opened the door, let me out, and relocked it.

I walked around the side of the building, intending to meet up with Fletcher on the deck, but he must have been watching for me through the window, because he met me halfway.

"Want to walk along the beach before heading home?" he asked.

Maybe he wanted to talk about something. I almost laughed. He didn't share things. Still, I said, "Sure."

I pulled off my shoes, dropped them in my bag, retrieved my flip-flops. The lights from the restaurant provided enough faint light that we could see where we were going as we wandered over the dunes to the beach area. Sandpipers scurried along on spindly legs. The tide was low, leaving a lot of beach area.

"You seem to have recovered from your drinking spree," I said lightly.

He groaned. "I don't know why people get drunk."

"I heard you leave early Friday morning. Did you actually go to class?"

"Had to turn in my homework."

"I'm impressed."

"You'd be even more impressed if you'd met the guys with sledgehammers inside my head."

"I met them the morning after Scooter's party."

He chuckled low. "I bet you did."

We continued on in silence until we reached the water's edge.

"So I never asked: how was your date?" I asked.

"It wasn't a date."

"The booty call then."

His smile flashed in the darkness. "It wasn't a booty call either. It was just . . . her name is Raven. We went out a couple of times last year. When she called and wanted to hook up, it sounded like a good idea."

I slipped my foot out of my flip-flop, squiggled my toes in the wet sand. "Do you like her?"

"She's nice."

"That's good."

"I'm not going to see her again, though."

"Thought you liked her."

"I said she was nice."

"What's not to like about nice?"

"She wasn't you."

My heart went into a hard gallop.

"How was your date with Marc?" he asked.

"He wasn't you," I said quietly.

Fletcher moved in, cradled my face. "I've missed you. That's crazy. I've never missed anyone before. You'll be leaving soon and this is going nowhere, but I can't seem to stop thinking about you."

"Why weren't you waiting for me when I got home last night?"

"Thought if I went a little bit longer without seeing you then I'd stop missing you."

I couldn't stop myself from smiling. "Didn't work, huh?"

"Don't look so happy."

"I'm sorry. It's just nice to be missed. I missed you, too."

"So maybe we can be friends," he said.

"Gee, you made that sound really enticing. Where do I sign up?"

"Right here." Then he kissed me.

The kiss was slow and hot, had the potential to go on into tomorrow. But I had the nagging thought that a few days earlier he'd kissed someone else. So had I—not so much to make him jealous but to make him realize other guys would kiss me. But Fletcher kissed girls because he liked to. I deserved loyalty. I was worth being considered special.

Breaking off from his lips, I backed away. While there wasn't a lot of light, I could tell that he was confused.

"You can't tell me a few days ago that you're going to be seeing other girls, then kiss me tonight and think everything is going to be okay. If you want to be friends, we'll be friends, but I don't kiss my friends."

"I kiss my friends," he said impatiently.

"Not if you're kissing me," I said. "I like you, Fletcher. I like you a lot. I want to explore these feelings, see where they take us, but you want easy, and I'm not. I want a boyfriend. I want a guy who isn't trying to get together with other girls."

"You're talking about a commitment."

"It doesn't have to be forever. But yes, if you want to be more than friends then I need to know I'm the only one you're spending time with. Otherwise, we can just be friends. Late-night walks and talks. No kissing, no snuggling, no skinny-dipping."

"Like you'd go skinny-dipping."

"You're right. I probably wouldn't. But I'm not just someone to kiss when you're in the mood for a kiss."

He looked disgruntled and frustrated, which made two of us. I wanted more with him, but I needed for him to want more with me, too. More than he'd ever had with any other girl.

"I don't know how to be a boyfriend," he finally stated flatly.

"I've never been a girlfriend, so it would be new to me, too. Maybe we could figure out how to be a couple together. But I can't pretend our kisses don't mean something. Every time we kiss, I fall just a little bit more."

"You're so open about it."

"I'm not afraid of falling. I am afraid of being a fool, of getting hurt. You said you didn't want to hurt me. Then don't kiss me anymore unless you're willing not to kiss anyone else."

Shoving his hands in his pockets, Fletcher stared out at the water.

"You don't have to decide tonight," I told him. "Just know that I'm a no-kiss zone as long as you're seeing other girls."

He faced me. "I guess that means no kiss for the road."

"No kiss for the road. But I will hold your hand if you want to walk me to the car."

He wrapped his hand around mine and we headed

299

back toward the dunes. It wasn't a lot, but I couldn't help thinking that maybe it was a start.

The next afternoon, after lunch, I was basking in a lounge chair by the pool. Although my eyes were closed, I was aware of a shadow crossing over my face, someone blocking out the sun. I expected to find Fletcher there. Instead, it was my dad.

"Your mother and I need to have a talk with you and Fletcher."

My dad wasn't the sort who did a lot of joking around, but he sounded way too serious. As I got up and followed him into the house, several possibilities went through my head. That the kiss-cam had been posted to the Internet, gone viral, and my parents had seen it. That they knew about the walk I took with Fletcher along the beach last night. Or that maybe it went even further back than that. Maybe they found out about everything that had happened at Scooter's party.

When we walked into the den, I saw Fletcher standing beside Mom. I knew him well enough now to recognize the wariness in his eyes and I figured all the thoughts that had gone through my head had gone through his as well.

"Have a seat," Dad ordered.

Fletcher and I sat on the couch. I resisted the urge to grab his hand, squeeze it in reassurance as we faced together whatever horrible thing had come to pass that had brought us to this moment.

"As you know," Dad began, "on Wednesday, your mom and I will be celebrating twenty years of marriage."

I blinked, looked at Fletcher, blinked again. I wasn't quite certain why this required a conversation—unless they were calling it quits after twenty years. In the back of my mind, I'd known their anniversary was coming, and I'd been vaguely aware that it was one of the ones that came with rules about the gift, but I hadn't gotten around to Googling it yet.

"I was going to surprise your mom and take her to New Orleans for a couple of days, starting Tuesday."

She smiled, rubbed his shoulder.

"I'd made arrangements for your aunt Beth to come and watch you while we were away."

"Oh, Dad, I don't need a babysitter. I'll be eighteen in August and I'm going to college."

"I know, I know. But we were going to be gone for three nights—"

"What do you mean were going to be?" I asked.

"Something came up at work and Beth can't come."

"Like I said, I don't need a babysitter. Fletcher could totally watch Tyler if I need to work."

"The plan was to come back Friday morning."

"Do it."

Dad looked at Fletcher, studied me. "I was a kid once. I know that when parents are away, teens tend to party and go crazy, but you have Tyler to think about."

"Dad." I got up and walked over to him. "Go to New Orleans. We'll be fine here."

He looked over my shoulder at Fletcher. "I expect you to be responsible."

"I will," Fletcher said, coming to his feet.

I could tell by his tone that he was a little offended. Not that I blamed him.

"No partying," Dad continued, "no sex, no drinking—"

"We'll dehydrate if we don't drink," I said.

Dad scowled at me. "You know what I mean. No booze."

"Dad, you've always trusted me before. Why not now?"

"We've just never left you alone this long before," Mom said.

"We'll be fine," I assured her. "Go have some fun."

Tuesday morning after they left—and after they'd provided a list of rules, reminders, and phone numbers—I drove Fletcher and Tyler to the grocery store so we could stock up. Because it was going to be unlimited junk food time for the three of us.

I knew there was a rule that those who eat healthy shop around the outer edge of the grocery store. We headed straight for the center and the three C's: cookies, chips, candy. We bought sodas and dips. Mom had left some frozen dinners in the freezer with instructions for thawing and heating. She'd also left money for pizza. The pizza we would order, but I didn't see us cooking the dinners.

When we got home, I called Kendall to see if she and Jeremy wanted to join us for No Parents Night. I stressed heavily that only they were invited. We were not throwing a party. We were not welcoming other people.

Fletcher and I were opening the snacks, setting them out on the island. Tyler was our taste-tester. The key to success without having my parents around was to keep him occupied. I didn't want him missing them or whining for them. The last time they'd taken a night out together, Tyler had been afraid they were never coming back. He still had separation-anxiety issues sometimes.

It was odd, though, just having the three of us in the house. Or maybe the oddity was having Fletcher in the house without my parents around.

"I've gone off on field trips and taken trips with Kendall where I haven't seen my parents for days," I began, "so it's not like I miss them. But I've never been here without them overnight."

"Are you scared?" Fletcher asked as he came up behind me where I was stirring a package of ranch dip into sour cream. He moved my hair aside and pressed a kiss to the back of my neck. "Don't worry. I'll protect you."

I turned in the circle of his arms until I was facing him. I placed my hands on his shoulders and said in a very low voice, "I'm a no-kiss zone, remember?"

"But that was just a harmless peck."

Not so harmless when it shot pleasure through me and made my toes curl. I glanced quickly at Tyler who was absorbed in eating chips while playing a handheld game. I gave my attention back to Fletcher. "You know the rules."

His gaze held mine. "I want to break them."

My heart was pounding. "I deserve someone who follows them."

He sighed. "Yeah, you do."

"Okay, we brought munchies," Kendall announced as she and Jeremy walked into the kitchen. "Oops, sorry." She grimaced.

Fletcher reached for a chip, dipped it, and popped it into his mouth. "I was just taste-testing. Betty Crocker here was in the way."

"Yeah, right. Should we come back later?" she asked.

I pointed at Tyler to indicate that she wasn't interrupting any making out because he was here. I wasn't exactly sure what she was interrupting. It was all bad timing.

"Hey, squirt, look who's here," I said to Tyler. He was unusually quiet. Normally he welcomed anyone who came to the house.

He scrunched up his face. "I don't feel so good."

"Probably ate too much candy. Come on, we're going out to the pool for a while."

"Skinny-dipping, right?" Fletcher asked with ease. I thought I'd probably been misreading whatever he'd been trying to tell me.

I slapped playfully at his arm. "No."

The guys took Tyler out to play in the pool while I helped Kendall unpack what she'd brought. Most of it was homemade: fudge, peanut butter-chocolate bars, chocolate chip cookies. She loved to bake, especially when she was stressed.

"This is a lot. Is everything okay?"

"Oh, yeah, just needed some time away from my mom. Maybe we could turn this into a sleepover." She winked at me. "I told my mom we might be over here all night."

"Really?"

"Yeah. Jeremy and I just haven't had a lot of time together lately. My mom is always at home. His parents are usually around. I cannot wait until we are off at college and each have a dorm room—"

"And a roommate," I felt obligated to point out.

She groaned. "Yeah. Wish you and I were going to the same college. I'm going to miss you."

"We won't be that far away," I told her.

"I know, but it'll be weird. Anyway"—she spread out her hands—"we have a feast."

The guys were playing some form of keep-away with a small inflatable beach ball. I thought the object was to keep it away from everyone except Tyler. Kendall and I stretched out on the lounge chairs.

"I'm afraid he's going to grow up believing that he can win at everything," I said.

"Is that a bad thing?" Kendall asked.

"I don't know. It's just that you don't always win. You need to learn how to handle disappointment."

"Life's harsh lessons," she said. "Seems like they need to be put off as long as possible. Speaking of harsh lessons, what's the status of you and hotcakes? Did we interrupt something?"

"How could we have been doing anything? Tyler was at the island."

"Absorbed in junk food. You're avoiding the question. If we were in a courtroom, you'd be a hostile witness."

I laughed. "Oh my God, have you been spending time in a courtroom this summer?"

"A couple of hours. I knew Jeremy was going to be there. And he was right. It was *so* boring. Something about some terms in an agreement not being honored and the need for restitution. I nearly fell asleep and slipped off the bench. But then we went for lunch afterward and that made it worth it. But then being with him is always worth it. How about Fletcher?"

"How about Fletcher what?"

"Is it worth it to be with him?"

I watched him bouncing in the pool, the water sluicing over his skin. He went to toss the ball to Jeremy. It fell short. Tyler shrieked and laughed as he caught it. No way Fletcher hadn't deliberately given it to my brother.

"I like him, Kendall, but we're still working things out. He's not used to commitment."

"Told you. Way back in the beginning. Commitment-phobe. You're going to get hurt."

"I don't think he's afraid of commitment. I think the whole idea of it is just new to him."

He of whom we were speaking glided over to the edge of the pool. "Come on in. The munchkin is killing us. We need some help."

"Put more air under the ball," I told him.

With a devilish grin, he placed his hands on the ground, lifted himself up—

And I knew he was coming for me. I jumped up, ran forward, catapulted myself over his head, brought my legs up, wrapped my arms tightly around them, forcing them closer to my chest, curled forward, and landed like a cannonball. Kendall joined us. We had a splash fight, girls against guys. In spite of my worries about Tyler never knowing what it was to lose, I declared his team the winner.

As the sun went down, we sat on the lounge chairs and

watched the fireflies. Tyler wanted to capture some, but I explained to him as I had before, they were meant to be free. He was curled against me. He was warm and I figured he'd had too much sun today.

After we went inside, we ordered pizza, scarfed it down, and played Candy Land until Tyler got bored with it, stretched out on the floor, and fell asleep. He'd wanted to stay up all night. I'd told him he could, but I'd known eventually he'd conk out. I remembered when I was younger, I'd thought the best thing in the world would be not to have to go to bed. I put a pillow beneath his head and draped an afghan over him. He'd be just as happy to wake up in the morning, realizing he hadn't technically gone to bed.

"So do you guys want to watch a movie?" I asked.

Fletcher was sitting on the couch. Kendall was curled on Jeremy's lap in one of the recliners. She looked at him. He shrugged. She nodded, turned her attention back to me.

"Listen, we're going to go," she said quietly. "But if my mom should ask, I was here with you all night."

"Are you sure?" I asked.

"Uh, yeah," she answered, somewhat sarcastically.

Jeremy lowered the footrest and they clambered out of the chair. "Thanks for all the food," he said.

And the alibi, which remained unsaid.

I followed them out to the entryway, aware that Fletcher was behind me.

At the door, Kendall hugged me. "Seriously, we just don't get enough alone time together, so . . ."

Yeah, so I was going to lie to her mother if she asked. But what were the odds of her asking? One in a gazillion. Because she'd have no reason to suspect her well-behaved daughter wasn't behaving. I didn't want to judge Kendall. I didn't have a boyfriend. I didn't know what it was like to want to spend every hour of every day with him and not be able to.

"Just be careful," I whispered.

She smiled softly. "We will."

They left. I closed and locked the door, and turned to Fletcher. "Want to watch a movie?"

Chapter 34

FLETCHER

Watching a movie was the very last thing that I wanted to do with Avery. But I understood her rules. Even respected them. I'd never had a girl set down conditions before. To be honest, I found it a little hot.

But then I found everything about her hot.

We sat beside each other on the couch. She put on some movie that had Sandra Bullock and the guy who played Green Lantern. Just based on the first couple of minutes, I knew I'd rather be watching *The Green Lantern*.

"I guess boyfriend types are supposed to sit through movies like this," I said. Earlier I'd put my arm along the back of the couch. Now I took advantage of my positioning to toy with strands of her hair. They were so thick and silky. The only light in the room came from the flickering TV. It illuminated her hair, made it look like moonbeams.

"It's better than shark-wielding tornadoes," she said.

"Yeah, that is a pretty silly movie. Giant crocs is more believable."

"Nothing in those movies is believable."

"And what happens in these movies is?" I asked, pointing at the screen.

"Romance movies guarantee a happy ending."

"There's a happy ending in monster flicks. The good guys always win out."

"Yeah, after much blood and gore."

I slipped my hand beneath the curtain of her hair and began kneading her neck. She didn't object, but kept her gaze on the movie. I darted a quick look at the munchkin. "Should I take him up to his bed?"

"He's fine where he is. He'll think it's an adventure that he slept on the floor."

I couldn't remember being young enough to think something so simple was an adventure.

"So, this boyfriend thing," I began. "What are the other rules?"

She shifted around until she was perpendicular to me, her lower leg pressed against my thigh. She had changed into a tank top after we went swimming. I skimmed my fingers up and down her bare arm.

"You have to share things with me," she said.

I stilled, grinned. "I have something to share." I leaned in—

She shoved me back. "Not a kiss. Nothing physical. Something personal. Tell me about your mom."

What could I say to that? I barely remembered her. Made me feel like a jerk. But I could spout facts, which would probably make me seem like more of an ass. "She died when I was eight. Think it was cancer. Not sure. Just remember her being sick for a long time, not having any hair. My dad would never talk about it."

She combed her fingers through my hair. I liked the way it felt.

"That had to be hard," she said.

"I don't really remember. It makes me an ass, I know. Sometime after that my dad went all psycho."

"I'm so sorry."

"Look, this is why I don't talk about all this stuff. I don't want your pity or your sympathy or your sad eyes."

"Because you're so tough?"

"Yeah, pretty much. Sometimes life is rough. You get through it."

Her gaze wandered over my face. I felt like she could see every bruise I ever sported.

"How did you meet my dad?" she asked.

"Are we going to do twenty questions again?"

"This will be the last one."

I sighed. I hated answering questions. Probably the reason that I hated taking tests. They were nothing but questions.

"Met him when I got caught stealing some stuff from a convenience store a few years back."

She didn't seem surprised so she probably knew about my shoplifting, not that I thought her dad had told her. But the store hadn't been empty. Anyone could have been the snitch.

"What made you steal stuff?" she asked.

I was hungry. My dad had disappeared for a couple of weeks. I didn't have any money. Not that I was going to tell her that. I didn't want to see the puppy dog look again. Which I figured made me awful boyfriend material. "Why do you think? I wanted it."

"What did you take?"

Twinkies, peanut butter crackers, M&M's. "Can't even remember now."

"I shoplifted once," she said with her usual straight-forwardness.

I wasn't expecting that. "You're kidding?"

"Nope. A pack of gum. Mom doesn't believe in chewing gum. I was about six. I waited until she put me to bed, then I snuck it out of its hiding place, and chewed the whole pack. Don't know how I got all of it in my mouth, but I did. I was still chewing it when I fell asleep. And when I woke up in the morning it was all in my hair."

I stared at her. "What did you do?"

"What could I do? I took scissors to it." She shook her head. "I looked like a freak. She made me go to school with my hair sticking out all over the place. There was still gum in it. Which Kendall, thankfully, cut out during recess. You know, with those little paper scissors that don't really cut well. Then she decided to play beautician, and I ended up with bald spots."

I wanted to laugh, but I imagined this little kid paying for her crime in such a public way.

"After school, Mom took me back to the store. I had to apologize to the owner and pay for the gum with my tooth fairy money, which I had been saving for Disney World. Then Mom took me to her stylist to see if she could do anything with my hair, so it got cut even shorter. That was my last foray into crime."

I skimmed my knuckles along her cheek. "I thought you were born obeying the rules."

"No, but I learned pretty early on that disobeying them came with consequences. Never chewed gum again. Not even when I played softball my sophomore year."

"I watched you play," I said, and wondered why I'd confessed that.

"You were just checking out the girls."

"Yeah." But she was the only one I remembered. "So maybe I'm thinking about not checking out other girls anymore."

"How seriously are you thinking about it?"

"Pretty seriously." I cupped my hand around the back of her head. "Really seriously."

I leaned in—

"Avery?" a little voice whined.

Not now, munchkin, I thought. *Not now.*

Avery waited. The voice came again. She unfolded that long, slender body of hers and went over to where her brother was stretched out on the floor. He'd kicked off the afghan.

"Hey, squirt," she said. "Ready to go to bed?"

"Don't . . . feel good."

"Told you not to eat all that junk. You'll be fine in the morning. Let's go on upstairs."

"I'll get him," I said as she started to lift him.

Then she put him back down and looked up at me. "He's burning up. Watch him. I'm going to get the thermometer."

"How can he be burning up? He was fine earlier."

"I know," was all she said before dashing out of the room. I crouched down, touched the kid's forehead. Even to me, he felt way too hot.

"I want Mommy," he murmured in a sad way.

"She's not here, but you have me and Avery."

She came back and took his temperature. "Hundred and four," she announced. "I'm taking him to the emergency room."

"I'm going with you."

Chapter 35

AVERY

I'm going with you.

Not a *do you want me to go with you*, but *I'm going with you.*

It's what people who cared about you said. They didn't ask if you wanted them to be with you. They just made sure that they were.

Fletcher had driven Trooper, while I'd been in the back with Tyler and comforted him. Now as we sat under the fluorescent lighting in the waiting room of the ER, he was curled on my lap, moaning, asking for Mom. Fletcher was beside us, bent forward, his elbows on his thighs. Every now and then he looked over at us, his brow furrowed deeply.

"Why's it taking them so long?" he asked.

"Sick people ahead of us." I combed my fingers through

Tyler's hair, hoping to keep us both calm. My worry was escalating as the minutes passed. I needed something to take my mind off it, because I felt like I could hear each second ticking by.

"So how many times have you been to the emergency room?" I asked Fletcher, my tone casual, conversational.

"Too many to count." He stiffened, closed his eyes, shook his head. When he opened his eyes, to my surprise, he grinned slightly. "You and the questions."

"I want to know everything about you."

"Not everything. But I will tell you that one night I was here with a broken arm and your dad came in to talk to me. I'd already been here a couple of times before that: cracked rib, another broken arm, bruises, you know. Anyway, I guess someone had called the cops because I was becoming a frequent flyer. I think he wanted me to point the finger at my dad. The irony was: that time, I'd broken it skateboarding."

I never would have taken him for a skateboarder. I loved discovering all these little tidbits about him.

I looked down at Tyler. He was flushed and was having trouble keeping his eyes open. I told myself it was because it was so late, but what if it was another reason?

"He's going to be all right," Fletcher assured me.

They called for us, finally. Fletcher took Tyler from me and carried him, following the nurse down the hallway to a room of beds, separated by curtains. He set Tyler on a bed, then moved aside. The nurse questioned me, got all the information she needed, then took Tyler's vitals.

"The doctor will be here shortly," the nurse said before walking out.

I moved up and took Tyler's hand.

The curtains opened, closed, and a short, stout man set a laptop on a table beside the bed. "I'm Dr. Zachary," he said.

"Avery Watkins. Tyler's my brother. My parents are out of town."

He looked at me, looked at the computer. "Looks like we have a medical treatment form on record authorizing you to oversee your brother's medical care."

"Yes, sir." Mom was extra cautious but she'd never really expected that I'd have to use it. I was a little nervous that I'd had to.

"Okay, little guy, let's see what we have going on," Dr. Zachary said, checking his ears and his throat, listening to his heart and lungs.

I smiled at the tiny stuffed bear clipped to his stethoscope. Tyler didn't notice it. It was so unusual for him not to notice anything.

"My guess is strep," Dr. Zachary said. He swabbed Tyler's throat. "I'll call you with the results tomorrow. Meanwhile, I want to give him an injection of antibiotics and then I'll give you a prescription you can start him on tomorrow."

My head was spinning. I had to remember all this. "Okay."

"He's also a little dehydrated. I'd like to get some fluids into him before I release him."

"Okay." That one word seemed to be the extent of my vocabulary.

The doctor left and a nurse came in. She gave Tyler the shot and then hooked him up to an IV. When she left, Fletcher scooted a chair toward me.

"Sit down," he said. "You look like you're about to collapse."

"I should have paid more attention when he said he wasn't feeling well."

"Avery, there were three other people there and none of us thought anything about what he said. He'd been eating junk food. It was natural to think that was the problem."

"He just looks so . . . fragile."

Fletcher sat in the chair, pulled me onto his lap, and held me. "He's not. If anyone should have noticed he was sick it was me when we were goofing in the pool. But he didn't feel fevered."

"But he probably was. It couldn't have come on this fast."

He cupped my cheek, turned my face, made me look at

him. "You brought him as soon as you knew he was sick. They've given him medicine. He's going to be okay. You did everything right."

"I'm so glad you're here with me. I was so scared."

"You didn't act scared. You kept cool. You were in control. No panic. You were great."

Fletcher had been great, too.

It was nearly three in the morning when we got home. Fletcher carried a sleeping Tyler to his bed. I removed his clothes, slipped on his pajamas. I left his Spider-Man lamp on. I didn't close his door. I wanted to be able to hear him if he called for me.

Fletcher was standing in the hallway when I walked out. I went up to him and placed my hands on his shoulders. "It meant a lot to me that you were there tonight."

"I wasn't going to leave you to take care of him on your own."

"I know. You say you don't know how to be a boyfriend. I think maybe you just don't know that you do."

"You really need that label, don't you?"

"Not right away. Not if it's too soon, but to be a kiss zone I have to know I'm the only one you're spending time with."

"You are." Then he was kissing me, and it was like everything just overflowed into the kiss. The worry for Tyler. The long wait. The exhaustion. The quiet talks we'd had. The things we'd shared.

I understood him now like I hadn't before, understood his doubts, his inability to believe in permanence. I could be patient. I could give him the time he needed to get used to the idea of being a boyfriend.

Taking his hand, I led him into my bedroom. I kicked off my sandals and climbed onto the bed. Fletcher stretched out beside me. I snuggled up against him.

"This is all I want for now," I said quietly.

"I know."

His arms closed around me, and I drifted off to sleep.

The next two days were pretty much spent entertaining Tyler, retrieving Popsicles for him, playing games, putting on movies, and watching them with him because he didn't want to be alone.

When Fletcher got home from work, he'd take over for a while so I could go for a run, get out of the house for a bit. It was funny how I didn't have to ask him to do any of that. It just happened. And at night, we'd cuddle in my bed, kissing and talking low. Or mostly I talked. Sometimes Fletcher would share something. He wasn't as guarded as he'd been that first day when he came to live with us, but I could tell when he was watching his words, when he was hesitant to reveal too much.

But we were making progress.

He was at work when Mom and Dad got home early Friday afternoon. I could see Dad examining things with a cop's eye as he walked into the house, like he expected to find evidence of a crime.

With a croaky voice, Tyler yelled when they came in, rushed forward, and leaped on Mom. She swung him up like he was a little monkey. I explained about the strep, the trip to the ER.

Mom touched his brow. "No fever now."

"No," I assured her. "But the doctor called with the lab results and it was strep."

"You should have called us," Dad said.

"Why? We had it under control," I told him.

Mom leaned in, kissed me on the cheek. "You did good."

"Me and Fletcher. Fletcher and I."

"I'll have to fix him something special for dinner," she said.

"Tell me about your trip."

Mom blushed, Dad grinned.

"It was fun," Mom said. "We'll tell you all about it later."

Friday night, after I got in from work, I thought it was weird to sleep alone in my bed. I almost went out and knocked on Fletcher's door, but I figured my parents were paying attention to things, trying to figure out if anything had happened between Fletcher and me. Something had happened, but it wasn't something I could explain. I was definitely no longer a no-kiss zone. But exactly what were we? We were exclusive, but not using labels. Without labels, how did I describe us?

We needed more time together. We needed more time to figure things out.

Saturday, since Smiley's was only open until noon, Fletcher got home in time for lunch. As we enjoyed the pralines she'd brought us from New Orleans, Mom got out her tablet and flipped through the pictures they'd taken. She told us about the decadent food, the beignets, and the carriage ride Dad had taken her on. It all sounded wonderfully romantic.

Fletcher and I spent a lot of time avoiding looking at each other, as though we thought they would see everything that had happened in our expressions. As if they'd know about every kiss, every whispered conversation, every cuddle in my bed.

I knew they might be okay with the kiss part, but they definitely wouldn't approve of the bed part. Or maybe they wouldn't approve of the kiss part either. They wanted me to find someone like Jeremy. Fletcher wasn't Jeremy. I was okay with that.

I just didn't know if they would be.

When we were finished with lunch, Fletcher excused

himself. I got ready for work. I halfway thought he might come by the Shrimp Hut but he didn't. I tried not to be disappointed. I'd gotten so used to having him around while Mom and Dad were gone that I was really missing him.

It was after one when I got home, nearly one-thirty when my phone chirped. I smiled when I saw the caller's name. "Hey," I said in a low, what I hoped was sexy, voice.

"What are you doing?" Fletcher asked.

"I'm in bed."

"Come over."

I got up, walked to the window, pulled back the curtain, and looked out. Fletcher stood in the doorway, backlit by one of the lights in the apartment. Since it wasn't very bright, I figured it was a lamp. "You know I can't."

"I'll answer a question," he said softly.

I released a light laugh. "Are you bribing me?"

"If that's what it takes."

Oh, I was tempted, so tempted. But one of us had to stay rational. "Fletcher, if my dad discovered me over there, he'd kick you out." Not to mention that he'd be disappointed in me.

"It'd be worth it," Fletcher said.

My heart did this quick little flutter with his willingness to risk so much. Why was I so afraid of taking a chance? I wanted to be with him. I just had this crazy idea that my parents would be able to sense if I were in the FROG. I'd always been the good, obedient daughter. Tonight I wanted to be with Fletcher more than I wanted to be good. I just didn't want to get caught. "What if we went to the beach?"

"Now?" he asked.

I nodded, realized he probably couldn't see subtle movements in the shadows. "Yes." Did I have to sound so breathless when I said it? Was this any different than Kendall telling her mom she was spending the night here when she wasn't? When you loved someone you took risks. I didn't know if I loved Fletcher but I did know that I wanted to explore these feelings I had for him. I wanted to know more about his feelings for me.

"Okay," he said. "Meet me down here. I'll push my bike to the end of the street so we don't disturb anyone. I'll have you home before dawn, before they wake up."

"I'll be down in ten."

My nerves were so jittery that my hands barely cooperated as I changed into a pair of black shorts, a pink tank, and pink sneakers. I couldn't believe I was doing this, risking my parents' wrath. They'd eased up on the curfews in anticipation of my going off to college—but I couldn't tell them where I was going without telling them who I was going with. I just didn't know how they would feel about that. They'd blame Fletcher, but as long as we didn't get caught, who were we hurting?

I braided my hair so it would get less tangled during the ride. I slipped my keys into one pocket, my cell phone into another. I stuffed an old blanket into a tote bag.

Then I eased my door open, crept out, closed it behind me. I stood still, listened to the creak of the house and the air conditioner coming on. I slowly tiptoed down the stairs. No TV sounds coming from the den. The only light was the one coming from over the stove that Mom left on to serve as a night-light. The alarm was the tricky thing. It beeped when I turned it off, beeped again when I reset it and closed the door behind me.

I scrambled quickly over the front yard to where Fletcher was already waiting on the street. He flashed a quick grin. My chest tightened. I didn't know exactly where we were going in our relationship. I just knew we were getting there fast.

When I reached him, he held out his helmet to me. I took it, then realized it wasn't his. His was black. This one—I held it up to a streetlight—was red. I looked at him. "Where did you get this?"

"A store. Figured you should have your own, you know, if we're going to be doing more things together."

Deeply touched, I said, "Thank you."

"So what's your question?" he asked as he began guiding the bike down the street.

"It'll keep," I said. "Until we get where we're going."

"What are your plans for the future?" I asked.

We were lying on our sides, facing each other, on the blanket on the beach. Fletcher had built a fire with driftwood that he'd gathered up. As far as I could see there was no one else out here. The stars were diamonds on velvet. The moon was a slender crescent. The tide lulled us as it rolled in and out.

"I thought you'd ask a question about my past," he said.

"Is there something you want to share?" I asked.

"Ah, trying to get two answers out of me tonight, huh?" Leaning in, he kissed the tip of my nose, my chin.

"I wouldn't be that deceptive." I wondered if a time would ever come when we discussed movies, music, TV shows. When we talked about other people. When we speculated about the royal family or the Hollywood elite. Right now it seemed like I could fill a lifetime just getting to know Fletcher.

"My immediate future involves kissing you," he said.

It was like he couldn't go two minutes without kissing me, which was good because two was a stretch for me.

"Seriously, Fletcher. When I asked you about your future before, you said you were going to get a haircut after graduation. Which I assume you'll do as soon as you pass this summer class and officially graduate. But what are you going to do after that?"

He laughed. I loved his laugh. I wanted to hear it every hour of every day. Then he sobered. "I don't know, Avery. God, I miss you." He rolled over until he was half covering me and started nibbling on my neck. "Which is silly because I see you every day."

I wound my arms around him. "I miss you, too."

He rose up slightly, brushed strands of hair from my face. The braid could only hold so many captive for so long. "What am I going to do when you go to school?"

"You could go, too."

He scoffed. "Yeah, right."

"You're smart, Fletcher. Lots of people who don't do well in high school succeed in college."

"I hate studying."

"Maybe you're studying the wrong thing. What interests you?"

He grinned. "You."

He kissed me again, only this time he was slow and deliberate. He really didn't like it when the conversation turned to the future. Not that I blamed him. I thought I wouldn't fall in love until I went to college and here I was beginning to do it way ahead of schedule. I couldn't imagine leaving him. But then neither could I imagine not going to school the way I'd always planned.

Time was running out. I knew I needed to get home before the sun was peering over the horizon, before anyone saw me arrive, could report that I'd been out all night.

"We need to go," I said, not bothering to hide my disappointment.

Fletcher got up. I folded up the blanket, stuffed it into the tote. When I looked over, he was crouched at the water's edge, stick in hand.

"What are you doing?" I asked as I walked over.

"Giving you something."

I looked down. Within a heart, he'd written:

Avery
+
Fletcher

"Oh, Fletcher." Tears stung my eyes.

"I've never done that for anyone," he said. "I want you to know that you're different, that what I feel for you is different."

As he stood up, he pulled me near. He folded his hands around my shoulders, held my gaze. "With the helmet and the sand . . . I'm trying to let you know that I'm committed to you. I want to be your boyfriend."

I smiled so brightly that I figured they could see it from the space station. "Oh, Fletcher, I want that so much."

Rising up on my toes, I kissed him, putting everything I felt into it. He made me so happy. He pulled me closer, his arms enveloping me. His mouth moved over mine, taking the kiss deeper. I warmed with the pleasure sweeping through me like the waves sweeping over the shore.

Drawing back, he pressed his forehead to mine. "There's no one else."

"I'm so glad."

"It's going to be light soon. We should go."

I wanted to stay here forever. But I knew we couldn't. I took my phone out of my pocket and snapped a picture of his artwork.

"The tide is going to wash it away," I said. "That's kinda sad."

"Maybe the tide is just going to carry it out to sea and it'll exist forever."

With a smile, I tilted my face up and met his gaze. "Are you a secret romantic?"

He scowled. "Hell, no."

"I'm crazy about you anyway." The words seemed to hang there. I didn't regret saying them, but I was nervous that they'd chase him away. But I wouldn't take them back, even if it meant they might end things between us. I wanted him—needed him—to know what he meant to me.

He didn't offer any sort of sentimental words in return. He just kissed me again.

For now, it was enough.

Chapter 36

FLETCHER

Avery had me wanting things, thinking things, dreaming of things that I had no business wanting, thinking, or dreaming of. She made me want to be the kind of guy she deserved. She made me spout romantic nonsense about the tide.

She almost made me confess that I'd fallen for her. Hard. But I knew once I said the words there would be no going back. And our lives were on different trajectories. She was traveling fast, far, and high, while I felt like I was standing still.

With her I laughed. I smiled more than I ever had in my life. I talked more about things that weren't really important. I revealed more about things that were important. It might not seem like much to her, but it was more than I'd ever revealed before.

I even thought about trading in the bike for a car, just so we could talk when we went places together.

Before her, no one asked me questions about myself. No one pried, no one dug for the answers. No one made me want to tear down the walls.

She did.

As we rode back to her house, I couldn't deny that I loved the way she pressed herself against me, wrapped her arms around, hung on as though she thought I'd disappear if she let go. With her I felt special. With her I felt . . . loved.

And that was scary. I worried about letting her down, disappointing her. Doing something that would make her wish she'd never met me.

I parked the bike at the end of the street and started walking her to her house. She wrapped her hand around mine. It was a small thing really, the way she always liked to touch, but it was incredible, too. Amazing.

"Now that you know I'm committed, I guess you'll want to let your parents know." I looked over at Avery. "Maybe you could tell them that you have a date. When they answer the door, it's me."

"I'm not sure that's a good idea," she said.

I didn't blame her. It had sounded a little hokey when I said it out loud, and I'd never really cared about getting parents' approval, but I had to admit that seeing the way they'd greeted Marc had made me think it wouldn't be so bad.

"You just want to tell them during dinner? Hold a special family meeting? However you want to do it is fine."

She stopped walking. I did, too. A streetlight was casting its glow over her. Although her face was cast in shadows and light, I could see it pretty clearly. She was obviously troubled. "Avery?"

"I don't know that we should tell them yet that we're going to be seeing each other."

"Why not?"

"Don't take this wrong, but Mom and Dad have certain expectations where I'm concerned."

I felt like she'd punched me. "And I don't meet those expectations." How was I not supposed to take that wrong? "You're ashamed of me."

"No, I'm not." She grabbed my arm for emphasis. I pulled it away. She sighed. "It's just that I know the kind of guy they've always seen me with."

"A guy who wears yellow shirts with button-down collars and loafers?"

"You noticed what Marc was wearing?"

I'd noticed everything. His haircut, his height. The way her parents smiled at him like he was surrounded by rainbows. "Is that what you want?" I asked.

"No, of course not." She wrapped her fingers around my arm again. "I want you."

"Then why not tell them that?"

"What if they don't approve? What if Dad kicks you out?"

"There's a break room at Smiley's. I'll sleep there."

"What if things don't work out between us? Neither of us has ever been part of a couple."

"You said we could learn together."

"But what if we fail?"

"When was the last time you failed at anything?" She didn't answer, and I got it then. "But you think I'll fail."

"No, you're twisting everything around. I just don't want to set up expectations and feel like everyone is watching us. If we wait until I go to college—"

"Are their *expectations* going to be different then?"

"No, but at least I won't be living with them if they're disappointed." Her eyes widened. "I didn't mean that the way it sounded. Of course they're not going to be disappointed—"

"If your equation contains expectations, then yeah, you gotta factor in disappointment. But the variable is: why do you care so much?"

"You know how important their opinion of me is."

"So important that you're going to become a doctor when you really want to be a teacher." Then I thought of something else and it sent a chill down my back. "Let me ask you this. You were upset when kids at school thought we'd made out."

"Of course, I was upset. My reputation—"

I pressed my finger to her lips, my gut clenching because I was pretty sure I knew the answer. "What if the rumor had been that you'd made out with Scooter Gibson? Rich kid with upstanding parents involved in the community who own a huge house in town and one on the lake. Football star who got a full scholarship. Would you have been so worried about it then?"

"Of course. I still would have been upset."

"But not as much. You wouldn't have poured tea over his head. But instead the rumor was that you'd been with a guy who came from a trailer park, wasn't smart enough to make the grades, probably destined for prison. Yeah, Avery, I was well aware of what people thought about me. I didn't care. But I cared about what you thought. I'm an idiot."

"No, you're not, Fletcher. You're smart, funny, good—"

"Save it for the next guy. I'm outta here."

Spinning on my heel, I trotted back to get my bike. Glad that she didn't follow. Hurt that she didn't try to stop me. Angry that she mattered enough to hurt me.

When I reached my bike, I was tempted to get on it and ride off into the sunrise. But I'd been up all night and was tired. I might be an idiot to think I mattered to Avery, but I wasn't stupid enough to risk having an accident.

I revved my bike and rode it the short distance to

Avery's house. I was grateful and disappointed she wasn't waiting there to confront me. I wanted her to grill me. I wanted to grill her. I wanted to know the exact reason why she was ashamed of me. I'd tried to straighten up my act, had been working hard to conquer algebra—I just couldn't seem to conquer the demons that labeled me a loser.

It was one thing to sneak around with the town bad boy. Something else entirely to stand beside him.

I jogged up the stairs to my place. Looking over my shoulder at her window, I saw only darkness. I thought about calling her, about telling her that I wanted to talk. For the first time in my life I really wanted to talk to someone. I just didn't think anything good would come of it.

I opened the door, walked in, staggered to a stop.

Avery's dad was sitting on the couch. Slowly he came to his feet.

"Want to explain where you've been?" he asked.

Chapter 37

AVERY

What had just happened?

I sat on my bed, stunned. I kept replaying the conversation, but it was disjointed; pieces of it were missing. Because it made no sense in my head.

I'd been so concerned with having a boyfriend, with how a boy should treat me, that I hadn't given any thought to how I should act as a girlfriend. Kendall made it seem so easy. She and Jeremy never fought. They got along great. I'd assumed when a guy wanted to be my boyfriend that it would be the same. He'd step into the role and everything would be perfect.

Shoving myself off the bed, I went into my bathroom and turned on the shower. I was feeling sticky and sandy. And confused. I knew I'd hurt Fletcher's feelings, but he just didn't understand about expectations. He'd never had any thrust on him.

After removing my clothes, I stepped into the shower and let the hot water wash away the sand, brine, and my tears. I hadn't even realized that I was crying.

Mom had said she wanted me to find someone like Jeremy. Jeremy with his buttoned shirts, his good grades, his college aspirations. Jeremy who never showed up with bruises, who had a steadfast family, who was dependable.

But Fletcher was dependable. He'd been there when Tyler was sick. He'd made sure the rumors about us at school had stopped. He'd made my car purr on his own time. He'd fixed Mrs. Ellis's car on his own time. He'd bought me a helmet so I'd be safe.

I'd been so afraid that he'd hurt me that I hadn't considered that I would hurt him. I also hadn't realized that he would want my parents to know about us. I'd thought he'd prefer sneaking around, thinking we were getting away with something.

I was going to lose him if I didn't tell them. And I didn't want to lose him.

When I got out of the shower, I dried off and slipped on a tank and some shorts. I walked to my window and looked out. I was so glad to see Fletcher's bike was parked near the stairs. The lights in the FROG were out. I guessed Fletcher hadn't had any trouble going to sleep. Or was he sitting over there in the graying dawn like me?

Dad's car was gone, which was odd because it had been there when I got home. Maybe he got called out while I was in the shower.

I grabbed my phone and hit Photos. The flash had illuminated our names in the sand. The exact moment that I took the picture, the foamy tide was tickling the edge of the heart. I wanted to think that they would still be there when I returned to work tonight, but I knew they would probably be gone. If not by the tide, then by the beachgoers who walked and played along the edge of the beach.

But it didn't matter. Tough-guy-of-few-words Fletcher had drawn our names in the sand. They'd been part of the earth and now they'd be part of the ocean, traveling the world.

Such fanciful thoughts, but I guess they came from being in love. And I did love him. What if my parents' expectations were only that I be happy? Fletcher met those expectations exceedingly well. And if they were disappointed, I'd deal with it, because Fletcher was worth it.

I needed to let him know.

I trotted down the stairs. I heard movement in the kitchen. Probably Mom. I tiptoed to the front door and slipped out. Dawn was arriving, painting the sky in a vibrant hue of pinks and oranges. I dashed across the driveway and up the stairs.

I knocked on the door. Waited. Knocked again. "Fletcher?"

Nothing. No sound. No movement. But he had to be here. His bike was here.

I knocked again. Silence. "I know you're mad, but we need to talk. Or I need to talk. You don't have to say anything, but please listen. I can explain why I said what I did. I know it was wrong and stupid—" I sighed heavily. "Fletcher, open the door. Please."

Only he didn't. I tried the handle. The door was locked. Frustration slammed into me. I wanted to fix things. I knew there was an extra key in a drawer in the kitchen. Would it be wrong of me to use it?

Yes.

"You can't avoid me forever," I called out. At some point he would eat with the family. Mom and Dad would insist. He couldn't stay in there forever. I thought about sitting on the steps and waiting. Probably better to leave him alone to mope for a bit. I didn't know how to handle a fight with a guy. I'd never had one.

As a matter of fact, I couldn't recall ever having a fight with anyone.

I wandered back to the house and walked into the kitchen. Mom was sitting at the island.

"Hey, honey," she said, but she sounded . . . off.

"Where's Dad?" I asked as I took the stool beside her.

She gave me an odd smile, one of reassurance and maybe embarrassment. "There was a robbery last night. He got the call around three."

I sat up straighter. "He's okay, right?"

Reaching across, Mom squeezed my arm. "He's fine. I'm sorry. I should have led with that. He's fine, but they have a person of interest and he's dealing with that."

Relief washed through me and I sat back. "Thank goodness." I thought about making some tea, but I didn't feel like drinking anything. I wasn't interested in breakfast either. I was worried about how upset Fletcher was. Maybe I should ask my mom for advice.

"Avery," Mom said softly.

I looked back at her. All the lines in her face had deepened with worry. "Mom, what's wrong?"

"The person of interest . . . it's Fletcher."

I stared at her as though she'd suddenly started speaking in Klingon. I pushed myself off the stool. "Wait a minute."

Was that why Fletcher didn't open the door? Why Dad's car was there when I got home but wasn't there now? He'd taken Fletcher in? "What are you talking about? Why would Fletcher be a person of interest?"

"Smiley's was robbed."

"So?"

"Apparently the evidence points to Fletcher."

"That's crazy! He loves working there. He wouldn't do something like that."

"Calm down."

"Calm down? This is Fletcher we're talking about."

"I know. I don't want to believe it either. I don't know the details. Only that your dad took him in for questioning."

Took him in for questioning. I'd never before realized how ominous those words sounded. "Why would Dad do that? It couldn't have been Fletcher."

She held up her hands. "I know you like him . . ."

I more than liked him. I loved him. I believed in him. And I knew he couldn't have done it, because he'd been with me. All night.

Neither of my parents was going to be happy about that. I had been the girl who followed the straight and narrow, who never got into trouble, was never late with her homework, never did anything she wasn't supposed to do. Until Fletcher.

They'd blame him, even though it had been my idea. Right from the start we were going to be announcing loud and clear that they couldn't trust us. But Fletcher would have no choice except to tell my dad everything. Dad would know where I'd been, who I'd been with. What we'd been up to.

All their expectations regarding me were about to be

crushed. I was so terrified of what their reaction might be, but I was more worried about Fletcher. Surely he had told my dad before he'd been taken to the station. Had Dad not believed him because it seemed like something so out of character for me? Fletcher had to be so scared.

I heard a car pull into the drive. I rushed through the house, raced through the front door, and staggered to a stop when Dad got out of his car—alone. "Where's Fletcher?" I demanded.

Dad heaved a heavy sigh. "Still at the station."

"You can't possibly think he robbed the shop."

"About three o'clock this morning, a tow truck driver was dropping off a car. He noticed lights on in the office. Found Smiley. He was mumbling Fletcher's name. Unfortunately he's now in a coma, so we're short on details. Don Johnson confirmed money was missing and that Fletcher has a key."

"None of that proves anything," I said indignantly.

"He doesn't have an alibi. I know he wasn't here most of the night, because they called me when they realized what Smiley had been saying. I went to his room and waited until he showed up at dawn. When he walked through his door and saw me sitting on the couch, the guilt washing over his face—I've never in my life seen anyone look so guilty."

He was looking guilty because he'd been out with me

and thought he'd gotten caught. But something else Dad said struck me as more important. "What do you mean he didn't have an alibi?"

"He said he was alone last night. No one can vouch for his whereabouts."

I felt as though I'd taken a solid blow to the chest. Fletcher had lied. But why? Because I'd told him that I didn't want my parents to know about us? Because I'd made him think I was ashamed of him? My knees grew weak. I staggered back.

Dad grabbed my arm, stopped me from falling down. "Avery?"

I shook my head, the words lodged in my throat. Fletcher must have thought I'd rather let him go to jail than back up his alibi. Did he really think I'd do that?

He'd been concerned that he wouldn't know how to be a boyfriend. He'd cared enough about me to worry about it. When the truth was: I didn't know how to be a girlfriend. He deserved a lot better than me.

He'd once told me that easy wasn't always the right choice. He didn't always choose easy. Until this moment I had.

"He does have an alibi, Dad."

My dad arched his brow. "Oh?"

Swallowing hard, I nodded. "He was with me."

"When?"

The word came out like a gunshot. Harsh. Short.

"Shortly after I got in from work. We went to the beach. We were there together until almost dawn."

"Jack?" Mom said hesitantly, and I looked over to see her arms crossed over her chest, not like she was mad, but like she wanted to hug me but wasn't sure she should.

"Avery says she was with Fletcher last night," Dad said.

"I can prove it," I said quickly, and dug my phone out of my pocket. I went to my photos and brought up the one of our names in the sand. "See the properties? It's dated and timed." Of course that didn't mean Fletcher was with me. I didn't have a picture of us together last night. We hadn't been hanging out with people so no one had seen us.

Dad studied it before giving me the hard cop glare. "You left without letting us know."

I nodded. "I know it was wrong. I wanted to be with him, which I realize isn't a good excuse, but I knew you'd say no."

"To you going to the beach, in the middle of the night— of course I'd say no," Dad said.

"Can you yell at me later? Punish me, whatever you think is fair, I won't object, but can we go get Fletcher? Please?"

"You should have told us," Dad said. "And we will definitely discuss this later. What I don't understand, though, is why Fletcher didn't tell me he was with you."

"Maybe he didn't want me to get into trouble." I shook my head. "I don't know, Dad."

Although I was afraid I did know. Maybe he was afraid that if he told Dad he was with me that I would deny it. That thought nearly broke my heart.

I'd been to the police station countless times on school field trips. Sometimes Dad would bring me and show me around. But I'd never noticed how loudly the hallways echoed or how glaringly bright the lights were. Or how noisy it was with fingers clicking over keyboards, people talking, business getting done.

Dad had let me look through the observation mirror into an interrogation room before, but no one had been inside. I'd thought it was fun, interesting. But not now, as I observed Fletcher sitting there studying his hands. Tears burned my eyes. He was there because of me.

"He looks so alone," I said quietly.

Dad placed his broad hand on my shoulder. "Maybe he thinks he is."

I glanced up at Dad. "But he's not."

He slowly shook his head. "No, he's not. Why don't you try to convince him of that?"

If he'd even listen to me.

Nodding, I took a deep breath. Dad reached over and

opened the door. I stepped through into the big yawning abyss, and the door *snicked* closed behind me.

Fletcher lifted his eyes to me. "You shouldn't be here."

"Neither should you."

His gaze darted to the mirror before coming back to me. "Look, Law and Order—"

"Don't," I said softly. It had been so long since he'd called me anything except Avery. I understood what he was doing. All the times he'd referred to me with some stupid nickname had been because he wanted to keep distance between us. Using my name made things more personal. He'd been hurt so much that he didn't trust anyone. He didn't trust me. He didn't trust me to stand by him. But then why should he?

He'd asked me last night to stand by him and I'd been too afraid of what my parents might think. It hurt now, to realize that. I couldn't imagine how much I had hurt him.

"Don't make light of this or start putting up walls between us." I looked over at the mirror. "And, yes, my dad is standing out there, probably watching and listening. It's his job to get to the bottom of things."

I crossed the distance separating us, pulled out a chair, and sat.

"You need to go," he insisted. His eyes were dull, his expression flat. He wasn't at all glad to see me.

"Why did you tell my dad that you had no alibi?"

He studied me in that way he had that made it seem he was memorizing lines and curves, as though he thought he would need to recall them for later, as though he wanted the memory. He leaned forward slightly. "Look, you don't need to be dragged into this. They'll figure out it wasn't me."

"Fletcher, you're just making their job harder by not eliminating yourself as a suspect. Not to mention that you have to sit here while they ask you questions, while they make you feel as though you've done something wrong."

"I did do something wrong, just not what they think. I'm not good for you, Avery."

"That's true. But you are perfect for me."

"So perfect, let's keep it a secret."

"I know you're hurt and angry."

"You don't know anything about what I'm feeling."

"But you're still trying to protect me," I said. My chest tightened so painfully with the realization that he was more concerned about me than himself. It didn't matter if Mom and Dad were disappointed in my choice for a boyfriend. I knew I'd never find anyone better.

He shook his head. "Just looking out for myself. It's what I do best. Your dad would kill me if he learned about last night."

I lifted a shoulder. "He already knows, and you're still breathing."

His eyes shot to the mirror, before landing heavily on me. "You told him?"

"They think you robbed Smiley's. They think you hit Smiley on the head. I'm mad that they would even think you'd do those things, but I'm also mad that you didn't tell them you couldn't have done those things. Not because it's just not the kind of stuff you do, but because you were with me."

He released a long sigh that seemed to come from deep within his soul. "I know how important your reputation and their expectations are to you."

"I was wrong. I thought about it a lot after you went to get your bike. My parents are such good people, they do good things, but sometimes I think that they foster kids because I'm a disappointment."

"That's nuts." Fletcher didn't talk a lot but when he did, he got right to the point.

"I guess it's a little like thinking you'll be like your dad. We get these crazy thoughts and we can't shake them off. I've always tried so hard to be what they want me to be, to pick the right clothes and the right college, the right major. To get good grades, to not get into trouble. To make them proud."

"Avery, you just have to be you."

"I know that now. I thought about how you don't do things because of what people will think. You do them because of what you'll think. I'm at my best when I'm with you. I came over this morning to tell you that but you weren't there. I just thought you were too mad to open the door." I tentatively placed my hand over his, grateful when he didn't jerk free. "Before I knew what had happened, where you were, I came to the realization that nothing is more important than you. Not my reputation, not what my parents think. The only thing that matters is how much I love you. I love you so much, Fletcher."

He lowered his head, groaned. "You kill me, you know that?"

"Not literally, I hope."

Chuckling low, he turned his hand palm up, closed his fingers around mine, and I felt the touch deep inside, near my heart.

"I do love you, Fletcher, and I'm so, so sorry that I made you feel like I didn't. I don't blame you for being upset with me, but you have to tell them the truth." I glanced back at the mirror and nodded.

Less than a second later, Dad opened the door and signaled for me. I squeezed Fletcher's hand, stood, and walked out.

Dad closed the door—with him on my side.

"Aren't you going to talk to him?" I asked.

"Avery," Dad said quietly, "our taking in foster kids wasn't because of any kind of disappointment in you."

"Dad—"

He cupped my face. "Your mom and I love you. You bring us such joy. We're so fortunate to have you. Helping other kids is kind of our way of sharing our happiness. That's all."

"Oh, Dad." Tears rolled down my cheeks.

"Fletcher's right, sweetie. Just be yourself. You'll never disappoint us." He hugged me tightly and I wound my arms around him.

"I love you, Dad." I leaned back. "Will you let Fletcher out now?"

We were all silent in the car on the drive home. I sat in the front with Dad; Fletcher rode in the back.

When we arrived at the house, we all climbed out of the car. I walked over to Fletcher and wrapped my hand around his. Dad stood there and looked hard at me.

I tilted up my chin. "I love him."

I knew he'd probably heard everything I'd said to Fletcher but it was important that he hear it now, that he knew I'd meant the words. That Fletcher understood I'd meant the words. I was going to stand beside him, no matter what.

"Well, then, I guess we need to have a little talk," Dad said.

"Actually, sir," Fletcher began, "it's really between me

and Avery." He grimaced. "Avery and me."

Dad arched a brow. "Oh?"

"Yes, sir. I know you won't approve, so I'll be moving out."

"Where are you going to go?"

Fletcher hesitated. "I'll find someplace."

"I don't think that'll be necessary," Dad said. "Although we may need to revisit the rules."

Mom came flying out through the front door. She staggered to a stop beside Dad. I figured she was about to hug us, but then she saw our joined hands. "What happened?"

Dad nodded at us. "Fletcher corroborated Avery's story that they were at the beach."

"Well, that's good news," Mom said. "From the police perspective."

"I love him," I told her. "He's my boyfriend. And I'm proud of him." I squeezed his hand.

Mom smiled. "We know that, sweetie."

I stared at her. "You do?"

"Your dad's a cop. I'm a mom. Not much gets by us." She looked at Fletcher. "We're thrilled."

"But I thought . . ." I began.

"Thought what?" Dad asked.

"I thought you expected me to love someone like Jeremy."

"Someone who can make you as happy as Jeremy

makes Kendall. That's all I meant. We don't have any other expectations," Mom said. "If Fletcher makes you happy, that's all that matters. Lunch is ready. Grilled cheese and tomato basil soup."

Mom and Dad started to walk off like it was all settled.

"You should know," Fletcher began.

They stopped, looked back at him.

Still holding my hand, he shifted his stance. "I care for Avery."

"Care?" Dad echoed.

Fletcher looked at me, and I saw everything he felt for me in his eyes. "More than care. I just haven't told her that yet."

"They're not easy words to say the first time," Dad told him. "I understand you wanting it to be a private moment." Then he and Mom went into the house.

I swung around and faced Fletcher. "You don't have to say the words. I know how you feel."

"You deserve the words."

"I don't know that I do. I hurt you. You mean so much to me. I was afraid to trust what we were feeling and that I might lose you. That maybe it wasn't permanent. I was afraid if I told them that I might lose them, too."

He cradled my cheek. "You're not going to lose me, Avery. I like being your boyfriend."

He kissed me, and it was better than any other kiss

we'd shared. It was out in the open; we were out in the open.

I heard a door close, then Dad clearing his voice. Fletcher and I drew apart.

Dad held up his phone. "They just called me. Smiley's awake."

"That's great," Fletcher said.

"But do they know why he said it was Fletcher?" I asked.

Dad rubbed his chin with his thumb. "Apparently, he was trying to say 'Fletcher's dad.'"

Fletcher stiffened beside me. "My dad robbed Smiley's?"

Dad nodded. "The evidence is pointing that way. They just arrested him. Found Smiley's cash bag in his car. Most of the money is still there."

"I need to see him," Fletcher said.

"I'm on my way to the station now," Dad told him.

"I'm going with you," I said, but I wasn't sure if Fletcher heard me. He was already heading for the car.

Chapter 38

FLETCHER

I stood outside the window looking into the interrogation room where I'd been sitting a short time ago. Now my father was sitting there, slouched back in the chair, his handcuffed wrists resting on the table. I didn't know if I'd ever felt more ashamed.

Avery was beside me, holding my hand. Every couple of minutes she squeezed my fingers. That was the only thing that stopped me from feeling completely dead inside.

"You're not responsible for his actions," Avery's dad said.

"Why would he do everything he did?"

"Sometimes there's no explanation that makes any sense."

"Can I talk to him?"

"Do you think that's a good idea?" Avery asked.

"Probably not, but I need to talk to him. He's my father."

"I'll go in with you," she said.

I was so glad she was here, but I couldn't expose her to him. Shaking my head, I touched her cheek. "I need to do this alone."

"You won't be completely alone," Avery's dad said. "I'll be in the room."

"I'll wait out here," Avery said.

I looked back at the man in the room and realized that I didn't really know him. We'd shared a trailer for most of my life, but it was like looking at a stranger.

Avery's dad placed his hand on my shoulder. "Ready?"

Not really, but I needed to do this. I took a deep breath, nodded, and followed him into the room.

My father glanced up, sneered. "Got nothing to say."

I took the chair across from him, while Avery's dad leaned against a wall.

"Why'd you do it?" I asked.

He looked at me with dead eyes. "I ain't talking until my lawyer gets here."

"This is unofficial," Avery's dad said. "Talk to your son. I'm not recording anything."

My father curled up a lip, lifted a shoulder. "Okay, then, sure, why not?"

At least I realized where I'd learned the art of conversation. I'd once revealed as little. Until Avery.

I knew no matter what I asked, he wasn't going to give me an honest answer. That didn't mean I couldn't talk to him honestly.

"When you used to hit me, I thought it was because I did something wrong."

"You gonna cry about it now?"

"No. I didn't cry when your fists came down. I'm not going to cry now. But I wanted you to know that I can't seem to not love you. I guess because you're my father. But I don't like you. I don't know if I ever liked you. But I do know that I'm not going to be like you."

I leaned forward. "I'm going to make something of myself."

"Make me proud?" he mocked.

"It's got nothing to do with you. I'm doing it for me, because I deserve it. When I walk out of here, I hope I never see you again. But I wanted you to know that if you ever come at me again, I will flatten you."

"You couldn't—"

My fist hit his face so quick, so hard that I felt the force of it shimmering up my arm and through my chest. "That was for Smiley."

Gerald Thomas—I no longer thought of him as my dad; I didn't want anything more to do with him—was moaning, cursing, rolling on the floor.

I didn't remember coming out of the chair to strike

him, but Avery's dad had his arms around me and was pulling me back.

I was breathing harshly, my body was coiled.

"Got anything else you want to say?" Avery's dad asked.

I shook my head.

He pushed me gently in the direction of the door. "Then get on out of here."

I put my hand on the knob, looked back over my shoulder.

Avery's dad was crouched near Gerald Thomas. "You need to watch how you sit in the chairs, Mr. Thomas. It's very easy to topple yourself over and break your nose on the floor."

I opened the door and walked out without another backward glance.

Chapter 39

AVERY

I almost cheered when Fletcher walked out. His father had so deserved that.

But Fletcher didn't even look at me. His face set in a stony mask, he simply walked by. I followed. Normally I could keep up with his stride but he was moving too fast.

By the time I did catch up with him, he was outside, standing on the front lawn by the flagpole. His back was tense, his hands fisted.

My heart ached for him. "He deserved that, Fletcher."

He shook his head. "I never hit anyone before. It didn't feel good, I'm not proud of what I did, but I'm glad I did it. I didn't even think about. I just did it."

"You're not your father," I said as I pressed my hand to his back.

He spun around, and I could see the anguish on his

face. "He hit Smiley over the head with a wrench. He could have killed him. What did Smiley ever do to him?"

"What did you ever do to him? He's just a horrible person." I took a step closer. "But you're good."

"Avery—"

"You helped me with Tyler when he was sick. You didn't have to do that. He's not your responsibility. You repaired Mrs. Ellis's car because her husband isn't here to do it for her. On your own time. Again, not your responsibility. You made my car purr like a contented cat. You made sure no one took advantage of me when I was drunk. You can say it was because of the bet, and that you took me home because of the bet, but I think you did it because you knew I was vulnerable. You're a good guy, Fletcher. You're tough on the outside, but inside you're a marshmallow."

"I'm not a marshmallow," he groused.

I pressed up against him, wrapped my arms around him, and held his gaze. "Am I right, Fletcher, about Scooter's party, about the reason behind the bet?"

"I needed a few bucks," he said. He cradled my face. "And yeah, I was standing with a group of idiots who noticed you weaving around the patio, knew you'd been drinking, and were trying to decide who should make the first move on you. Made me mad. I thought, 'Einstein's got nobody watching out for her.' I've loved you, Avery, for longer than you know."

He kissed me. I wound my arms around his neck and kissed him back. I loved the way he held me, the slow sweep of his tongue. He pressed me closer, and it was just the two of us, melting into each other. He loved me. I loved him. The kiss was a little different with the words said, but it was also the same. We had cared for each other longer than either of us had known. Now we were together and everything felt right.

Chapter 40

FLETCHER

FOUR WEEKS LATER

I was sitting on the couch, flipping through channels, searching for a baseball game. I'd finished summer school three days ago. This was my first Sunday when I didn't need to work on algebra problems. Since Avery had left for work an hour ago, I wasn't quite sure what to do with my spare time. Maybe I'd take Tyler to get some ice cream.

A knock sounded on my door. I got up and opened it. Avery smiled up at me.

"Hey," I said, slipping an arm around her and bringing her in close. "Thought you were working."

"That's what I wanted you to think." She held up a blindfold and wiggled her eyebrows.

"Are we about to get into something kinky?" I asked.

"Not too kinky." Reaching up, she tied the cloth over my eyes. "I want to show you something, but I want to unveil it."

"I love it when you're mysterious."

She brushed her lips over mine. "You're really going to love this," she whispered.

Taking my arm, she led me slowly down the steps. When we reached the bottom, she spun me around several times until I was disoriented, then she was leading me again but I couldn't figure out where we were going, but it seemed farther away than the house.

"I know you're backtracking," I said. "Going in circles."

"You do not."

"I do now."

She playfully slapped my arm. "So clever."

We moved off the driveway or sidewalk onto springy grass. I heard a little giggle, followed by a shush. I was pretty sure it was Tyler's giggle. Maybe her mother shushing him.

"I'm not going to be embarrassed, am I?" I asked.

"Trust me."

"I do."

She squeezed my arm. A few steps later we stopped. She let go. "Okay, you can take off the blindfold."

I dragged it off.

"Surprise!" Avery, her parents, Tyler, Kendall, and Jeremy shouted.

We were all standing near a table set up by the pool. Balloons at each corner of the table were bouncing in the breeze. In the center of the table sat a white cake and written in purple icing was:

Congratulations, Graduate!

I was overcome with emotions. I didn't know that many existed in the world.

Avery slipped in against my side. "I'm so proud of you for acing that algebra class."

"I had a great tutor," I told her.

"But you got the work done. Ready for some cake?"

"Absolutely."

Avery began slicing up the cake.

"I'm going to get started grilling the steaks," Avery's dad said. He stopped by me and patted my shoulder. "Knew you could do it. I'm proud of you."

My throat knotted up at the words my own father had never spoken to me. "Thank you, sir. That means a lot."

He sobered a bit. "Got word that your dad took a plea bargain. He's going away for a while."

"That's the best news I could get today." Smiley had recovered from his injuries. Had even given me a raise. I wasn't sure why, but I appreciated it.

"Thought it might make your day. Sure as hell made mine." He headed for the deck and the grill.

Tyler rushed over and held up a paper plate with a corner piece of cake on it. "Avery says you get the first one," he said.

"Too much icing for me. Why don't you take that one?"

"Yes!" He raced off.

Avery's mother wandered over and handed me a small card. "Just a little something for your college fund."

"You don't have to do that. You've done so much for me already."

"You've made our daughter happy. That's all we've ever wanted for her. We want that for you, too." She hugged me, and I folded my arms around her. "You deserve it, Fletcher. Don't let anyone ever convince you otherwise."

Moving back, she patted my arm. "We're going to miss you."

"I'm not leaving for a few more weeks."

"They'll go fast. And now I'd better check on the potatoes." She walked off.

I strolled over to the pool where Kendall, Jeremy, and Avery were waiting. I sat in a chair beside Avery. She handed me a piece of cake. "Thanks."

Jeremy lifted a glass of lemonade. "A toast: to your graduation. Cheers!"

"Cheers!" Avery and Kendall said.

I clicked my glass to everyone's and drank deeply.

"So now that you're finally finished with high school,

what are you going to do?" Kendall asked.

I looked at Avery. "You didn't tell her?"

She smiled. "It's your news."

"Come on, spill it," Kendall said.

I took a deep breath, couldn't believe the words I was about to utter. "Going to school."

Kendall looked as shell-shocked as I'd felt when I made the decision. "It's a little late to apply, isn't it? At least for the fall."

"Not to apply to a community college," Avery said. "He's been accepted to one in Austin. Which works out great for us since we'll be in the same city. And his grades there will help when he's ready to transfer to a four-year school."

"What are you going to major in?" Jeremy asked.

"Law enforcement." I'd spent considerable time getting advice from Avery's dad regarding the path I should take to becoming a police offer.

"A cop and a doctor," Kendall said.

"Actually," Avery began, "a cop and a teacher."

Kendall's mouth dropped open. "When did you decide this?"

"A couple of weeks ago."

"Thought your mom wanted you to be a doctor."

"That's what I thought. Seems I misjudged her expectations."

"I can't believe you didn't share all this news with me!"

Avery leaned against me, her smile bright. "I've been a little busy."

"We need to schedule a spa day or a girls' weekend or something, so we can catch up."

"We should, we really should."

"Hey, guys, steaks are ready!" Avery's dad yelled.

Jeremy and Kendall headed over to the deck. Avery held me back, moved in close, and held my gaze.

"Was it a nice surprise?" she asked.

"The best."

I lowered my mouth as she lifted up on her toes and met me halfway. I wrapped my arms around her as she pressed her body to mine. Her fingers combed through my hair. Her mouth moved over mine, slowly, seductively.

I loved kissing her, loved talking with her, loved being with her.

With her in my life, my world was a little bit brighter. With her at my side, I could do anything.

Read a sneak peek
of Kendall and Jeremy's story in

Chapter 1

KENDALL

I loved Jeremy Swanson.

I loved his long, slow kisses, his dimpled smile. I loved the way one of his hands always came to rest on the small of my back when we walked.

"I love you, Kendall," he whispered breathlessly as he trailed his mouth along my neck before returning it to my lips for another searing kiss.

I loved that most of all. That he loved me, quirks included.

We were doing our contortionist impression, as we struggled to find a comfortable position in the cramped backseat of his car that was quickly turning into a sauna. Because of all the mosquitoes, we had the windows rolled up. Because of the price of gas, the car wasn't running, the air conditioner wasn't blowing.

But neither of us cared about the discomforts. We were together. That was all that mattered.

Jeremy shifted, lost his precarious perch on the edge of the seat and, with a yelp, tumbled the few inches to the floor.

I laughed, held up a hand. "Sorry."

"No, I'm sorry," he said, moaning as he shoved himself into a sitting position. "I don't know why my parents had to get me such a small car for a graduation present."

"Probably because they knew this is what you'd be doing with it."

He grinned. The shadows stopped me from seeing the little dimple that I knew had formed in his left cheek. "Probably. Dad worries that I'll do something stupid before I even get to college."

"Like fall in love," I teased.

He leaned forward and gave me a quick kiss. "That's the smartest thing I've done so far."

He tried to get up but he was wedged between the front seat and the back. "This is ridiculous. I'm glad you love me. These moves wouldn't impress a date."

I placed my hand against his cheek, leaned in, and let my mouth play over his. "Your moves impress me."

They always had. We'd been together for nearly four months, longer if I counted the friendship phase that had begun at the start of our senior year just after his family moved to town. Over spring break when my best friend, Avery Watkins, hadn't been able to go to a movie with us, Jeremy had kissed me for the first time. It had been a sweet kiss, a tentative brushing of his lips over mine as though he were afraid I'd take offense and slap him or something. I hadn't taken offense. Instead I'd moved in to welcome his advance. He'd taken the kiss deeper and I'd fallen hard.

Now, without breaking off the kiss, he tried to smoothly get back onto the seat. He grunted, shifted, pulled away, and sighed. "I'm stuck."

Ruffling my fingers through his short, blond hair, I laughed again. "And I intend to take advantage of that."

I kissed him again. He cupped my face, his thumb stroking the underside of my chin where the skin was soft and sensitive. Shivers went through me. He skipped his tongue over my lips before slipping it inside to dance with mine. He always took his time. He always went slow.

Sometimes slower than I wanted.

I tugged his shirt out of his jeans, glided my hand beneath the soft material, and skimmed my palm up his back. He groaned low, began pushing himself up—

"Oh, God! Oh, God! My back's cramping." His hand flew to his side, his head reared back.

"Okay, hold on." I opened the door and clambered out of the car, trying to give him more room to maneuver. I pulled on his legs. He really was wedged in there. We'd already moved the seats up as far as they would go. "Here, take my hand."

Finally he was able to shift slightly so he could crawl backward out of the car. Arching with his hands pressed to his spine, he paced back and forth several times. With a look of contrition, he finally straightened and laughed with an exaggerated roll of his eyes. "That car has got to go."

Although it was relatively new, it was the unsexiest thing I'd ever seen and looked like something my grandmother would drive to church. Walking over to him, I flattened my palms against his chest. "Maybe you could trade it in for a motorcycle."

"Where would we make out?"

Good question. I'd have to talk to Avery about that. She pretty much became a motorcycle expert when she started dating Fletcher Thomas.

I heard the beep of an incoming text on my phone. I opened the front door, reached in, and grabbed my phone from where it rested on the console. Speak of the devil.

Avery:

Going to B.S. Meet us?

I almost said no but I was tired of the cramped backseat. I looked over my shoulder. "Want to meet Avery and Fletcher at the Burger Shack?"

"Guess I kinda ruined the mood with my old guy, back-out-of-whack impersonation."

"It's more the heat." I slapped at a mosquito. "The bugs. And I'm a little hungry."

"Okay, let's go." He slammed the back door while I slid into the passenger seat. Then he closed my door before jogging around and slipping behind the wheel.

He started off, slow and careful, backing away from the lake until we reached the road. I didn't look to see what other cars were out there. This area was pretty much make-out central, but couples deserved their privacy.

"You know," he began, "you don't have to say Avery *and Fletcher*. If it's Avery, I assume it's Fletcher, too, now."

Avery and Fletcher had started dating seriously just a few weeks ago. "I'm so glad she got a boyfriend," I said. "I think she was starting to get a little uncomfortable hanging around with us all the time." She'd been my best friend forever and Jeremy had always been good about inviting her to go places with us. I loved how considerate he was, but I had to admit it was nice that Jeremy and I had more time alone now.

"The right boyfriend." Jeremy cast a quick glance my way. "You didn't just want a boyfriend, did you? You wanted the right one."

"Totally." Reaching across the console, I touched his arm. "And you're the right one for me. That's what I wanted for Avery. Just didn't expect the right one to be him." Fletcher had a bad-boy reputation, had needed to take a summer class to graduate from high school. Avery was all smarts, ranked third in our class, and nearly always followed the rules. The ones she broke were harmless.

"I like him," Jeremy said.

"He's a lot different than I thought." I knew Fletcher as a tough guy who often came to school looking like he'd been in a brawl. After getting to know him, though, I realized how sweet he could be—at least where Avery was concerned. The guy would do anything for her.

Jeremy pulled into the B.S. parking lot, came around, and opened the car door for me. It had taken me a while to get used to him doing that. I'd never had anyone open the door for me, but his dad had taught him to be courteous. It was a little old-fashioned, but I liked it. When we got to the front door of the restaurant, he held it open while I walked through.

Avery wasn't here yet, so we settled in a booth near the back by the window so we had a view of the parking lot. We'd barely sat down, when I saw a motorcycle with two people on it roar into the lot. My heart skipped a beat at the recklessness. Jeremy would never take a risk like that. He was sure and steady—just like me. But I couldn't help thinking about the thrill of the ride, noticing how brightly Avery was smiling as she got off the bike. Joy and happiness radiated off her.

"Is that why you suggested I trade in my car for a

motorcycle?" Jeremy asked.

I'd been so absorbed watching them that I jerked with a little guilt at Jeremy's question. "It just looks like it would be fun, doesn't it?"

"A car is more practical. What do they do if they have to haul a bunch of stuff?"

Turning slightly, I looked at Jeremy with his conservative haircut. I put my hand over his, and he immediately turned his palm up and threaded our fingers together. I didn't know why our mode of transportation was suddenly nagging at me. "But it would be exciting."

"As long as you don't smile while you're whipping along and get bugs between your teeth."

"I've never seen Fletcher with bugs."

"He doesn't smile all that much, either."

"True." Leaning in, I gave him a quick kiss. "And I love your smile."

"Love yours, too. Bet I wouldn't see it at all if we got caught in a rainstorm while riding that thing. We'd be like drowned cats."

"I hadn't considered that. It's not very practical, is it?"

"Not that I can see."

I wasn't quite ready to give up on the thrill of having one. "Good gas mileage, maybe?"

"Drowned cat," he repeated.

"Maybe we're being too practical." And boring.

Hearing the door open, I looked back. Avery was walking in, Fletcher right on her heels. I couldn't be sure but I wouldn't have been surprised if she'd opened the door for herself. Fletcher was not as polite as Jeremy, not that Avery seemed to mind. She slid into the booth, sitting across from me.

"Hey, guys," she said, smiling brightly.

Dropping onto the bench seat, Fletcher immediately put his arm around her shoulders and acknowledged us with a nod. Fletcher Thomas was a guy of few words.

"What were you up to?" Avery asked.

I felt myself grow warm, knew I was blushing. "Nothing special."

Fletcher studied me, shifted his gaze to Jeremy, and hitched up a corner of his mouth. I figured he knew exactly what we'd been doing.

"We were down by the lake," Jeremy said, and I wondered if I'd wounded his pride, if he felt a need to prove something with Fletcher around.

"Skinny-dipping?" Fletcher asked, a devilish twinkle in his eyes.

"Absolutely not," I said with conviction. I gave Avery a pointed look meant to convey the question: *Have you skinny-dipped?*

Laughing, she rubbed his arm. "He's always trying to talk me into trying it."

"You don't know what you're missing," Fletcher assured us.

"Fish nibbling at things I don't want them nibbling at," Jeremy said.

I loved that he considered all the ramifications of his actions. Which was one of the reasons he'd make a good lawyer. And one of the reasons that he hadn't quite landed safely on second base yet. He put his hands under my shirt, but he never moved past my lower ribs. Limiting temptation and showing respect for me.

That's how he had explained it the night I thought we'd be going further, possibly even all the way. I'd told my mom that I was sleeping over at Avery's and instead had spent the entire night with Jeremy. We'd checked into a motel at the edge of town, walked into our room, and watched a roach crawl across the wall.

"This is not what I want for our first time," he'd told me.

It hadn't been what I wanted, either. We were both virgins . . . and too broke to afford anything nicer. So we'd left, driven to the lake, spent the night in his car talking about what our first time would be like. And he'd told me that he had too much respect for me not to make sure that it was special. That he knew I loved him and we didn't have to have sex to prove that.

I knew our first time was going to be awesome, but

until then, all I could do was admire his control. I always knew exactly where we stood, what to expect. No surprises.

Although as my mom was fond of saying: "Life without surprises is kind of boring."

"Never found fish to be an issue," Fletcher said now, bringing my thoughts back to the present.

"You've really gone skinny-dipping?" I asked.

Fletcher lifted a broad shoulder, moved a saltshaker to the center of the table for no apparent reason. "Sure. You should try it sometime. Seriously."

I stared at the shaker he'd abandoned, moved it back where it belonged, before answering in a way that wouldn't make me seem like a prude. "We'll think about it. Now what do we want to eat?"

Avery and I told the guys what we wanted. They headed to the counter to place our orders. Leaning forward, I held Avery's blue gaze. "Don't take this wrong, but I'm still having a difficult time seeing you two together."

"Maybe you need glasses," she said, a teasing tone to her voice.

"What?"

"If you can't see us."

Avery only responded to the literal meaning of what I said when she was bothered by what I was trying to say, so I knew I'd hit on something that upset her. I probably wasn't the only one who thought she and Fletcher were an odd match. "I didn't mean that in a bad way," I assured her. "It's just that you're so opposite."

"Not as much as you think. But that's what makes it fun."

I looked toward the counter. I'd never seen Fletcher in anything except a black T-shirt that looked like it had shrunk in the wash. Even after our session in the car, Jeremy's light-blue shirt was barely wrinkled. "Do you think we're boring?"

"What? No." Avery touched my arm, brought my attention back to her. "What brought that on?"

"You've gone skinny-dipping, haven't you?"

"No." She took a sugar packet and tapped it repeatedly as though she was trying to stir up her answer. "Although I probably will before summer's over—or maybe once Fletcher and I get to Austin."

"You've changed since you got together with him," I said.

"A little, I guess. Don't you think you've changed since you started dating Jeremy?"

"Not really. We're the same as we were when it was just the three of us hanging together."

"You're cute together."

Inwardly I cringed. "Cute" sounded like we were in elementary school or something.

Two girls got in the line and immediately started talking to Fletcher. His shadowed jaw made him look older, more dangerous. He'd always drawn girls' attention. Jeremy, who had shaved before he picked me up, stood there trying not to look awkward, because they were ignoring him.

"What's wrong?" Avery asked.

"Those girls." I bit on my lower lip. "It's stupid, but it bothers me that they aren't talking to Jeremy. Like maybe they don't think they could be into him." I shook my head. "See, that is so shallow and stupid. I don't want to be jealous, but I wouldn't mind if girls were jealous of me." Because if they were, then I'd know that they knew I had a terrific guy. I didn't know why I needed that validation.

"I was," Avery said quickly. "Jealous of you. Before I had Fletcher. I know that's awful because you're my best friend, but for a long time I wished that Jeremy had wanted to be my boyfriend instead of yours. I mean, the three of us hung out together. What was wrong with me that he didn't choose me?"

"Nothing was wrong with you," I reassured her. Then I added, "But I didn't know you wanted him for a boyfriend."

"Now I can see that we wouldn't have been right together, but I would have said yes in a heartbeat if he'd asked me out. He's so nice."

He was nice. But was he too nice?

The guys returned to the table. Avery dropped that bag of sugar. I snatched it up and placed it back into its holder, noticed a yellow packet mixed in with the blue ones, plucked it out, and inserted it in its proper place. Then I smiled at Jeremy—a little guiltily because we'd been talking about him—as he set a cheeseburger and shake in front of me, and a basket of fries between us.

"Thanks." He knew exactly how I liked my burger and he didn't mind ordering it medium well, with a slice of cheese on top and a slice on the bottom, pickle, and tomato that wasn't from the ends. Mustard on the bottom of the bun, mayo on the top, and the B. S. special sauce on top of the mayo. My mom always made me order my own burger. She was embarrassed that I couldn't just order a burger by calling out a number or saying *all the way*. But I was particular. What was wrong with that? I knew what I wanted.

Avery and Fletcher had cheeseburgers, too, but they were sharing a basket of onion rings. I carefully unwrapped my burger, peered beneath the top bun to see everything exactly as I liked it, and bit into it.

"So . . ." Avery said as she dipped an onion ring into ketchup. "You know Dot, the owner of the Shrimp Hut?"

The Shrimp Hut was the restaurant on the beach where Avery worked on the weekends. "Yeah," I said.

"Her mom is having some surgery so she's going to be out of town for a few days next week and she asked me to house-sit, take care of her cat and dogs. The cool thing is, her house is on the beach. It has three bedrooms, and she said I could have company. Interested in joining us?"

Us? I looked at her, shifted my gaze to Fletcher, back to her. "The two of you?"

Grinning, she nodded.

"Your parents are okay with this?" I asked, stunned. Her dad was a cop who kept a pretty tight rein on things.

"I'm leaving for college in six weeks. They know they need to trust me. I'm officially curfew-less. They want me to let them know when I'll be home, but they know there is nothing I'm going to do right now that I won't do at college." She shrugged. "They're letting me grow up."

My mom hadn't given me a curfew in a while but I didn't know if she'd approve if she knew Jeremy was going to be there. I suppose I didn't have to tell her that he'd be there, although I'd felt so guilty about lying to her before that I'd confessed about our botched romantic night. Mom had just laughed and said, "Karma's a bitch." Now Karma was giving us a second chance with a bedroom on the beach. I couldn't hide my excitement about that as I looked at Jeremy. "What do you think?"

"Up to you."

He was always such a gentleman. Clearly he didn't want to push me into anything and would let it be my decision. Although I did wish I heard a little more enthusiasm in his voice. "Could be loads of fun. I just don't know if I can swing it with my mom."

"There's nothing you could do there that you can't do just as easily out by the lake," Fletcher pointed out.

I grimaced. "I don't exactly tell her we go to the lake. But you're right. I'll talk to her."

"Great!" Avery said. "We'll have a blast. It'll probably be two or three nights. Dot's still working out the details. I'll let you know when I have them."

"Sounds like a plan."

Beneath the table, I squeezed Jeremy's hand. We were getting an all-night-alone-in-a-bedroom-together do-over. This time I was determined we would round second base and head to third. I could hardly wait.

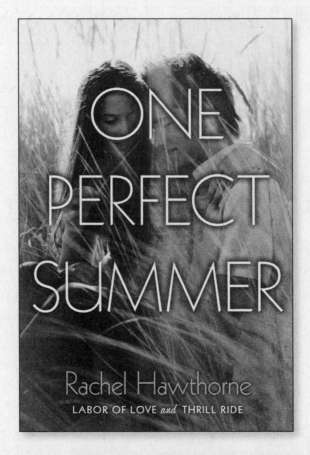